MURDER ON THE GRAND

Christopher H. Meehan

Published by Thunder Bay Press
Publisher: Sam Speigel
Designed and typeset by Maureen MacLaughlin-Morris
Cover by Aaron Phipps

ISBN: 1-882376-49-8

Printed in the United States of America

97 98 99 2000   1 2 3 4 5 6 7 8 9

"Deep calls to deep
    in the roar of your waterfalls;
all your waves and breakers
    have swept over me."

Psalm 42, Verse 7

To Jim and his brother, the real Bob

CHAPTER ONE

Huge flames billowed from the car, swirling from under the smashed hood, broiling the driver's body and pushing me back. I knew the person trapped in there. She was very close to me. Hands tried to grab me from behind, but I slogged forward, forcing myself in slow motion toward the fire.

Through a column of searing, bubbling smoke, I saw the woman's hair, dancing with tongues of fire, twisting with golden sparks. As I made my way helplessly to her, the face started to drip flesh, long fluid strands. Tendons unwinding. Engulfed in her own hell, she began to melt. I had to save her, drag her free, onto the desert floor, and smother the heat with my body.

Try as I might, I only moved inches across the sandy ground. My feet felt buried in muck; my heart slammed my chest; my eyes were riveted to the fire. Sinking into quicksand, I reached out and felt a wall of heat stab my palms like nails. Behind the steering wheel, I saw movement, the body crumbling, brittle as paper. Then suddenly the door exploded and pieces of the woman flew out, blasting into the sky like the sparks of a thousand blackbirds.

Which is when I struggled awake. From the dream. That dream. The dream of Ruth.

Barely conscious, I scrambled out of bed, fumbled for the door, yanked it open and stumbled outside. Curling my fingers on the bone-cold balcony rail, I gulped air, my mind filled with the familiar terror.

It was below freezing but that was OK. I reminded myself: I was not in the New Mexico badlands, racing to the wreck. I was outside Three Rivers, Michigan, at a Benedictine monastery. I was no longer a paramedic in a town called Gallup. I was a Christian Reformed Church minister in Grand Rapids. Chill out, I told myself.

That's when I became aware of the wind coming hard across the brittle winter cornfield, sweeping toward me with an icy vengeance. Standing on a second-floor balcony at the Abbey of Saint Gregory, I turned up my face and let the cold slap me awake. It felt good to be out here, still a couple hours before dawn, even if I only wore sweatpants and a baggy Redeemer College T-shirt.

I shook my head, rattling the colliding, crackling cells that wanted to drag me back to sleep. My eyes focused on a swoop of white powder swirling out there, looking like a figure whose arms swirled madly in the wind. There was no one—just tiny tornadoes of snow funneling up in the midnight glare of a full moon.

Feeling chilled fingers slide through the thin fabric of my shirt, I shivered, but did not go back in. I rolled the weariness out of my neck. I was aware the dream of Ruth was connected to Monica, my fiancée. It dealt with unfinished business.

I willed the nightmare back into its cage and paid closer attention to my surroundings. I loved this Episcopalian monastery, especially in the dim hours before sunrise. I had been trying to get away for months, since before Thanksgiving. But, as always, the world had pressed down on me. Pastoring an inner city church was busy enough. Then came that business with one of my fiancée's students drowning herself in the Grand River, followed by sensational news stories, tying the death with women trying to be preachers in our small, conservative denomination. Once that had eased, Christmas arrived, followed by January and February. Here it was the first week of March.

I closed my eyes and felt the chill wash around me. I emptied my mind; uttered a few prayers.

Soon enough, the banging of the 4 a.m. gong resounded in the crisp air, calling us to the first psalm service of the day. Good, I thought, time to get away from me. From the past and the future. Be with God and the black robes.

Crisp snow slanted from the dark, starry sky. Stuffing my hands in the pockets of my Chicago Bulls parka—I told the teens in my storefront church I was a gang member for Christ—I started along the stone path toward the church. After a moment, I paused to take in the solitude, the fields, the huge sky. A snowy cornfield rose to my right; the monastery buildings stood to the left. The barn-like church was behind. Few other places gave me such a powerful sense of God's force and grand designs.

Starting up, I was halfway to church when I heard a door creak open in the monks' quarters. A hooded figure emerged. "Reverend Turkstra?"

I paused, wiping wet flakes from my cheek and squinted in his direction. "Father Mica?"

"You have an emergency call."

My feet turned numb; my underarms prickled with fear. Gone was serenity and communion with my higher power. That world, the one of harsh responsibility, beckoned. I felt my feet sinking in sand, a door about to burst with birds of fire. "Who is it?"

"He didn't say."

I took the call in the waiting area outside the dining room. Father Mica had switched on a lamp on an end table by the completely black window looking out on the yard. "Hello?"

"Truman, Pete." Pete Hathaway was a colleague of mine in the Christian Reformed Church ministry. I had assumed his duties as pastor of Heartside Community Church not long after he was elected mayor of Grand Rapids a year or so before. "We've got trouble," he said.

In my downtown parish, trouble could take many forms. I waited to see how it happened.

"Monica's been hurt."

Father Mica hovered in the doorway. I was glad he was there, as if his monkly presence might protect me. This was trouble of the worst kind.

3

"The police gave me the call about a half-hour ago. I'm at the hospital now."

"Police?"

"Truman, meet me at Butterworth soon as you can," he said.

"What happened?"

"We'll talk then."

"Now, damn it!"

Father Mica didn't flinch. Maybe he heard preachers swear all the time.

"Someone assaulted her."

My mind scrambled as my heart did a dance in my throat. "In her apartment?"

"She was at a house on the West Side. Her brother, Bob, was with her."

Her retarded brother. It was Saturday, actually Sunday morning. He would have been spending the night. "Was he hurt, too?"

"He scared the attacker off."

I leaned a shoulder against the wall. The monk had folded his hands inside the sleeves of his tunic. He gazed at me solemnly.

"What was she doing, Pete?"

"That's what I want to talk to the police about."

"Did they catch who did it?"

"I don't think so."

I took in three deep breaths, tried to hold the last one, hoping this trouble evaporated into the stuffy heat of the dim room. "How bad is she?"

"I don't know."

"Whose house was she at?"

"Tina Martin. You know her?"

I swallowed a hard marshmallow of anxiety. Another of Monica's students, in her Women in the Church class at the seminary. She was around the night the other one drowned. "What was Monica doing there?"

"Don't know."

"Has anyone talked to her?"

"I don't think so."

"What about Tina?"

Another pause, during which the monk cleared his throat and stepped into the hall. Enough of the high drama already, I imagined him thinking, although he was probably being kind. "No, Truman, they can't."

"Pete?" I asked.

"Police found her strangled in bed."

CHAPTER TWO

After all the racing I'd done on U.S. 131 to get here, my body could hardly stand still. I composed myself as best I could and approached the nurses' desk in the waiting area of the emergency room at Butterworth. I didn't recognize the woman who was on, but I did know the man standing at a file cabinet behind her, drinking coffee. It was Tom Schooner, the midnight social worker.

Given my line of work, I'd been in this place often. Tom told me they had taken Monica to surgery to repair a broken leg and check for a ruptured spleen. As far as he knew, she was now in intensive care. I wanted to pump him, but needed to see Monica more. So I turned and headed for the stairs.

On the fifth floor, I asked a nurse where the new patient was and followed her directions to a room in which people in scrubs bustled around a bed. I looked for Pete, but he was nowhere near. Still shaking from the drive and the quick climb up the stairs, I stepped in.

At first no one noticed me. Or if they did, they were too busy to care. I glimpsed Monica as they jostled around her bed. From what I could tell, she was asleep. But what I was able to see amid the movement of doctors and nurses made me weak all over.

Half-open mouth, through which a hose was jammed; bruised, swollen eyelids, swelling out like moons; pale skin; matted, undistinguished, pulled-back hair. Monitors blinked and beeped and buzzed above and beside her. I saw one thickly bandaged and splinted arm. Wires sprung from the wrist under bunched gauze. A leg was elevated and attached to a pulley. I groaned.

A bearded doctor turned. Short and authoritative-looking, he stuck his hands in the deep side pockets of his white lab coat and stepped over. "You are . . .?" he asked.

I told him.

"Let's go outside."

I remained where I was, gazing at the puffy face. Discolored cheeks; distended mouth. I smelled something acrid in the air, a warm licorice odor. "How is she?" I asked, forcing myself to act calm.

"Please," he said with a firmness he expected me to obey.

We faced off in the middle of the large busy hallway. "I'm Don Schumaker, the trauma surgeon."

"You're in charge?"

He tried to smile, but the gesture died in process, as if he didn't have time for pleasantries. "She's a lucky lady," he said.

I glanced through the wall of glass. "That's lucky?"

He frowned, squeezing a hand down his beard. "It could have been much worse, Reverend." I'd seen him around the hospital, especially in the ER during hectic times when all the forces were mustered to respond to a crisis.

"How bad is she?" I asked, wanting to whop him one, if only to relieve my racing fear.

"The fall down the stairs broke the leg and caused contusions on her face. She has three broken ribs as well, most likely from the fall."

I winced, as if someone had kicked me in the rib cage, aware the injuries, serious enough, didn't sound life threatening. "Fall?"

"However she was hurt." The doctor stared at me, his eyes weary and sad. He said a few other medical things, but I didn't listen.

Immobile on the bed, Monica reminded me of so many others I'd visited over the years as a pastor. People who had been happy and healthy one minute and devastated by an accident or assault the next. But this was different. I didn't have the luxury of looking at her from a distance. "Why was she at that house?"

The doctor shrugged, keeping his yap zipped.

"How about Bob, her brother?"

"I think they're in the waiting room, Reverend. Why don't you go down. I'll be there in a few minutes."

Bob blinked when he saw me come in. He sat next to a lamp which threw down a circle of light onto a white-painted end table. He wore baggy blue jeans and a T-shirt. On the chest an angry-looking tiger leapt from inside a broken base-ball. A blue baseball cap, decorated on the front with the English D of the Detroit Tigers, had been shoved down on his head.

On the left on the couch were Pete Hathaway and Manny Rodriguez, a Grand Rapids Police detective. Both stopped talking when Bob made a sound in his throat and pointed a gun barrel finger in my direction.

The mayor and the cop stood. Still seated, Bob looked around anxiously. A large notepad, its pages twisted, sat on the floor by his feet, which were jammed in black-and-white Nikes I got him for Christmas.

We didn't spend much time saying hello. The two of them returned to the couch. I sat in a chair next to Bob. One of his huge hands reached over and clasped mine.

Rodriguez glanced at Bob with expressionless eyes, then looked at me. The detective wore tight jeans, shiny brown boots, and a thick leather jacket with a fleece collar. His swarthy face showed its usual dose of cynicism and anger. He undoubtedly did not like sitting in a warm hospital waiting room with a retarded kid and two pastors.

Pete told me Monica's parents were on their way from Iron Mountain in the Upper Peninsula. They would be here in a few hours. We then briefly discussed Monica's condition.

"Doctor says she's going to be fine, thank God," said Pete.

Rodriguez scowled at the mention of the deity. In our few encounters, I sized him up as an agnostic. The cop was in his late thirties.

Pete and I were about the same age. We shared many things, among them that we both came to the ministry in our late twenties. We'd been preachers a decade. "What happened?" I asked.

"Manny was out there," said Pete.

The detective leaned back, his head against the wall. He sniffed and wiped a hand over his mouth. A painting of a clown holding balloons hung from the wall above his head. "We don't know much until Miss Smit wakes up."

Pete leaned forward, fingers linked between his knees, and looked at the detective. "Manny, at least tell Truman what you can."

The detective's eyes rolled down. He had a bushy black mustache and nose decorated with blossoms of scar tissue. He cupped his thick-fingered hands in his lap. "She and her brother went to a house on Courtney, behind the Buttercup Bakery, about 11 p.m.. Miss Smit apparently left him in the car and entered the residence. When she did, she was attacked and thrown down the stairs into the basement." Simple, flat, police talk.

"How do you know this?" I asked. Bob's hand felt cold and clammy in mine.

"Tried and true police work, Turkstra," he said, giving me a chilly smile.

"How was it the police were called out, Manny?" said Pete, an edge in his voice.

Rodriguez rolled his shoulders, like a boxer about to bash his way into the ring. "The other woman. Called it in."

"Which woman?" I asked, sliding forward in my seat.

The detective cupped his hands over his crotch. The toes of his boots were tapping. I suspected he longed for a smoke. "Ditzy broad, works at the incense place."

"Aurora?"

Rodriguez nodded into his chest.

I knew her as another student of that class. I waited, letting go of Bob's clutch, listening to a faint hum in his throat. He smelled of stale sweat. "What was she doing there?"

"Far as we know, the three of them were on a mission of mercy."

I wanted to count to ten before speaking, but got to about two before blurting: "Why're you being such an ass?"

The detective's head lolled back, as if I'd landed a glancing punch.

"Please, Manny, this is Truman's fiancée," said Pete, whose firm, square face offered a weak smile. Always the peacemaker, I thought.

"Bottom line, investigation's just starting. I'd as soon wait before blabbing to the whole world what we know."

Pete nodded, his green-gray eyes prickling with anger. "Neither of us is the whole world."

The cop shrugged, not up to disagreeing.

We slouched into silence. I felt the hospital, coming alive for the day's duties, murmur around us. I wanted to know more and didn't like his predictable know-it-all attitude. "What did Tina Martin want?" I asked.

"You know her?" asked Rodriguez, perking up.

"It's not something I'd want anyone to know." As soon as I said it, I felt childish. But that didn't stop me from adding: "Everything being so frigging hush-hush."

Rodriguez sighed, looking away, ignoring me, staring at Bob. "Wish he could talk," he commented.

Aware he was being singled out, Bob smiled, then covered his mouth with his hand. He had a large square jaw, with no beard. It never grew on his smooth, milky skin.

"What did he see?" I asked.

"Maybe the whole kit and caboodle."

The detective stuck a finger in an ear, scraped around, leaned forward, glanced at the notebook on the floor. "Mayor says he likes to draw. I was hoping he could do a little Picasso of the killer."

"Not on demand," I said.

Rodriguez gave me a blistering look. Pinched together his mouth under the bush of his mustache.

The door to the room opened a few inches and the doctor dipped in his head. "Miss Smit is coming around." He addressed this to all of us. Then to Rodriguez: "But if you want to talk with her, detective, it's going to be a couple hours."

As the surgeon left, the cop slapped his knees and stood. He sniffed the room, as if checking for unseen clues, still eyeing Bob. "I'll be back."

My fiancée's brother, who had a syndrome that read like alphabet soup, blew out his lips. "Eat my shorts," he said.

The cop grinned, shook his head. "I'm hungry, bub, but not that hungry."

CHAPTER THREE

We watched Bob beat a frantic path through a leaning tower of hot cakes, two orders of sausage, a pile of hash browns and a bowl of mixed fruit.

"Nothing seems to have affected his appetite," observed Pete, hunched over a cup of tea. His garlic bagel sat untouched by his elbow. I'd eaten a bowl of cornflakes and an English muffin. I was on my third cup of coffee.

"Bob likes to eat," I said.

Pete smiled, a singular gesture that made his eyes squint and revealed a fine pair of white teeth. Beard stubbled his chin and cheeks. He looked tired. "Thanks," I said to him.

He lifted his head and looked at me curiously. "For being there," I added. He shrugged slightly, hands still around his cup. Finally, he took a sip, wrinkled his nose, shook his head. "Cold," he said.

Once Rodriguez left, Pete had watched Bob as I spent an hour hovering in Monica's room. But since she was still out of it, and doctors and nurses hadn't finished their tests and probes and whatever else, I left. We came to Prisms, the hospital's up-scale cafeteria, bustling with business at 8 a.m. on a Sunday.

Bob wiped a finger through syrup. If Monica was here, she would have grabbed his wrist and told him to stop. Bob had been living at a group home in Grand Rapids for the last three years, since Monica moved here from Chicago, where we had met. She had come to West Michigan to become youth pastor at an non-denominational church that allowed women to be ministers. I had followed and took a job, as it turned out, in the Christian Reformed Church congregation in which I'd grown up. Our relationship had been put on hold for a time and had only heated up again after a tragedy involving her former employer, a glitzy TV-style preacher who committed murder.

"I wish Rodriguez was more help," said Pete.

"He's just doing his job." It sounded as if I was defending him. Which I was. It turned out he had warmed up in the hallway outside the waiting room before he left. He said something that got me wondering. He told me no way was he going to let this one pass. Meaning what, I didn't know. Except I had an idea he was referring to Janet VanTol, Monica's student who drowned in the river. He hinted that others, including maybe Pete, had done some political covering up on that.

"You know," said Pete, "I'm going to ride him real hard to get to the bottom of this." His green eyes flashed, a sign he was angry. Or hiding something.

"I don't think he's going to need that."

Pete shook his head, not catching my drift.

"He as much as told me this is connected to Janet VanTol."

The mayor looked surprised, maybe a tad bothered.

"Rodriguez said things got swept under the rug with that." When he didn't react, I added: "That ring any bells?"

"What got swept under the rug?"

"Her drowning."

My head hurt. It was horrible seeing Monica on that bed; as bad to think about one of her students strangled. Then to also recall Janet. Her body floating in the river, pulled out by late-night salmon fishermen. Supposedly drunk and distraught, she'd plunged off the Sixth Street Bridge. No one saw it, but that was the story. Until TV grabbed it and tried to make it more. "What do you think, Pete?"

"What do you mean?"

"Did what happened to Janet turn into this?"

He spoke to the table. "We need to talk to Monica."

I sipped tepid coffee. Bob tapped a spoon against his empty juice glass, as if trying to get newlyweds to smooch. I sensed my friend avoiding me; his mind closing.

"Do you think the cops dropped the ball with Janet VanTol?" That had been the focus of the news stories on TV-8. Crystal Franklin, a reporter who knew Monica, had hammered hard on a supposed connection between the death and an underground movement of angry men in our church trying to prevent women from being preachers. For years women in our small conservative denomination had been trying to win approval to be ministers. I had dismissed Crystal's comments as hogwash. Monica had said there was something to it. Since she was hoping to get ordained in our church, and had been thwarted, I thought she had been blowing it out of proportion. There was no underground group, I had thought. Until now.

"Is there something here, Pete?" I added.

He shook his head, still not looking at me. "We need to see how this washes out," he said, like a good politician.

Bob spun his empty plate, picked up the fruit bowl, licked the inside. He said, "Jelly bellies for Nancy."

I took the bowl from him, handed him a napkin, which he started to shred into tiny pieces. "Any chance you can take Tarzan to church with you?" I asked.

Pete had already been planning, since I was supposed to be at the monastery until late afternoon, to preach at the storefront, his old stomping grounds. As for Bob, he loved church, especially the singing. He swayed and smiled and clapped like a charismatic with ants in his pants.

"No problem," said Pete.

I drank the muddy dregs of my coffee. Pete swirled tea in its cup. Bob started to stick wads of napkin in his pocket. I let him go and stretched back in my chair, watching white-clad men and women carry trays heaped with food to nearby tables. I knew my friend was holding something back. I thought about the course Monica taught. She talked about it a lot, particularly the powerful emotions the dozen or so students, all women, shared. I believed the course turned into group therapy as well as became a profound exercise for them in debating how they could assume a place in a church that for 130 years had essentially ignored their gifts.

"Do you think, Pete, there's some group responsible for this?"

The mayor's eyes rolled toward the ceiling. He rubbed his chin. Bob rocked back and forth in his chair, fingers splayed on his chest. It looked as though he was riding an imaginary Ferris wheel. "Like they said on TV?" Pete's face was sharp-edged, the eyes defeated, as he looked at me.

"For the sake of argument, let's say TV had it right."

He gave me a funny look, as if he had a bad taste in his mouth. His eyes grew intense. He glanced at his tea and bagel. He seemed uncertain, mulling thoughts. Finally, he said: "A cop I know, not Rodriguez, saw something last night."

When I said nothing, my friend went on: "He was at that house. Where Monica went. In fact, he found Tina. He told me, and this shook him up almost as much as seeing the body. He said someone wrote, in lipstick, the letters 'p' and 'k' on the wall above her bed."

I didn't get it at first, or if I did it struck me as crazy. But I caught on, or so I figured. "Promise Keepers?"

"The thought comes to mind."

"Why didn't you tell me this before?"

"I just remembered."

I was familiar with the PKs. I'd been to their first big rally in Michigan a year before at the Pontiac Silverdome. They were a group of good men trying to do right, by themselves and by the women they loved, with the help of God. "C'mon, Pete. How would they be involved?"

The mayor shook his head.

"No, really. Someone is dragging them in?"

"Truman, I'm just telling you what I heard."

We were silent a minute or so. Bob had climbed off the carnival ride and picked up his plate again. He now pretended to doll up his face, using the plate for a mirror. He licked a

15

finger, wiped it under one eye. I leaned across toward Pete. As mayor, I knew he was close to the murkier inner workings of our city, a place that Dutch immigrants in our church had helped shaped. "I suppose this will be on TV on the noon news. The PKs are killing and maiming our women?"

He stuck a finger in the hole of his bagel, as if probing for something. Then he picked it up and took a dry crunch. Mouth moving in slow-motion, he said: "I wouldn't put it past some to organize and . . ."

"Kill women?"

Pete sighed. I saw a hint of guilt in his eyes. I ignored the faces from surrounding tables that turned our way. Even Bob stopped brushing his teeth with a forefinger to give me a listen. I said in a softer voice: "I'm not buying conspiracy theories."

"A couple minutes ago, you talked about sweeping things under the rug."

"Not the same as pretending the Promise Keepers are the KKK."

Pete hunched over the table, as if drawn down by heavy thoughts. "Then who is doing it?"

I bobbed my head, side to side, thinking on it. There were rich men in the CRC, some of them PKs, who wouldn't lose sleep if the women kept their aprons on until Christ came back and maybe longer. But turning to murder to stop the changes that were undoubtedly coming, no way. "Doesn't compute."

Pete gave me a helpless, remorseful look.

I was going to ask him something else, but Bob took that moment to pick up his water and pour it on his head.

CHAPTER FOUR

I couldn't help thinking about Homer Simpson as Monica answered the questions posed by the Grand Rapids Police detective. In one of the cartoon shows, Homer, the patriarch of his laughably dysfunctional family, was asked by son Bart what religion he belonged to. Taking ice cream out of the freezer, Homer paused to think, then answered: "The one with all the well-meaning rules that don't work in reality—Christianity."

I had laughed when Monica and I watched the show. But I wasn't smiling now. Her story, related as she lay prostrate and battered on the ICU bed, was about her faith, our church, and how the profane world often made a mockery out of our "love-thy-neighbor, turn-the-other-cheek" beliefs.

Pete had taken Bob to church and I had been sitting with Monica for an hour or so when Rodriguez returned. Poked his head in the door with an "is-it-OK-if -we-talk" look on his face. Monica had been awake since I'd come in from breakfast and I'd warned her he'd be back. She had given me a shrug. So, I motioned him in.

He had stood at the head of the bed. I remained in a chair by the front, holding Monica's free hand, which was much smaller and colder than her brother's.

In fits and starts, with one warning from a nurse to make it quick and not tire herself out, she told him what she knew. As she spoke, her face turned to the detective, I kept marveling at her strength, even in this situation. But I knew she was mad. Even beaten as she was, she mustered all her energy to communicate the story.

It boiled down to this: She had taken Bob from the group home for dinner on 28th Street. When they finished, they

17

drove to her apartment. They were watching Olympic try-outs for swimming on ESPN about 11 p.m. when she got a call from Tina Martin. Her former student. She wanted to talk. She was in trouble. Bad trouble. Could Monica please come over? she asked. Monica didn't want to go out. What did she need to talk about?

"Tina said it was about Janet. She knew something and had to get it off her chest," relayed Monica, her hand pressing mine, her voice shaky, eyes half-lidded, probably from the drugs for pain.

"What did she need to . . . get off her chest?" asked Rodriguez in a quiet voice.

Monica shook her head. "She said she'd tell me when I got there."

At his end of the bed, Rodriguez leaned one arm on a rail that rose up and anchored the pulley helping to hold Monica's broken leg. He'd been watching her as she spoke, every so often checking me out, as if asking was it all right to let her keep talking. "There was nothing else?" he prodded.

"Not really. Except . . ." Monica bit her lip, her swollen face showing no expression I found familiar. "There was something about a boyfriend. That they had seen something involving Janet."

The cop nodded. "She name this boyfriend?"

"Billy something."

I wanted to jump in with my own questions. What had they seen? Had they been by the bridge that night? I recalled that someone had mentioned that Janet was driven there and dropped off by a person she'd been drinking with at a bar. Had that been Tina and maybe this boyfriend?

"Why did she call you, Miss Smit?"

Monica shook her head, slowly, side to side, the discolored cheeks and puffy eyes making my stomach clench. With anger. With fear. "Maybe because she trusted me?" As her voice trailed off, it cracked.

Rodriguez nodded, his face impassive, his leather jacket

18

unzipped, revealing a plaid shirt with a button-down collar. He seemed to be taking in every word and nuance. I was impressed with the calm, kind way he had with her. "This boyfriend, she say where he was?"

"I think gone. That was part of what was scaring her, I think."

Rodriguez wiped a finger along his mustache. Soft light fell in the window behind him. "Nothing on where he was?"

"No." Monica's eyes then rolled in my direction. Her face was swollen, the lips parched, but the tubes were gone. "How's Bob?"

"He thinks he's on vacation."

She smiled, but winced. Her hand still in mine, Monica lapsed into silence, her eye lids fluttering. Her hand slowly released its grasp. Her eyes flipped open a second. "Anything else, detective?"

"Not now."

Monica sighed long and hard, turned toward me and gave me a weak smile, as if pleased I was there. I cupped the side of her face gently, and felt the anger, no, it was rage, thud in me. Which is when I thought about Homer. Because by then I was thinking how this woman, my future wife, held to Christianity at its prickly core. Even though she was tired last night, even though she wasn't sure what she faced, she went out on a winter night to help someone else. A former student. A woman torn up, it sounded like, by something she saw.

No, Homer, I was also thinking. You got it wrong. This was a religion, at least when practiced by a few believers, that was no theory. It was real and it worked. It's just that at times you got broken but good for the reaching out you did.

The detective now stepped away from his perch by her elevated leg. "Some woman you have there, Reverend." He stared at her with respect and even a kind of longing on his slingshot of a face.

"You married?" I asked.

"Twice."

"Kids?"

"One."

"Living with you?"

He gave me a cross-eyed glance. Looked almost defensive. "Macho man like me playing Mr. Mom?"

I chuckled, heard Monica sniff and mumble.

"She dropped right off, didn't she?" said the detective.

"I'm surprised you got as much as you did."

"Without even having to take out the rubber hose."

I stood. A nurse had come in and was checking the monitor bolted to the ceiling and blinking out Monica's vital signs.

We stepped into the hall, where late morning rounds were in full progress. The floor looked shiny as an ice rink. "Where is Bob?"

"At church."

"Quite the kid."

We leaned side by side against the wall on the other side of Monica's room, which was separated from us by a thick pane of glass. After a moment, we strolled to the end of the hall to a window that looked out at the north end of the city. The view showed the Belknap/Lookout Neighborhood, a tumble-down collection of houses situated across the concrete ditch of I-196, the Gerald R. Ford Expressway, named after our former President. A mural of former city fathers graced the side of the cemented hill across the way.

"What do you figure happened once Monica got there?" I asked. The neighborhood in which she had been hurt was a mile or so to our left, across another freeway, in another part of the city where poverty smoldered.

Rodriguez's face was brutally cleanshaven around the cheeks and chin. It looked as if he plucked his beard stubble by stubble, unlike Pete who always wore a shadow of bristly hair. He folded his arms over his chest, turned from the window. Spoke to the hallway in front of him. "I think she went in just after our

20

perpetrator got done with Tina. I think Monica saw him. He went after her and shoved her down the steps. I'm thinking he would have gone down there to finish her off expect for Mr. Big coming in and scaring him off. This Aurora babe wasn't far behind by that time either. Looks like the killer went out the side door and didn't look back."

"Monica didn't say anything about seeing the guy. You think she did?" If so, I was thinking the madman might try coming to the hospital for another house call.

The cop shrugged, turning in on himself again, brushing me off.

"Pete said earlier that Monica told the officers this guy had a ski mask on?"

"It's what we hear."

"So no one saw him?"

"Looks like."

"How's Aurora fit in?" I asked.

"Need to talk to her."

I watched trucks and cars zip by on the road named after the guy who was in Nixon's back pocket. I had to be thankful for Bob and Aurora. Without them, Monica would have been killed. But this made me boil even more. Then I thought of Pete: What did he know? "What about this boyfriend, any sign of him?" I asked.

"None."

"How's he fit?"

The detective made a face. I was pushing it, his expression said. "We'll see."

I decided to try a theory I'd been cooking up. "You think he took the money and ran?"

"What money?"

"Sounding to me like Tina and whoever he is were putting the squeeze on someone. Likely the person who shoved Janet in the river. Blackmail, maybe?" I looked over my shoulder at him.

Rodriguez scraped the floor with the toe of his cowboy boot. A beeper on his belt went off. He checked the message. Seemed to ignore it. "Very astute, Reverend," he said. "Where you getting this bullshit speculation?"

I turned to face him, feeling the city rumble at the edges of the window, as if trying to break in on us with important information. As for blackmail, it fit. It was, after all, one of the longest standing of human activities. "You don't like me very much, do you?" I asked the cop.

"Murder investigations are not popularity contests."

"You consider me a suspect?"

"I'll double-check this monastery story."

I felt blood rush up my neck, throttling into my head. "You've got to be kidding?"

A flurry of nurses and doctors trotted past, pushing a gurney on which an old man with a huge bandage over his chest was strapped. IV bottles swung from a pole being rolled by a young woman bringing up the rear. They adeptly turned into a room at the end of the hall and began plugging the patient into machines.

"Does it look like I'm joking?" His jaw tilted in my direction. I thought of clipping it with an elbow. A fine basketball move, one for which I was noted, and for which I fouled out many times at Redeemer College. Rodriguez looked so smug, I wanted to hack him off even more. I thought of a way. It had to do with shoving my way in on him, but not with arms flying. "You might want to know something. The mayor asked me to help you guys out." Which wasn't exactly true.

"Oh?" A nasty twist in his voice and curl in his mouth.

"He's convinced it's all tied to our church and that it involves someone, or a group, who are trying to keep women from having any say so."

Rodriguez chuckled, not happily. "I grew up Seventh Day Adventist. Women mostly run that church."

"It's not happening in the CRC."

22

Rodriguez examined his nails, lifted and brushed something off the toe of his boot. "Cute theory."

"But holds no weight?"

"You tell me."

"I will, after I look into it."

The cop licked his lips, as if he wanted to bite me. "I gotta go. Tell your girlfriend I'll be back?" Icy, his tone now.

"Of course."

He tugged up the zipper of his jacket, stuck his hands in the front pockets of his jeans. "Just one thing."

I waited.

"We really don't need your help, especially if it's coming from the mayor."

"Why are you so hard on him?"

Rodriguez shifted side to side, as if showing off his tight jeans, or maybe finding room in them for his thick leg muscles. "Ask Joan of Arc why he tried to put the lid on that floater."

CHAPTER FIVE

Sliding along the winding asphalt road in Allendale, I noticed a few bands of orange hanging in the sky above the rolling countryside in the west. On my left I caught glimpses of lights flickering across the flat campus of Grand Valley State University. Free-ranging weariness, heavy as a log, filled my head. It had been a long day. "Bob, you up?"

I heard deep breath suck in, coarse, rattle-sounding and noticed Bob's head hanging limp over his chest in the seat beside me. "We're nearly there," I told him.

His Indian-head-nickel face, in profile, was a fallen slab of flesh. He smelled a little like a wet tarp. Pete and his wife had taken him to their place after church and had brought him back to the hospital about 4 p.m. I wanted to talk to Pete then, but he rushed off. But my friend did tell me that from the time he left until he returned, Bob had been hard to handle. Normally excited in church, he'd sat on a chair and tried to rip up the mimeographed song books. At Pete's house for lunch, he didn't eat, just stared at his food. Once he got to the hospital, he spent awhile with his father and stepmother and then I offered to bring him back here.

"You know, Bob, your stepmom's a real piece of work." He mumbled something into his chest, his shoulders turned down like falling rocks. "You ever see the soap opera she was in?"

Miranda Moss—she still went by her stage name—returned a few years ago to her home in the Upper Peninsula, where she met Ron Smit, a widower who'd just retired from his job as a biology professor at Michigan Technological University. Back then, Bob lived in a foster home near Baraga. Soon after the marriage, Monica convinced her dad to move her brother to

Grand Rapids to be closer to her.

"Didn't she play some kind of vampire?" I asked Bob.

He stirred slightly, raised his head and looked around, dopey-eyed.

I slowed and turned up a long driveway toward a house set atop a small hill surrounded by evergreens. "In fact, she looked a little like Morticia today, don't you think?"

Bob gurgled in his throat. "Jesus shaves," he replied.

"Got a point."

"Born to boogie," he added, his blocky face drooping with seriousness.

"I may argue with you on that, partner," I said.

Laura Lee Jennings stepped onto the porch, arms folded, hair piled on top of her head as I stopped and turned off the engine.

"Big Hulk, kicking butt," said Bob, staring intently at me. One side of his face slumped, as if he'd had a stroke. Rolled in his fist was a comic book, entitled *The Prophet*. Pete's oldest son had given it to him.

"Hulk's not here right now," I told him.

"Drinking Coke?" he asked.

"That either."

I marveled at his mind. Monica told me several times the obscure name of the problem he had. I wondered if his twisted brain was trying to form the proper words for him to tell me what happened on Courtney.

"Let's take you in." Getting out, I nearly bumped into Laura Lee, who was Monica's third cousin.

"Reverend," she said in a breathy voice.

"I've got Bob," I told her needlessly, feeling the evening chill snap around us, noticing that my passenger had opened his comic book.

"How's Monica?"

"Up and eating and in a different room talking to her dad and Miranda when we left."

Laura made a face. "The actress is there?"

"In spades."

"We should be there for Monica."

I touched her shoulder, a pastor to the core, and told her to save it. A couple days from now Monica would want the company.

At that moment, the front door opened and her large husband loomed in the shadows. "Is that Calvin with Bob?" My first name was Calvin, after you-know-who from Geneva. The middle one came from my Roman Catholic mother, a die-hard Harry Truman fan. Quite the Democratic-Republican one-two punch, my parents. Election years were never dull around our farm.

"Hi, James."

"You need a hand?"

I checked. The lug had fallen asleep again, the comic book spread on his chest. Lips flapping. "Dynamite would help."

Sitting at the round wood table in their bright country-style kitchen, I watched Bob trundle off to bed, a monster of a man with a back that hardly fit the hallway. James led the way; his head nearly brushed the ceiling.

The smell of fresh-brewed coffee filled the room. I'd agreed to stay for a cup when it became clear the Jennings had something on their minds. "Cream and sugar, Reverend?"

"Black's fine."

She placed the cup in front of me. Steam rose in twisting fingers, scooting toward my nose. I realized again how tired I felt. Closed my eyes a second, saw a car in flames and Monica in distress. Got them open straight off.

"Would you like something to eat?" she asked.

I declined, even though my gut yawned, unfilled since a hamburger at the hospital in the afternoon.

James returned, his scrubbed, pink face glossy with sweat. "Greg's trying to find the dirty movies again," he told his wife.

She shot me a glance, a faint coloring in her cheeks. "We have cable, pastor, and there's a blacked-out station with lots of huffing and puffing in the background."

I smiled and shrugged. I'm not the Dove Foundation, the family group that makes sure the only movies we Christians watch are pale and drab as spilled milk.

She gave me a weak smile and turned to James. "Did you turn it off?"

He pulled the tuner box out of his back pocket. James then sat across from me. "What's this about the Hulk?" he asked.

"You tell me," I replied.

James shook his head. "He and Monica must have gone through hell."

"Not to mention that poor girl whose house it was," added his wife.

I drank coffee, scalding it down, wishing to keep my emotions at bay, just like my farmer dad. "I keep wondering if Bob's trying to tell us something, with this Hulk business?"

James shrugged. "Who knows?" He then folded his hands in front of him on the table. Laura Lee leaned against the sink, coffee cup in hand. I noticed pink stitching along the edges of the pockets of her jeans. She once told me I had a preaching voice that sounded a little like country singer George Jones when he was young, but she'd been tipsy at the time. Like George Jones was all of the time. Or had he kicked the habit?

There was a wariness in the air. Laura Lee gazed hard at her husband. "We were wondering, pastor," she said, without looking at me.

James nodded, as if he agreed that they were wondering.

I waited for them to tell me what.

"We thought about it when we saw the news," she said.

I heard voices in the back of the house, some laughter, a door shutting, water running.

"You see," she said, "it got us, especially James, thinking."

James gave me a guilty nod, refolding his nicked and dirt-

27

peppered hands. He worked full-time as a truck mechanic in a garage across from the university. "Well, you tell Calvin, hon."

James sat up straight, hung his arms behind him, and sighed through his fleshy nose. "The woman on there, the blonde one, mentioned there might be some group tied with what happened to Monica."

That would be Crystal. I had thought of turning on the evening news, but hadn't wanted to disturb Monica with it.

Laura Lee poured coffee in my empty cup with a waitressy flourish, one hand on her rump, the other deftly handling the pot. I sipped, eyeing James through the steam.

"She said men in our church, you know, are working in secret to, I guess they called it, thwart the women."

I watched him carefully, feeling warmth on my upper lip from the coffee. I wondered why this story had touched such a tender spot. I had the idea he was about to tell me.

"Anyhow, you see," he said, looking at his wife, as if for help. She had turned to the sink and was fiddling with dishes. When she didn't respond, he leaned forward in his chair and wiped a hand across the glossy top of the table, as if trying to rub clear the right words to say. "I'm wondering," he said, looking at me, "what you're thinking on that is, Pastor?"

I gave him a non-committal shrug.

"Doesn't it make sense?"

"I'm wondering why you're asking, James."

The hand kept rubbing. He peered at the smudges he made. "What it is, a year or so back I was on Synod, you know?"

Synod was the big bureaucratic blowout for our church, held every year at nearby Redeemer College in Holland. It was our annual business meeting, a time when a bunch of my brethren speechified at great length about how God wanted us to handle our affairs. Pastors and lay people went as elected delegates. I often considered it an early summer convention for well-meaning blowhards.

28

"I was there when we voted for the first time to let the women be ordained," James said, looking pale and stricken. Laura Lee had stepped over and stood behind him, a hand on his shoulder. Standing by her man. Like Tammy, who hung by George for a couple minutes.

I prodded him with a nod.

"Maybe this isn't related, and I'd never ever bring it up, except for that business on the TV." James wiped a stubby forefinger in a circle on the table top. "Anyhow, a couple weeks before Synod, I get this call. From a banker friend deciding a second mortgage for us."

I sat up, my attention keen.

"He more or less let me know the mortgage was a sure bet if I made sure to, you know, vote right."

Sitting at long tables, the delegates used their reading of the Bible to set church policy. For the better part of a decade, they'd been battling whether to let women preach. There had been one setback after another, but slowly the women had been gaining ground. Although we still had no women pastors in our church, the Synod before last had agreed to let women have some additional power, but still kept them muzzled from the pulpit. But this year's meeting was supposed to put the cap on the deal and finally let women preach. Monica was in line to become one of the first.

"He blackmailed you, James?" I asked, thinking about Tina's boyfriend.

"Something like that."

"For one vote?"

"Yes, sir."

I watched him. The hands linked, the knuckles stretched taut. Even though I'd been a CRC minister for a decade, I'd spent most of the time in Chicago, away from the political center of our denomination. Maybe, I began to wonder, I'd missed some of the more disgusting dirty dealings as a result. "This friend, who is it?" I asked.

"He died last spring."

"Who was it, James?"

He shook his head, not ready to offer everything.

"And he was part of a secret group?"

"He never said so."

"But you had the feeling?"

He made a sad gesture with his head, telling me yes.

Laura Lee put her other hand on her husband's shoulder. Protecting him. My mind raced to catch up with this development. I wondered if the TV reporter had talked to others, like James, who sketched such a tale. "This group formed to fight the women issue?"

He shrugged.

"How long had they been at it?"

James shook his head. "No idea, Calvin."

OK, I thought. We've got this group of malcontents, out buying votes on an issue they ultimately lost. It was possible. "Was this group into other things?"

"I don't know."

I nodded as I thought. But connections slipped away. We're talking about murder here, gentlemen, I said to myself. A key question had to be how many were in it, if there was a group, and who. I asked James.

"Sorry, I can't answer that."

I placed the cup in its saucer. Tried to see the shape of this in the whorled grain of the table. Maybe James saw answers in there. I sure didn't. I had another question. "Did you have any sense this group was tied to the Promise Keepers?"

James blinked, looking surprised.

Maybe we had two things at work, a couple groups, or maybe one, or maybe none. I knew of dark currents that ran under the surface of our church. I always hoped right thinking and true spirituality ruled the day, but conversations such as this made me sick. I wondered about any person or group who held a mortgage over someone's head to get them to vote the right

30

way. Which brought me to a final question. I didn't want to ask. But then again, I did. "So, did you get the mortgage?"

Both were silent a moment, as if rebuked, which made me feel petty. "Yes, pastor," said Laura Lee, "we did."

CHAPTER SIX

Rolling into the S-curve going south on U.S. 131, I noticed a swooping rainbow of color on my left. Blues, yellows, and reds above the old buildings down there.

Sliding off the Wealthy Street exit, I caught a glimpse of police, rescue and fire vehicles behind the new arena. Once off and stopped at the light, I could see better. A crowd had formed around the flashing lights, traffic had backed up on Ionia Avenue, and cops were directing cars up Weston Street and onto South Division.

On the way here, I'd gotten tacos at a restaurant in Standale. As I swallowed the last bite, I decided to take a look. Some sixth sense, plus the fact that my ministry center wasn't too far from the commotion, convinced me to stick my nose in this stew.

By the clock on my dashboard, I saw it was almost 8 p.m. I'd called Monica's room on the way in from the foster home. Her father answered and said she was sleeping. I told him I had to stop at the church and would be there by 9. He said fine.

Parking along Ionia, I wiped taco sauce from my mouth with a napkin and started along the sidewalk toward the activity. I drew my Bulls parka around me and yanked my Promise Keepers baseball cap down on my head. I was aware that I had grabbed the hat out of the back of my truck and stuck it on almost as a way of showing the world I didn't buy them being involved.

The air held a sharp chill. Brittle chunks of snow clung to the ground and in doorways of buildings. This was one of the oldest parts of Grand Rapids, the old railroad yards. Lately, it had been undergoing a massive transition, with the work on a new arena and opening of yuppie coffee houses and swinging bars. I didn't like it, since the gentrification was pushing the poor people, the ones who lived here, out.

Looking ahead at the cars, lights and people, I saw a man approach. Swaying slightly, his coat billowing behind him. One of the urban refugees. "Hey, Ramon," I said.

He stopped a couple feet from me. The tar-colored eyes tried to focus. He had the slow, tentative presence of a guy trying to protect his high. "S'up," he replied.

He'd been in our storefront for a few services and occasionally, by court order, attended the AA meetings in the sanctuary. "What's going on?"

"I'm cool."

"I mean down there."

Ramon stared at me a couple seconds, as if waiting for my mouth to move again. He blew on his hands, puffing out steam. His coat hung around him like a Darth Vader cape. "They found a body."

"Where?"

"In a dumspter."

Eerie lights continued to twist, throwing elongated shadows on the buildings and streets. I shivered, hands inside my jacket pockets. I didn't like the sound of this. "Preacher's down there," said Ramon. "Says it's all cut up in packages, like."

"What is?"

Ramon kept blowing on his hands. His smoothed-back black hair shone with a slick sheen. He had thick, Mick Jagger lips and a forehead crisscrossed with scars marks from, he once told me, being shoved through a window in a bar in Topeka, Kansas.

"What's cut up?"

"The body, man. Preacher says it's chopped up for the meat market."

I tried to imagine something so gruesome. Found it hard to figure, although I'd seen a lot as a paramedic. "Preacher saw something?" I asked.

"Says the devil did it."

Par for the course. Preacher, a gimpy street person, was big on devils. "Who is it?"

"Got me."

I noticed a flash of anxiety, maybe the drugs dimming, in his eyes. "You OK, Ramon?"

He held the hands before his mouth, no longer blowing. "You got a buck?"

"Stop by the church. Have Florence give you one after AA."

He sniffed. Florence was our secretary. Ramon knew she'd make him pray before she gave him any money, even if that was contrary to AA rules. He continued on, swaying as he went, the long coat spread out behind him like the wings of a Stealth bomber.

Preacher was talking to Manny Rodriguez, peering up from his wheelchair with a beaked nose, pointed chin and predatory eyes. I couldn't push through the crowd to get near enough to hear what was being said. The detective's body language told me their conversation wasn't going very well.

Beyond them, flush against the back of the building that housed the Herkimer Hotel, I saw a swarm of cops and other official-looking folks at work around a dumpster. A great deal of milling was going on. People drawn to gore, gawking, maybe trying to get their own thoughts around a body in butcher paper. I took a moment to look at the blank city sky. There was nothing up there for me.

I looked back to the activity and saw Dr. Bernie Fritz, a medical examiner. He worked during the day as a pediatrician and moonlighted at night by pronouncing dead people dead.

I heard a beep behind me as an ambulance wove through the crowd of mostly inner city loners, dopers, down-and-outers and a few lower-class working stiffs. Among them, I also spotted a couple skinny prostitutes, a fat pimp and the custodian at the Indian Assemblies of God church. I stood to the side to let the Mercy emergency rig wind through, on its way to the dumpster.

I sidled over to Frank, the janitor at the Indian church, which worshipped in a former tuxedo shop down the street from my place. "What happened?"

Frank wore a bulky brown overcoat. He was an Odawa Indian who served time for murdering his ex-wife before coming to the Heartside area, where he got religion in our church and then wandered over to one that better suited his needs. "You know Esther?"

"Peoples?"

"She was looking in the garbage and saw the blood." Frank spoke in a low, melodious voice that made me think of soft drums thumping. He liked to dance in the pow-wows they had in the summer at Riverside Park.

"Where's she now?"

"Cops took her."

"Who's dead?" I asked.

Frank's bumpy face turned in my direction. His bad right eye wandered; the other settled on me with a question in it.

"The body?"

"I don't know, Calvin, but it is very bad."

I noticed Bernie Fritz hightailing it through the crowd, moving toward his black BMW, parked with one wheel up on the curb in front of an abandoned railroad depot. The city planned to tear it down for parking for the new arena, whose huge glassy skeleton stood down the way, brittle steel and a domed top.

I trotted over and intercepted Fritz a couple feet from his car. "What do you have, Bernie?"

We'd gone to high school together in Holland. He'd then gone to college and medical school and ended up as a doctor for kids. I took a much more roundabout path before returning to the old sod. "Turkstra."

"You mind filling me in?" I added.

35

He turned toward his fancy car, flicked electricity at it from a little device in his hand. The lock on his door snapped. Back to me, he smiled, then frowned. "Hey, I'm sorry. I heard about your girlfriend. That's her, isn't it, got hurt?"

"Monica. She's my fiancée."

"Is she all right?"

"She will be, the doctors say."

He nodded, a doctor himself, and glanced behind me toward the dumpster.

"What's in there?" I asked.

The chill air felt heavy and damp. The cobblestone street on which we stood was glossy with the makings of ice. He nibbled his lower lip and bent back his head before fixing me with a full frontal stare. Then he nodded, as if agreeing to some inner urge. "You should talk to the detectives, Calvin."

"Why?"

His jawed twitched. He was dressed in a puffy bluish parka, a stocking cap, dark slacks and running shoes. "You just should."

"Why?" I heard my voice echo in the air.

Fritz shoved his hands deep in the pockets of his overcoat. He shook his head. "Sounds like the body, what there is of it, belongs to the kid involved in the deal where your fiancée was hurt."

"What?"

He nodded solemnly, gazing back to the dumpster.

I turned to the crowd, now dispersing, and watched the ambulance jockeying for better position. "The boyfriend?"

"Ask Rodriguez."

The ambulance had stopped, its lights sweeping the area, and I saw Rodriguez step up the talk to the driver. Preacher was a bent form, riding across the street in his wheelchair, about twenty yards from us. I looked back at Bernie. "It's an ugly one," he said.

After he climbed in his car to go, I edged closer to the scene. Rodriguez glanced at me. I looked away. A few seconds

36

later a uniform cop approached and told me the detective wanted to talk to me.

I glanced back. Rodriguez was on his haunches, facing away from me. The cop led me to the yellow crime scene tape, looped it up and let me enter their inner sanctum, where clues lay and the blood congealed.

My feet crunched stones as I stepped behind the detective. He remained still, looking down at something on the ground. The ambulance idled to our right. The dumpster stood to the left, its lid open. Someone snapped a couple pictures, the flash popping like quick flames. The dream licked my memory.

Rodriguez turned and squinted up at me. His expression changed suddenly, grew grim. "Very nice, Turkstra."

"What?'

"The hat."

I took it off, examined it. The logo showed two hands, one black and one white clenching in a Christian male power embrace. The letters PK were stenciled in the background. "What about it?"

Rodriguez jerked his neck, ordering me to join him, close to the ground. The night fell around us, driving down a wet chill. One knee on the cold stones, as if praying but not really, I could see a dim lump. Next to it, something was laid out. It was brighter. Soiled clothing, maybe.

"Look familiar," he said, switching on a flashlight.

At first, I couldn't tell what he was showing me. Then it clicked. Hair, stunned features, a sheer flat cut. A piece of clothing nearby. Much of it stained. But the logo smoothed out for the world to see. My stomach swayed, but held. So did I. Had he done this as a test? "Recognize it?" he asked.

"You spoil a crime scene just to get my goat?" I asked.

Rodriguez shot me an angry glance. His face was full of fury and yet also a calm commitment. "Answer me, goddammit!"

"Which," I said, trying not to gag, "the T-shirt or the head?"

CHAPTER SEVEN

The room was quiet except for the occasional click and faint beeping of the machine monitoring Monica's vital signs. In a tall-backed chair by the head of her bed, I watched her sleep, calm and innocent-looking in the awful aftermath of her battering. It had been a long day. I had arrived at the hospital more than a dozen hours before. My head hammered with sluggishness; my body ached for sleep. But those lights from the vehicles by the dumpster, and especially that expressionless head and blood-sopped T-shirt, kept me awake.

I'd been in the room with her for a half-hour. Her father left almost as soon as I'd arrived. His wife was already back at their motel. He told me he'd go take a shower and be right back. I said not to bother; I'd stay the night. He could return in the morning.

I yawned and stretched in the chair, allowing my legs to unravel a bit. In doing so, I kicked the side of Monica's bed, making metal rattle. Her eyes opened and turned to me. "Hi." She smiled faintly.

"Sorry."

"What?"

"I didn't mean to wake you."

She watched me with mild amusement. "What time is it?"

"Almost midnight."

"What day?"

"Be Monday morning soon."

Her eyes closed. A man in a bluish uniform came in and checked Monica's pulse and the bandage on her stomach. He then gently re-positioned the sling that held her leg in place.

"My name's Tom, by the way," he said in a soft voice. "I'll be her nurse tonight."

I nodded. "Her father said the doctor told him she's doing well."

"That's right." He measured the amount of liquid in Monica's IV bottle, paused, gazed at me with steady eyes. "I couldn't help seeing the news. About the dumpster."

I put a finger to my lips.

Tom checked Monica, realizing what I was trying to say. He gestured with his eyes to the hallway.

I checked Monica, slipped out, wondering what he wanted. "She doesn't know about it yet," I told him.

He gave me an apologetic nod, pressed his lips together. He had long brown hair, tied in back in a ponytail, small eyes and a pointed nose. A studded diamond, or facsimile thereof, decorated his left earlobe.

"I think she's been through enough for the time being."

He glanced down the hall and back at me. "I know what you mean. Only thing I'm wondering. Do you think it would be wise to have one of our security people sit outside her room?"

One of the doctors asked earlier in the afternoon and I'd said no. I had been planning to do that, more or less. But, that head in the dumpster put an even more sinister slant on things. I had to admit: The killer might think Monica could identify him and come looking for her.

I knew that neither the hospital nor the cops were telling anyone for now that Monica was even at Butterworth. Still, getting more security didn't sound like a bad idea. I don't know why it happened then, but it hit me like a ton of broken concrete how vicious this killer was. Assuming it was one person. I nearly lost my balance, as if punched in the stomach by this realization, and had to lean against the wall for support. "We can use all the help we can get."

"Let me check."

As he bustled off, I took a few minutes to get my composure.

Back inside, Monica turned to me as I sat. In the dim light, her face looked puffy and gray. "What dumpster?"

I couldn't speak for a moment. I thought of the time more than a year before when I had been shot in the shoulder by a renegade sheriff's detective named Slade. Monica had been there. Another cop had then shot Slade. What I recall was the stark fear on Monica's face that night when it seemed that Slade was going to kill us. The fear was back now, showing through the bruises and the swelling. I felt a knot of emotion rise in my throat; my eyes got hot. I took in a few breaths to steady myself.

"Turk?" she said. "What dumpster?"

I didn't want to tell her, not tonight at least. Let her sleep. Deal with it in the morning. "They found some clothes that might've belonged to Janet's boyfriend."

I had no idea if she believed me or not. I've always been terrible at lying, so I looked away at the window, against which fat fists of snow were smacking.

"Do you think he's dead, too?"

Taking her hand in mine, I shook my head. "Who knows?"

Monica, rolling her face forward and staring at the ceiling, said: "Dear God."

Lethal silence filled the room. I watched the monitor glow as it soundlessly reflected the beating of her heart. Then it beeped and clicked again. But Monica still said nothing. I felt a little helpless in my chair. I leaned closer, thinking of how I followed Monica to West Michigan after she finished seminary at the University of Chicago. She came here to take a job at the huge non-denominational church that allowed women to be ministers. But soon after I arrived, we broke up.

Instead of returning to Chicago, where I did storefront ministry work, I took a temporary position in a church in Overisel, a farming community near where I grew up. The deal involving the crooked sheriff's detective Slade drew us back together. "Monica?"

She spoke to the ceiling in a surprisingly firm voice: "You've got to do something, Turkstra."

I glanced around the room, afraid she meant something medical.

"You can't let this go on." Her head flopped in my direction. Even in the darkly lit room, her green eyes shone and danced with, I sensed, love for me. Or maybe it was the morphine dripping into her arm.

"What?"

"All of this killing."

Hospital rooms can be so private and yet so public all at once. Right then, it seemed as if we were the only ones in the world, and she was trying with all of her energy to communicate to me her needs.

"You have to help that detective," she said. "Rodriguez. The one in the leather coat," she added for some reason.

I touched her cheek as tenderly as I could, felt its heat and drew back. "My place is here."

"No!"

I had to hand it to her. Even in a leg splint and with broken ribs, Monica could muster the passion that both attracted me to her and at the same time caused so many of our struggles. After all, we were both galloping into middle age and had been hardpressed to make decisions about a life together.

"They're going to need your help, Truman, if this is going to turn out like we think it is."

"Which is how?"

"Some crazy person hurting women in our church."

"Janet's boyfriend's not."

"He might just as well have been."

I sat back and set my palms on the thighs of my jeans. The black window seemed to stare mockingly at me. I heard the squeak of hospital shoes on the hallway outside the partially open door. I thought of Laura Lee Jennings and her husband

41

telling me about a group of men behind the scenes, pulling strings to keep the status quo. "What can I do?" I asked.

"Don't let them get away with this any longer."

"Just like that?"

Her eyes closed, opened, closed again. She just lay there, breathing softly. We intended to marry in the fall. About that time, Monica might land a job as pastor of a church. A thought that at this moment didn't sound at all pleasing, given the wild card of the violence that had just showed its awful face. We said nothing for many minutes.

"Truman?"

I blinked awake. Had to focus to find her, right where she had been. My mouth didn't work for a second.

"I was just wondering." Monica had purplish hollows under her eyes, the mouth was swollen, the nose taped. Even in that state, she struck me as the sort of woman who had beauty beyond all measure. I liked the sound of that, figured I ought to share it with her. But then again, maybe it would sound too sentimental to her. "Did you slay those dragons in Three Rivers?"

"Pardon?"

"Get the garbage out of the way, like you were hoping?"

Part of my trip to the monastery had been to sort through some business. There had been things, experiences, that blocked the way between us. Monica saw it and didn't shy from telling me I closed up like a clam when it got down to being truly intimate together. Not sex. But the kind that entailed talking, sharing, maybe telling her to her face about that immeasurable beauty she had. "Sure," I said. "All taken care of."

She smiled, not believing me for a second, let her eyes close and was soon asleep. I sat there awhile, my eyes heavy, my chest tight, the black window alive again with scraps of snow.

I was at the Silverdome for the first frantic Promise Keepers' convention. One man among thousands. Hugging, crying, swaying to a fierce evangelical beat, the lot of us were happy to be male. It was somewhere during the middle part of the day-long gathering, I could feel that the intensity was rising to a fever pitch. Row after row of us stood in our seats, a vast human wave of longing.

Gathered among my brothers, I wanted to escape, to run from all of that furious virility. I pitched one way and then the other, shoving someone aside. Was it Pete? I wanted to be there at the rally. It gave me something. But it also was offering too much. I needed to escape for a time.

Down the steep steps I went, wanting out, aware of the longing that the place represented, this desperate hunger for God to come to us as men. I hadn't gone far when music erupted from the stage and the men began to dance, like idolaters in the aisle. Stomping, swinging, yelling out for glory. Unable to move, I froze. All around me bodies began to crash, to swarm over me and force me floundering to the sticky wet cement. On my face, a crush of masculinity atop me, I wanted to cry. I squirmed, flopped on my back and was drawn under. The waters of Zion, a rush of rivers raging from many sources, tumbled in and swept me away.

At first, I was happy; the relief was enormous. But then the churn of the waters, the falling of the waves, drove me deeper, further down then I wanted to go. I spun in a swirl of sinking, aiming straight for an open dumpster. Unable to breathe, trying to summon a helpful presence from below me in the even darker waters, I coughed myself awake. Or so I thought.

Because I wasn't awake, not yet. I stood in the middle of the stadium, staring at the stage. Two men, one black and one white in a leather coat, spoke from the stage. One of them ripped open a curtain to show a car. He poured gas on it and lit a match. I knew I had to get up there to stop it. But I couldn't move. In the moments before the flames rose, I knew someone was behind the wheel. Someone I knew. Monica. She gazed out at me in terror, across a barrier I had to cross.

Cold sweat dripping, my heart slamming the anvil of my rib cage, I sat there. Straight-backed in the chair. Absolutely petrified, bereft of hope, a garbage bag before my Lord. I slapped hands on my face. Noticed the sickly green glow from the machines plugged into Monica. She lay there awash in the dire light from the monitors, asleep, lost in a slumber of dread. I shook my head and stood, suddenly aware of a faint stink, an undercurrent of cigarette smoke, damp wool, nose spray.

I swiveled from side to side, but there was no one, just me and Monica and the machines. I stepped over and looked down on her. She had asked me to help. Fat chance, me being such a nocturnal basket case.

In the hall, I saw a chubby, uniformed man waddling my way with a cup of steaming liquid in his hand. I blinked; it was the security guard. He'd checked in awhile ago, before I'd fallen asleep and into the clammy arms of the nightmare.

"Get some shut-eye, Reverend?"

I moved my shoulders, felt the firm grip of reality return.

"Cup of Joe?"

I squinted at him, his round sunny face, flecked with liver spots on the cheeks. He smiled at me through the rising stream of his coffee. I looked beyond him. He turned to follow my gaze. "Something wrong?" he asked.

"I could have sworn someone came in the room."

He looked a little worried. "I wasn't gone a couple minutes. Didn't see anyone on the elevator."

I sighed, feeling a hot molten movement in my gut. "Must've been my dream."

"Bad one?"

"What I remember of it." The roar of the Promise Keepers, those men I called my own, sang on the edge of my consciousness. My id is getting out of line. Thank you, Dr. Freud, I thought.

"Maybe you ought to stretch out on one of them couches down the hall," he suggested.

That was an idea. I nodded, just standing there, a little numb from troubled sleeping. Still, the dream and something else, gripped me.

"One thing," the guard said.

I swallowed my anxiety, trying to face the world and what it wrought, thinking, Monica is right. I know this church. If it's going screwy, which it undoubtedly was, I could help figure out who was at the controls, bringing on the latest run of chaos.

"You got a message. From Detective Rodriguez. Says there's a press conference at 8 o'clock on Calder Plaza."

"He wants me there?"

"That's the gist of what I got."

CHAPTER EIGHT

The ongoing battle between the mayor and the police chief may have been why they called a press conference on the neutral ground of Calder Plaza. Or maybe they did it in rotten weather to get it over with, to discourage too many questions.

Sporting a large orange metal sculpture called La Grande Vitesse, the slab-stone outdoor meeting place was alive through the better months with festivals and concerts. This morning the plaza was full of a bitter wind, driven down from gray clouds amassed low over West Michigan. But this area was neither City Hall, nor was it the Police Department. Exactly why they didn't hold their deal inside the Press Club or some other much warmer, neutral spot eluded me.

But there I was, sharp on 8 o'clock, wrapped in my parka, hardly with it after a night of lousy dreams. Monica, as it turned out, slept fine. She awakened only to smile a good-bye at me, ask me to buy her a lottery ticket (the Lotto being $22 mil) and to give her arriving father and flouncy stepmother a weak nod of the head.

I had forgotten to tell her the truth about the dumpster and thought of going back, but decided not to. I figured the former actress would blab about it soon enough. I just hoped Monica's dad kept his bride from decorating the walls with toilet paper prom flowers.

With that sardonic thought, as wind razored the plaza, I realized I hadn't said my morning prayers. As the mayor, the chief, and Rodriguez gathered on the pavement just below the looming riveted sculpture, I closed my eyes and talked a couple moments to God. Mostly asked him to stay with Monica and keep me from popping my mouth off at people today.

"Reverend Turkstra?"

I stood in a clutch of people, most carrying mini-cams or holding tiny notepads. Hunched into the collar of my coat, I nodded at the slender blonde woman who had approached. She had one of those chintzy pads in the palm of her hand. She wore a camel hair coat and flung strands of hair from her face with a shake of the head. "Hi, Crystal," I said.

"Can I ask a question?"

The mayor and chief were conferring as everyone else froze their fingers to the bone. "Why don't they do this somewhere warm?" I asked.

She offered me a movie star's smile, buttering me up, I thought. "It is nippy." Crystal seemed no worse for the wear. I wondered if she had a different, more untouchable type of blood. "But first I wanted to say how sorry I am about Monica." She sounded serious.

"Thanks."

The TV reporter's eyes glittered a moment; her mouth pursed. A shadow of something crossed her glowing face. "Tell you the truth, I hope they catch the sorry son of a bitch who did this."

Such foul language from such a pretty mouth, I thought. Then caught myself. Sarcasm, when it started to clip through my mind at this pace, told me to watch out. There were other matters boiling below. "I hope so, too." Which is when I wondered: This press conference, were they announcing a development?

A whining sound ran from the mike by the bigwigs. Crystal checked it out, made a face, got down to business. "Reverend, are the people responsible the Promise Keepers?"

You've been peeking in my dreams, I thought. "What makes you ask that?"

"Rumors?"

"Who's saying this?" I asked.

She gave me a tight smile. She had her sources.

47

"That's not one I've heard," I lied.

"But some group's behind the attacks."

I thought of the Jennings. I suspected others had also gotten a pitch for Synod votes. Quite possibly, that was the source of her suspicions. I believed, however, it was a long way from stacking an election to murder. I shook my head, shrugged inside the padding of my coat, stomped my feet, felt wind pinch my nose.

"You don't see a connection?" she asked.

Before I could answer, there was another screech, a scratching whine and then the police chief's voice: "Good morning. How is everyone?"

"Hey, Chief, it's cold out here." That came from a *Press* reporter up front, a man I recognized as one of their top writers. He wore, you got it, a trench coat with military-looking epaulets.

Police Chief Baxter Bailey got busy giving the *Press* a stern look with his dark bushy eyebrows, feigning displeasure. Next to him, the mayor stood ramrod straight in a dark overcoat, his gloved hands clasped prayerfully in front of him. Rodriguez had the leather coat zipped way up, digging into his chin. His cheeks were almost purple, his eyes dots inside the folds of his skin. His hands were stuffed in the pockets of his jeans. I figured he hadn't slept.

"We don't have much, Sam," the police chief said to the *Press*, his normally sonorous voice scratchy in the wind and open-air space of the Calder.

Monday morning workers paused as they scooted across the plaza on their way to City Hall or the County Buildings, two dark-windowed structures that towered above us and served to bounce wind into the open canyon in which we stood.

"Mayor Hathaway and I simply want to announce we are mustering all of the resources available to meet the demands of this investigation." He wore a shark-skin coat with a velvet-black collar. It ballooned over his large, bulbous body. His sparse hair was combed back and sprayed in place.

"First, Chief, who was the guy you found in the dumpster last night?" asked the Press reporter.

Bailey arranged his features in a pleasant smirk and shook his head, as if amused by the question. "Whose press conference is this, Sam?"

"Can't you answer?"

Bailey let his face grow somber, the flesh hanging from the jowls. "We'll release a name as soon as he is identified and his next of kin are notified."

"We heard, Chief, his name's Johnny Keester, an ex-con from the West Side. That he's the boyfriend of Tina Martin, whose body was found in the house on Courtney Street Saturday." Again, the *Press*, rattling on for the otherwise frozen crowd. I assumed Sam had a deadline to meet and was trying to get the show on the road so he could make the city edition.

"We think the two are related."

More questions popped. The chief did most of the talking, flipping a couple to the detective, who spoke in monosyllables. The mayor hung back in his tailored coat, giving me the once over a couple times. I shivered, feeling my eyes water, realizing this news event held terribly important dimensions, all of them unsaid.

"Chief, can you tell us the condition of Monica Smit?"

Bailey eyed me then. "Critical but stable."

More questions, but not much more information. Finally, from behind me, Crystal Franklin had to know about the Promise Keepers.

Blustery wind swept from above City Hall, zeroing in on our group. We stood dwarfed by the huge orange sculpture, on a morning whose sky was pale as day-old pastry. The chief handed Crystal's question over to the mayor, who took the hand-held mike, stuck it to his face. "I hadn't heard that, Miss Franklin," he said.

"I'm hearing that a small breakoff group of PKs are to blame."

Pete gazed at her with a baleful expression, his slender face looking hangdog and depleted. "What would their motivation be?"

"To thwart the movement of women in your denomination."

Pete shook his head, eased a flat palm over his floppy, wind-tossed hair. His expression was strained. "It's hard to see where the Christian Reformed Church would be that important to the world at large." The mike screeched. He winced and went on. "But if there is anything involving my church, we'll make sure to turn over every stone."

"But last time . . ."

Bailey grabbed the microphone and cut in: "As I've said, we are doing all that we can. This is a horrible situation. But we don't need to be badmouthing anyone until we know more."

"But . . ." sputtered Crystal.

Rodriguez had crossed his arms over his chest, turned to the side and was gazing at the fast-filling Old Kent Bank parking lot. Theological motivation no doubt eluded him.

"So there is a tie in here with the Christians?" asked Sam King, notebook held high, pen poised to write down the goods.

"By Christians, you mean the CRC?"

"Is there another church in Grand Rapids," Sam responded.

The chief kept trying to moderate. "Right now, we're looking at all angles, folks. When we get something, you'll be the first to know."

"Chief," said Crystal. "Why did your department and the mayor ignore the first murder?"

Bailey glowered under his dark eyebrow, the sides of his coat billowing in the wind. "No one, Miss Franklin, ignored a damned thing." With that, he axed the dog- and-pony show, thumbed off his microphone and slipped it in his coat pocket.

50

I was left wondering what this had been all about. As far as I, a pastor and no journalist could tell, no news had been uttered by anyone. Just rumors and half facts.

I stepped over to Crystal who was conferring with her cameraman, a round, pony-tailed man in a pink parka. She turned to me as I approached, the wind whipping her hair in smooth snaky strands across her brow. She forearmed it down.

"Can you tell me your source on the PK rumor?"

She blinked mascara-rimmed eyes. "Monica hasn't heard it, too?"

"If so, she hasn't told me."

She gave me an insider's nod, as if to say keeping me in the dark was a woman's right. Still, I sensed a disturbance in her.

"If there was a weird group like that," I tried, "what would be their point?"

Her lips were red, her coat expensive, her skin looked soft as putty. "Keep the ladies under control."

"You really believe that?"

"Do you have any idea what they are like?" she asked fiercely.

I noticed Rodriguez heading my way. "What about the mayor and chief holding back on Janet VanTol?"

"I was hoping to ask you that on the air." Her eyes narrowed. I saw intensity on her face, a hard knowledge, a sharp edge that I liked. I wondered if this story grabbed her and wasn't just fodder for her to leapfrog to a bigger market. "You mind going on camera with me? Tell us what you think. Perhaps give us an update on Monica, if that doesn't feel too personal to you?"

I looked at the fat guy in the bright crossing guard's parka. "Do you really have a source?" I asked.

"People have talked to me, yes."

"Who?"

She shook her head, the hair flying. I felt the wind trying to slide down my neck. I wanted to help her out, but thought going on TV wasn't the way. So I declined.

51

She looked disappointed and I felt a little bad. But I wasn't up to it. Especially not on TV. I suspected I'd look like one of those family members after a plane crash, gawking vividly into the camera, doling out my grief in sound bites. I said maybe I'd talk to her later. She brushed me off and turned to Rodriguez, who also skipped away from her by passing questions off to the chief. Which is where she and the porky camera guy hustled off to.

"Give her credit," said Rodriguez. "She's got balls."

"Isn't that an oxymoron?"

"You're half right."

He walked beside me as I made my way toward City Hall. Circles of snow jigged at our feet. The sky was a huge and blank face of powdery gray. Once we were out of weather in the overheated foyer of the building, the cop sniffed, rubbed his nose and also asked me about the PKs. "Who's the head of the outfit?"

"There's several local coordinators. I used to be one."

"Used to be?"

"I gave it up. Got too busy. But I'm still connected."

He nodded a couple times and gazed out the frosted window at the plaza, now empty and barren. I thought of the guy's head sitting there, so stunningly out of place on the ground. A head that had been wrapped in a PK T-shirt. "Can you give me a couple names?" he asked.

"Sure, but why?"

He turned to me. I noticed a couple gray hairs in his mustache. He smelled like shoe polish and worn leather. "You saw what giftwrapped Keester's head."

"Have you decided it was his shirt?"

Rodriguez tapped his feet on the foyer floor, waited for three women to slip in and pass us. "Not sure."

"Not sure or not telling me?"

"Preacher, don't diddle me. I need some names."

The heater grate in the enclosed area in which we stood clicked and whistled, as if reacting to this new chunk of information. I leaned against a window, wondering about my dream. I was absolutely sure I wasn't psychic. But it sure seemed someone from the other world was trying darned hard to get my attention.

"Who're these people anyway?" he asked.

I told him the PKs were started by a former University of Colorado football coach. In some ways, it developed in reaction to feminism in the church and society-at-large. "If you ask me, this is a heckuva red herring," I said.

"How so." He stared outside, bored with me, ready to get on with more important matters. "Our killer is laying the blame." I told him.

"You sound sure of that."

I was aware he was listening to me, carefully for a change. "This is a new group on the scene, only a couple years old."

"This a test?"

"What I'm saying is that I really don't think it has been around long enough to spawn a violent group, or person, who would do something like this in their name."

"Then there's nothing to it."

I examined his face, the marks, faint scars, the hard eyes, the wiry hair. I wanted to help and sensed he was willing to accept it, on a limited basis. So I took a couple minutes to tell him about James and Laura Lee Jennings. How I thought this group was more homegrown, probably very small. The PKs didn't fit.

When I finished, he filled me in on the mayor.

CHAPTER NINE

Captured on the walls of the mayor's office, each in a silver frame, were the official posters of each of the twenty-two Festivals that had occurred on the streets below. Every year, the first full weekend in June, thousands of people flocked here to eat ethnic food at volunteer-run booths and to check out the local talent—dancers, singers and other performers—who took to one of several stages. It was the city's annual blast, a huge block party. A local artist won a competition for a sketch or drawing that best captured the flavor of each year's Festival and had his or her effort produced in posters. Each of them, from the first to the last, hung in neat rows on the paneling behind Pete Hathaway's desk. One of them, I think the poster showing lightning crackling over the Calder, had been created by my fellow pastor's wife.

I doubted that the mayor was pondering the sites and sounds of Festival, however, as he stood at his eighth-floor window, hands on the glass, his pinstripe suit hanging loose from his solid but bony frame.

"You know, Turkstra, it's those little things, the situations that happen in a flash and are gone, that can come back to bite you."

For some reason I thought of Ruth, the married woman with whom I was involved for nearly a decade first in Seattle, Washington; where I met her as I worked as an orderly in a hospital emergency room. Then continued the affair in Colorado and ended in New Mexico, where she had gone with her Baptist minister husband. Our relationship, which continued to stalk me, was no flash in the pan. But somehow it seemed it was that first moment I met her, in the ER over a heart attack patient, that stuck and caused us so much grief. If she hadn't died in a car crash, who knows what would have happened. "What are you saying, Pete?" I said to his back.

He looked at me over his shoulder. Stricken.

"Look, Pete, I don't know politics. I'm just checking this out."

The mayor sat on the window ledge. Outside, I could see the square shape of the National Bank of Detroit building. Above and to the left of that, on Michigan Street Hill, stood the towers of Butterworth Hospital. Not too long ago, just as I was leaving, Monica had called me to her side and whispered to check in her purse and get five bucks. The Lottery was up to $22 million, and she wanted a few fast picks. The Lottery was her obsession, even in her condition. I told her I had her covered. I made a mental note to stop at Elliott's after the mayor got done.

"Then just run it past me again, Calvin."

He called me Calvin when he was hot and bothered. His chin carried peppers of beard; his eyes drooped. I leaned against the wall, watching him wring his hands. "Hey, Pete. It's just a question."

His smile was sickly, more an inkling of humor than anything else. His hands washed themselves. He stood and paced the carpet. On another wall, opposite the posters, were photographs, some from South Africa, a couple from Bosnia, where he'd worked at an orphanage, and a few from around town. I knew this was a man who had a passion for the world, especially for those who had gotten a raw deal. So I was surprised to be having this discussion.

"Well, it was Herb Wierenga." Again, a pained expression, thrown toward me like a challenge.

"I know Herb."

"We all know Herb."

He was owner of a large local contracting firm, an elder in West Leonard CRC, and widower whose wife, as I recalled, died in an accident near Lake Michigan several years ago.

Pete stood by his photographs, wiping a finger on the glassy surface of one showing him campaigning outside St. Isidore's, a staunch Polish Catholic Church built on the hilly site of a former brickyard on the east edge of town. In it, he wore a madras shirt and jeans and was hugging a squat gray-haired woman who had one of those funny handkerchief's on her head. Pete, because of his platform for the working stiffs, was a hit in the blue-collar Catholic parishes. I'd been with him that day, just out of camera range, watching him work the grandmas and grandpas who still believed in a God who spoke Latin. "Herb came in here, blustering like he does, the day after Janet was found in the river."

I was listening as he wiped a photo of himself at the Shrine Circus, yukking it up with clowns. Putting a finger to his nose, as if smelling for dust, he turned to face me. "Herb, more or less asking a favor."

During the mayor's run for office, he'd been tireless. He showed up at weddings in Polish halls, spoken to Jewish women's groups, played in a firefighters handball tournament, addressed a huge missionary conference held by our church in the Welsh Auditorium. Weaving through it all had been his campaign pledge that a vote for him was a vote for the people, whoever they were. His ties, he told his audiences, were to the church, meaning the only special interest to whom he answered was God. Fixing me with his steely greens, he moved away from the wall of fame and stepped toward his desk. He stopped in mid-room and gandered down at his shiny loafers. "What favor?" I wondered.

My friend Pete didn't look up. He could have been trying to laser beam his gaze through the floor below into some bean counter's office. Or, possibly, considering the fires of hell. Or maybe wondering if he should tell me the truth. "He wanted to know if I could ask the police to go easy."

A cold trickle of air slipped down the back of my neck, even though I still had my bulky parka zipped tight. "Wierenga wanted that?"

He shook his head, tore his eyes from the floor and finished his trek across the room. Sitting gingerly on the edge of his desk, he thumbed open his suit coat and fired me an unfriendly stare. "Herb told me Janet's mother was being admitted to Pine Rest."

I wandered over to the window, unzipped the Bulls jacket. Painted across the roof of the next-door county building, in bold orange, black and white, was a rendition of the Calder sculpture. The city's symbol, from this bird's eye angle, looked like a squashed, long-legged spider, spread from end to end of the building. As for Pine Rest, it was a local psychiatric hospital, begun at the turn-of-the-century by members of our church for shell-shocked World War I vets too vain to ask the government for care.

"Herb told me she tried to kill herself with pills when she heard about her daughter."

A few people scurried across the plaza below, heads bent into the wind. "I hadn't heard that," I said softly.

Pete coughed, made a quick scraping sound in his throat. "Fears were any more publicity than necessary might drive her over the edge."

"How is she now?"

"Better."

I knew Branson VanTol was owner of VanTol & Sons Furniture Company, a high-end maker of fancy chairs, tables and so on for the cream of the crop. His wife, Audrey, was a nervous, wispy woman whose name and face appeared occasionally in the Press entertainment section as a patron of the arts, especially chamber music.

"She was at the funeral," I said, thinking back.

"Well-medicated and under psychiatric care."

It had been a fine late autumn day, the leaves at Oaklawn Cemetery aflame with color, the air crisp and cleansing. Monica had clasped my arm so hard she left bruises. Audrey VanTol, as I recalled, had stood by the grave in a black coat and hat and had little reaction. Her daughter Janet had been a young woman whom I'd met twice and pegged as emotionally abused in some hard to define way. "Just how much got shoved aside here, Pete?" I turned and saw the hurt in his eyes.

"Nothing," he said, mustering a bristle, "was shoved anywhere."

"That's not what Manny Rodriguez thinks."

His anger simmered into a righteous burn, but still his face held a tortured look. "What'd he say?"

"That it wasn't all green lights when it came to Janet VanTol."

He crossed his arms over his chest. The many Festival posters shone behind him, glass fronts catching creamy light from outside. "I asked Bailey to go easy, only if he was sure it wasn't foul play."

"What does that mean, Mayor?"

"Not to keep the family hanging in limbo, if there wasn't anything to it."

I sat on the window ledge, heard wind rattle. "Why Herb?"

"He's a good friend of Branson."

"Who asked him to come to you."

"He said no."

"So you asked Bailey to back off, which meant he stuck the investigation in the can?" I shuddered, thinking of last night's dumpster. More than that, I was mad. If this was connected, and the cops let the killer go, only for him to kill and attack again, even my politician friend would have hell to pay.

"That's not how I see it," he responded carefully.

"Pete. This guy could have gone back at it because you laid off him."

He blinked, settled his hands in his lap. Once in seminary, we got into a heated argument in class about New Age religion. Pete said it held some valuable beliefs and practices. I as much as said it was the work of Satan. I didn't really believe that. It was just his know-it-all attitude that got to me that morning.

We didn't speak for a week. Then, during a pick-up basketball game, we made up.

"I know that, Calvin," he said, a touch of remorse in his voice. "If I'd had any idea, I would never have talked to the chief."

He'd handed me his defeat. Now, I thought, what am I going to do with it. "But," I said, "from the look of it down there, Bailey's all gung-ho this time."

Pete stood. "Grant me this, friend. I made a mistake."

I stood as well. "What about Herb. Was he duped, too?"

"Look, Calvin, I'm not so sure there's a connection to Janet even now."

"You can't believe that?"

"You have proof, any shred at all?"

"Only that Tina Martin wanted to talk to Monica about that very thing. She knew, maybe even saw, something."

The mayor sighed, gazed past me at the window. I saw his face grow deadly serious, the eyes narrowed, the lips got thin. He was thinking, rolling those mental wheels, churning on to the next steps that he had to take. "That's the thing, Calvin. When I talked to Herb, I believed him."

"Maybe he came with good intentions?"

He gave me a doubtful look. "There's one way to find out for sure."

I waited, figuring what would come next.

"Go talk to him."

"Why me?"

"Because," said the mayor, "he's already played me for a horse's ass once."

CHAPTER TEN

I slapped down a five. Joe took it, punched the Lotto machine to life, and handed me five easy picks for that night's drawing. On this topic, as we did on many others, Monica and I differed. I didn't like the Lotto. Too many street people dribbled away food and bill money in hopes of hitting the jackpot. In Chicago, where I did inner city ministry for years, and now here, I never met anyone on welfare or a fixed income who won anything more than a few bucks, which they dumped right back down the drain for a few more fruitless tickets. My bleeding heart beliefs even got me in the paper a time or two.

But Monica, hers was a fine obsession. Even in the hospital, she was looking for the big payoff. She considered the Lotto a form of grace. It was, she really believed, controlled not by the rules of chance, but by some divine power, sort of a heavenly gambling commissioner. Especially with the easy picks, the numbers determined by the machine, the Lord's free offering of prosperity was evident, she figured. So far, she hadn't won more than a couple free ones. But she bought tickets and watched the chintzy nightly Lotto show on cable TV with a believer's true commitment. "Might be the big one," I said to Joe, sticking the tickets in my wallet.

"Up to $22 mil."

"That buys a lot of bread."

"You giving it a shot this time, Cal?"

"They're for Monica."

Joe gave me a sad smile. A large man with friendly eyes, he tipped toward me from behind the counter. He wore a polo shirt with the outline of an exotic dancer on the pocket. "How is she Reverend?"

"I think she'll be OK."

"Terrific."

A handful of customers looked through magazines and paperbacks shelved around Elliott's, his newsstand on Ottawa Avenue. Monica and I had been here often, her to purchase tickets, me to get newspapers and bestsellers. We often shot the breeze with him. Monica had told him more than once he ought to come to my church. Another agnostic, with only marginal ties to his Muslim family back in Lebanon, Joe always brushed her off. God, he once said, was a good idea for people who needed it.

"Preacher was in here awhile ago," said Joe.

"Buying tickets?"

"Wine."

"You don't sell wine, Joe."

"He wanted a donation."

"I thought he wasn't drinking anymore."

Joe shrugged. "Told me he's got to drink to forget."

Joe took care of a couple customers. I noticed the new Elmore Leonard novel racked next to another shiny book whose cover showed a long-haired, Italian-looking heartthrob clasping the Hollywood version of an Indian maiden to his bare chest. "He tell you about the dumpster?" I asked when Joe was free again.

Joe crossed his thick arms over the outline of the dancer. The shirt came from Fascinations, one of the strip bars in Grand Rapids. Many church folks had lately been trying to get it closed. Perhaps not a bad idea. But it wasn't the type of fight that came out of my Bible. "You know him," said Joe. "Who knows how much is bull."

I picked up *Riding the Rap*, Leonard's book. Set it down on the counter. "He say he saw something?"

"Couldn't tell. He was jabbering his jaw."

"So, what's new?"

Joe pulled on his nose, rolled his eyes.

61

Preacher lived part-time under the expressway that curved through Heartside, just downwind from the new arena. Cops had been fighting to evict him; he refused and threatened to sue. Even though he couldn't walk on his own, Preacher got around just fine in his wheelchair. As far as I could tell last night, he was talking pretty animatedly to Rodriguez. "Did he say he saw something or someone?" I asked.

"Hear him tell it, he was around when this guy with the horns dropped the stiff's pieces in the dumpster."

"Guy?"

"This demon," said Joe sarcastically.

"He tell the police?"

The phone rang. A few customers were starting to hover.

"Got to ask him," said Joe.

Preacher had helped the police nab some armed robbers who killed a man from Grandville in a downtown parking structure awhile back. Problem was one of the thieves' friends didn't like Preacher spouting off and zipped him open with a knife. Or so the story went. Preacher was a month in Saint Mary's Hospital with an infected gut wound, and never did testify about what he saw. Later, it was unclear exactly what he did come across. Except, he was always down there, plopped in the weeds, watching and ranting.

"Well, thanks, Joe," I said as he picked up the phone.

He palmed the receiver. "You want the book?"

I paused, eyed the colorful cover, and shook my head. "Maybe later." Sticking it back next to the lovestruck he-man and his true love, I left. Outside, the wind nibbling my cheeks, I figured I had some real-life detecting to do on my own, namely I wanted to see one Herbert J. Wierenga. Old Elmore would be there when I got back.

CHAPTER ELEVEN

Twenty some stories in the air, with the wind plowing through the open side of the building, I could see as far as the haze hovering over the far western suburbs of Grand Rapids. On a clear day, I bet the view might have included the mucklands rolling into Holland, my old proving grounds, which was tucked along the shore of Lake Michigan. Up here in the Eastbank Towers, I marveled at the spread of neighborhoods, the icy flow of the Grand River and the straight piercing of streets.

"Quite a sight, eh, Reverend?"

I turned to face Herb Wierenga, a huge stump of a man, his skin barked and ridged from years of hard labor.

We stood side by side, peering down. A plywood barrier prevented us from tumbling into the blustery winter air. Directly under us and across the river was the Gerald R. Ford Museum, a triangular tourist trap that housed memorabilia belonging to the native son president of the same name. To the left of that was the new public museum and next to that the downtown campus of Grand Valley State University. When I was done with Herb, I needed to pick up Bob, who was visiting the public museum with a group from the sheltered workshop where he went to school. Gazing out, I once again realized how much this part of Michigan was in transition. Buildings going up everywhere. But as for the one in which I stood, it was undergoing a rehab job.

"What can I do you for?" asked Herb.

I'd asked at the construction office on the ground if I could talk with Herb. The woman at the desk in the trailer said he was supervising work on the roof. She gave him a call and he said to meet me on the 20th floor, in this room.

"I've got a couple questions." I said to him. Wind whipped in and smacked our faces. We were in what was left of a condominium that was being refurbished. The entire structure, in fact, was being stripped bare and built again. The first contractors had done a shoddy job. Herb had been one of them. Walls had begun to crack, windows to fall, and outside sheeting to crumble within a couple years after this place opened. Everyone was moved out, so Herb's company could do the job right. This was a massive structure, one whose shape helped define the skyline of the city. Currently, it was like a sore, oozing from mistakes made by bankers to cut corners. Engines roared, workers hammered and sawed and drilled just outside the room. Herb put up quite a stink and show of breast beating to get part of the contract to fix the place up.

"Can we go some place quieter?" I asked

Herb smiled and wiped a gloved hand over his mouth. "Sorry, Reverend. This is as quiet as it gets."

A pile of plasterboard leaned against a far wall. A tarp covered a mound of something to our right. A table, a couple chairs, and a large cooler sat in an alcove on my right. "Fact is," said Herb, "I've got heating ducts coming up. Got to make this snappy."

Herb wore a brown denim jacket, jeans, and scuffed boots. His cheeks looked raw and rosy, his gray hair bristled around the flat plane of his skull. He had the type of nose, large, fleshy and flat, you see on men who have stuck it in enough places that it had gotten whopped a time or two. I figured, since he was being pushy, to cut the chatter. "I just talked to the mayor. He told me you leaned on him to put the lid on Janet VanTol's drowning."

He slipped off a glove and ran a hand through his hair. He smiled strangely, like he'd swallowed a golf ball in the middle of a joke. I also saw his jaw clench. "I wondered if that's why you were here." He sniffed into the wind, his nose set high in his face, almost even with the wide rudders of his cheeks.

Rich as he was, as owner of Master's Construction Company, he kept busy with his hands. Not one to sit behind a desk, Herb was an on-site sort of guy, always active. I had the sense I'd thrown him, even if he had been wondering. He stepped over and sat in a card table chair in the alcove at the edge of the window. He jerked his head at a chair. I took it, feeling the cold reach through my coat.

"Tell me what the mayor said."

I did, remembering how Herb had been involved in the early construction of this place. That to an extent, he was getting a second chance at doing things right. I also wondered why he'd been so hot on getting another chance at it.

Herb slouched forward, head bent toward the floor, large hands folded between his knees. Paint spattered the toes of his boots. Down the hall I heard the slamming of a dozen hammers. I also felt a few puffs of warmth, probably winding its way from the stationary heaters I'd seen when the elevator dumped me on this floor. "Sounds a little fishy, doesn't it?" He angled his head up at me.

"I'd say so."

Herb smiled again, that same sickly expression. "Just idle curiosity bring you up here to ask?" he said.

In the chair, out of the wind, the sounds were a little muffled. I had to tip my head toward him to listen. "Not really."

He rubbed his nose, as if getting its blood supply moving. "That was your girlfriend, wasn't it, who got hurt the other night?"

I watched him carefully, my senses picking things out of the frigid air. Maybe speculation, but maybe more than that. "That's right."

Herb leaned back, hands in his lap, and closed his eyes. The chill seeped up from the floor and in from the window, through which I could see a bland covering of gray clouds. Riffles of heat, more a smell than anything else, waffled around us. "Well, I did talk to Pete Hathaway."

I waited. The hard chair under me was like a brittle candle-stick, holding me up. I wanted to get someplace hot. "Why?"

Herb twisted slowly to me, about to answer, and then his attention turned beyond me to the doorway. He immediately stood and went over. A guy had entered, a troubled look on his beefy face. The two of them conferred. Wierenga's expression darkened, his words coming fast. I couldn't exactly hear. It was over in seconds. Herb motioned me. "Got a worker hurt on four. Let's talk on the way. "

I'm not sure why he didn't take the elevator. But he hit the nearby stairwell and began clattering down. It was warmer in here; the enclosed space was brightly lit. I followed his descending back. "Ask away, Reverend," he called over his shoulder.

"You were telling me about Pete Hathaway."

"What's to tell." His voice echoed off the sloping ceiling. "Branson's my neighbor. I've known him and his family for years." I noticed a bald spot, the size of a hardball, in the middle of his head "About dawn that morning, after Janet drowned, I was coming out for work, and there he was, on my front porch." My feet slapped stairs, busy behind him. "He told me what happened. But he wanted help with Audrey."

"What about her?" We were clipping off the floors.

"Said she was in a bad way. So, I went over. Found she'd locked herself in the bathroom. We got worried and broke in. She was on the floor."

We stopped on the landing to eight. I almost knocked into him. He was as tall as me. I could hear drilling and a muted roar come through the walls. Coins of color dotted his cheeks. His eyes, slightly bugged in their sockets, rolled across my face. As far as I knew, he'd never remarried after his wife's death. "She took a bunch of pills, Reverend."

I smelled stale coffee on his breath. Didn't react to his words, just returned his serious gaze.

"I wanted to call 911, but he said no. He wanted to take her to Pine Rest. I argued with him, but he had his mind set."

66

It figured. Keep the suicide try secret. Don't let on how awful your daughter's death made you feel. Don't even go to the hospital. Just whisk it away into the dark spaces of a psychiatric ward. If necessary, get your stomach pumped there. Or, I wondered, could they do it there? Wouldn't the psychiatrists send her to an ER? I filed that away, pressed on. "Where's the trip to the mayor come in?"

He started stomping down the stairs, me in hot pursuit. "My idea." Again, he gave me a look over his shoulder. "It was hard enough. It didn't seem right for the police to be badgering Branson."

"They were badgering him?"

His shoulders hunched, as if I'd slapped them from behind. "You know them, always stirring up trouble."

"Maybe they weren't so sure Janet's drowning was accidental?"

He stopped, turned, eyes sparking. "Bullshit, Reverend! That girl was in a bad way."

"How?"

"Who knows, lots of things."

Pausing, my hand on the rail, I nodded.

"Look, he was hoping, it being a tragedy, to keep it out of the public. He was afraid something sensational in the news would push Audrey over the edge."

"TV made a big deal of it anyhow."

He looked at his feet, switched around and kept walking. I wondered if the media attention, and not the police investigation, was what had been bugging him and VanTol.

We reached four. He shoved through a door into a carpeted hallway. There was a group of workers at the end of the hall. Herb shook his head, hands on his hips. "Is it bad?" I asked.

"Woman fell off a ladder."

A man down the hall looked to us. Herb waved at him. "Just a second, Reverend."

67

The two met halfway and conferred. It was hot in here. Closed doors ran along both sides of the corridor, leading to a large open space where the activity clustered. After a few moments, Herb returned, shaking his head, tugging his doeskin gloves back on. "She's all right."

I gazed behind him, saw a stocky woman in a bibbed coverall climbing to her feet, with help from a couple others. "Probably a workman's comp," he grumbled.

"What?"

He seemed unwilling to answer, but did. "Getting off work for free."

"Lot of people do that?"

"The women do."

He'd let me peek in his soul for a second, and I cringed a little. "So, Branson VanTol didn't ask you to pressure the mayor?"

We stepped aside as two men helped the woman limp past. She gave Herb an expectant, wincing look. He ignored her. He was too busy starting to fume at me. His mouth twitched, as if caught by a spasm. "Why are you here again, Pastor?"

I didn't answer him. "What did VanTol have to hide?"

He glowered. "Nothing."

"Then why put the police off track?"

Herb checked his watch and looked behind, where the men had gone back to work. I saw no more women. "Is that all?"

"You haven't answered my question."

"Ask Branson yourself." He turned and stalked off.

"Mr. Wierenga?" He paused in mid-stride, settled his foot and swiveled.

"Have you heard about a secret group in our church who might be involved with what happened to Janet VanTol?" Trundling out the TV rumor, more or less confirmed by the Jennings, was a shot in the dark.

He chewed me up with his eyes and spit me out without saying a word.

I decided to give him both barrels. "I'm also hearing this group might be tied with the Promise Keepers."

Wierenga shoved his gloved hands into the side pockets of his coat. His ridged and lumpy face flushed. "That's blasphemy, Reverend."

"Come on, Herb. The PKs aren't God."

"But they're of the Lord."

I had to laugh. Then I saw how deadly serious he was. Hulking in front of me in the hall, I suspected he wanted to put me away. To make me stop. To shut me up. Even it meant my destruction. "Are you a member?" I asked.

A quick, hard-to-read look flickered across his face. "Yes, I am."

"You don't believe they would be involved in something like this?"

"Like what, Reverend?"

"Murder."

I expected him to rant some more. Maybe even to waltz up and give me a shove. At the least stick that busted nose against mine. But he did none of that. Instead, those wide eyes misted for a second, a pool of what looked like remorse forming, then he glanced away. "Christ, Pastor, how could you even think such a thing." I waited. "That group, it's saved my life."

Having no answer, I watched him leave, his body slumping in ways that it wasn't when I first met with him less than a half hour before.

Before heading to the museum to pick up Bob, I dialed the hospital, identified myself, waited a moment while I was checked out, and got bumped to Monica's room.

"Hi," she said. "Any luck?"

"I'm finding out some things. But I really ought to be with you." I stood at a phone booth outside the towering condominium complex. A large white crane, built with a series of white cages one on top of the other, dragged a huge pile of material from the ground across a barren patch of lawn.

The building was gutted, its sides open, the windows removed, the face of the place a shattered remnant of itself. A vast building remaking itself. Inside, Herb was calling the shots and complaining about the female help. Refurbishing a place he helped put up wrong. A man who says he was saved by the PKs.

"You're where you have to be, Truman."

"How're you feeling?"

"Better than I thought."

"Sure that's not the Darvon?"

"Could be."

I smiled. "I'll get Bob and be back in a half-hour."

"Turk?"

The wind had died down. In its place was a chilly trough of air, bearing down on the city, making me crunch inside myself.

She seemed to be mustering strength. Then she asked: "Why didn't you tell me about the dumpster?"

Cars rolled by on Monroe Avenue. The clouds had merged into one drab mass of gray. "Sorry." I stood there, listening to the empty space between us.

"It's just," she said finally, "this is so ugly."

I agreed. I tried to think of words to cheer her up. But I realized how stupid levity would be. This was a woman who was shoved down the stairs by someone who strangled Tina Martin. May have drowned Janet VanTol. And butchered the body of a young man who got too greedy. Don't be worried, honey, I could tell her. This will all work out. Like hell.

High up on the Eastbank building, just barely in sight, I saw a few figures. They were waving the load of whatever it was, possibly heating ducts, to its berth on the roof.

"Turk?"

I grunted, feeling cold.

70

"I'm scared," she said.

"Ditto."

"I hope you can find out who's doing this."

"Me?"

"Or that cop. Or the both of you. Whatever."

I wanted to reassure her, but it wasn't in me. So I just said good-bye. Hanging up the phone, I gazed at the roof again. Heavy metal hung from the hooks of the crane. It spun, looped, tilted, as if ready to crash to the ground into a hundred brittle pieces.

CHAPTER TWELVE

I crossed the former railroad trestle that led from behind Old Rivertown Place, a refurbished brick office structure, to the elevated sidewalk that ran behind the downtown campus of Grand Valley State University. The sky spit a few flurries, the type of flakes that danced and spun in the air without sticking. Already my mind was tumbling ahead: Get Bob, drop him off, check on Monica, stop at church, answer messages, see about pulpit help for Sunday, reschedule a few meetings, call Rodriguez about Herb, maybe track down Branson VanTol. The list went on.

Skirting the side of the nearly windowless college building, I headed along a path that ran next to the slow-moving, ice-clogged Grand River to the promenade circling the Van Andel Museum Center. It was an impressive place that housed the history of our town. I stood at the rail for a few moments, back to the museum, watching the river roll, feeling the cold wrap around me, and thinking about Wierenga and the possibility of two groups, maybe one, turning to the worst kind of violence to reach their ends. Of the groups, maybe there was some off-the-wall one connected to our church. As for the PKs, I had no idea how they fit, if they fit at all. With Herb, lots about him stunk to high heaven. Yet, I saw sincerity in him. I wondered how the PKs helped him. Then there was VanTol. It was a soupy mix, brewing up bad things that I couldn't digest. I decided to shut out thought, just clear my head for now.

Stretching to my left upriver was the near West Side. Across the way was downtown, a solid, ever-growing skyline that bustled with late Monday morning activity. Traffic buzzed on U.S. 131 behind me. I took in deep gulps of the air, thinking of Monica, the energy in her voice, her fear mingled with my own. Her strength, even in her fear, bolstered me now. Her attitude, which was to always look on the bright side, contrasted with my much darker, cynical view of the world.

But better get going, I thought, and turned. Directly in front of me, through the large, sculpted windows of the museum, I saw the sparkling movement of the calliope, a circus attraction of horses and other hand-crafted wood animals. It twirled beyond the glass, a few kids waving and smiling out. I smiled and held a hand up to wave. Tentative, wondering if they were looking at me, or just thrilled to be on a merry-go-round. One kid, catching me gazing, scowled and flipped me the bird. I buried the urge to do the same and went inside.

In the museum, I looked for Bob and his group. They were supposed to be done at 11. I planned to meet them in the polished, airy lobby. But no one was there, which seemed odd. I wandered back into the main area of the museum, just beyond a display hailing Grand Rapids as the "Fluoride Capital of the World," this being the town in which dentists first poured the decay-fighting chemical into the water, and out into a wide open area that led to a swirling staircase.

Right off, I spotted a crush of people gathered near the far end, heads craned back, a few pointing up at a person I immediately recognized as Bob looming on a second-floor ledge, staring at bleached white whale bones suspended from wires attached to the ceiling a dozen feet from his head.

I pushed through a few people and took the stairs two at a time to the second floor, where a couple security guards chattered anxiously into walkie-talkies. I asked one what was going on. Sharp-nosed and nasty-looking, the guy growled and gestured. "One of the retarded kids is going bonkers."

I shouldered around them, hearing the other ask my business. Another security guard, this a woman, blocked my way with grim, pursed lips and an upper body the size of a doorway. "Ma'am," I said, trying to edge around her, noticing a side view of Monica's errant brother. I saw his round shoulder, part of his hip and a thatch of his dark hair. "That's my brother-in-law," I said by way of cutting through red tape.

She tapped a hand on her shiny black belt, just above a billy club and nodded solemnly.

"What's he doing?" I asked.

She had wide-set eyes, a small chin, and mobile mouth that worked freely without saying a word. Seemed she was mashing gum with her molars. Since she apparently didn't speak English, I swept passed her, too. "Hey!" she then said, the cat returning her tongue.

I stopped. "Let me talk to him."

A few of Bob's classmates stood nearby. A couple official-looking folks huddled below Bob's feet. He leaned against a pillar, facing the other way, the pale whale bones within feet of his reach. "You better check with them," she said, indicating the pair in business garb by Bob.

I stepped over, nudged between them, glanced up at him. He looked scared, arms tight to his chest, his square face squeezed shut. "Bob," I said. If I wasn't mistaken, his expression softened.

"Sir?" asked a man next to me in a checked three-piece suit, glasses and spray of freckles on milky cheeks. He wore a small sign on his lapel, informing me of his name and position at the museum.

"I know him," I said.

Bob wore baggy brown pants, a Detroit Pistons sweatshirt, white tennis shoes, and a string tie. His mouth was motoring, mumbling words.

"You are?"

I told him.

The man on the other side of me touched my shoulder. He was almost as tall as I am and had a strained, pinched demeanor. His neck seemed to twist toward me on a rusty socket. "You're Monica's fiancée?" A small smile wiggled onto his mouth, as if he was pleased he'd made the connection. "I'm Bob's teacher."

Now I recognized him from the time or two I'd dropped Bob at school. "What's going on?" I asked.

Bob was stiff as a stone, his chin on his chest. I noticed him looking down at me. His nostrils were flared, fists at his sides.

"I don't know, Reverend. We were nearly done with our field trip. I was corralling everyone and counting heads. We'd just come out of the furniture display and saw Bob."

A gawky girl with large eyes, flat, sloping forehead and small shoulders showed up next to the museum bigwig. She grinned at him and made a guttural noise that seemed to pour out of her nose. Her mouth open and her lips burbled nonsense words. "Dana, get back," snapped the teacher.

"Do something, either of you, please, before this man hurts himself, or makes a bigger scene," said the museum bigwig, tugging on the back flap of his suit coat.

I dragged myself onto the ledge next to Bob. Mr. Museum blustered a bit as I did. He trundled off a couple feet and asked the security guard to call the fire department or the police. As the guard sauntered away to make his wish her command, he rocked back on his heels and looked up at me.

Directly below a hundred expectant faces turned up at us. I heard the museum hotshot call to the guard to disperse the crowd. I wondered if the bird-flipping pre-schooler was down there. "What's wrong, big guy?"

"Sucks," he replied.

"What does?"

He didn't answer. His eyes rocketed back and forth, mostly on me, but flickering at the whale bones as well. "The whale?" I asked.

"Can't breathe," he answered.

I turned and slipped next to him, both of us eye-level with the bottom of the bones. We remained there a half minute or so. I noticed the guards in black ushering people away from the floor 25 feet beneath us. "You know, John Ball is the one who found these bones. I think in Australia," I said to Bob.

Arrayed in front of us was a perfect skeletal replica, from sharp forehead to pointed tail, with all of the bent vertebrae in between, of a huge mammal that had swum the deep oceans a couple hundred years before. "You like it?" I added.

"Slick," he observed.

I felt movement next to me. Glanced down to see the girl with the small shoulders trying to scoot up to be with us. I figured by the round tone of her features that she had Down syndrome. The teacher dragged her away. She started to whimper, eyes turned to Bob.

"Your girlfriend?" I wondered, recalling that he did have one at the workshop, which really wasn't school. They mostly made coat hangers and stuffed pillows for couches. If I had it right, Bob got into trouble last Christmas for necking and petting in a coat room with his main squeeze.

Bob took a deep breath and groaned.

"What, bud?"

More movement below. Great, I thought, spotting raincoat-clad firemen. One held an ax.

"We better go," I said to Bob. I touched his elbow. He winced and pressed it harder to his side. "Really," I added.

At that point, he smiled and reached out toward the bones. I noticed the massive half rings of ribs, the bumped and pitted spinal column, the jutting jaw. "Gruesome," I think he said.

"You mean awesome," I responded, slipping an arm behind him as he eased away from the pillar. I felt him tug further, fingers flicking at what was left of the water monster. But he was on the move, into thin air, on the way to meet the whale. With a hard pull, I yanked back and took him down with me. We both spilled on the carpeted floor. We tumbled hard, Bob on top of me.

Even in the moment of the fall, I wondered if I overreacted, but I thought not. I feared he was going to step into a void, and possibly take me with him.

76

On my back, I suspected the worst. Bob lay on me. I twisted and shoved him off. He flopped over and landed on his rear, in a sitting position, attention still on Moby Dick.

I waited a moment, but then saw a smiling face above me. Her tongue was out, lolling on the lower lip. Her huge eyes shone. She made nasal sounds again. But I was able to make out words nonetheless. "New dummmmmeee. New fell."

I had to laugh. She was right. I was a dummy. And, sure as shooting, I had fallen.

CHAPTER THIRTEEN

Baubles, bangles and bright shiny beads, ting-a-lingle. That's what went through my head as I stepped into The Goddess Creations in Eastown. A sharp snooker of incense and whisper of flute music greeted me once I'd scraped the door shut with the back of my boot. I'd dropped Monica off a couple times for meetings in this place, and for some counseling sessions she held upstairs, but I'd never been inside.

Standing there, flower-scented warmth reached out to me. The weather outside was filthy with sheets of snow. Glancing at shelves stacked with dried flowers, posters, books, and jewelry made of stones and shiny silver, I thought this is definitely a woman's place. It had a soft overly feminine feel to it. A counter stacked with magazines, a bulletin board advertising all sorts of self-improvement workshops and seminars. To my left, beyond a rack of long-hemmed dresses like my grandma used to wear, was the front window, on which the model of a nude goddess, long hair flowing, was painted.

I rubbed my hands together and thought of calling out. After all, Aurora Benchley had said not more than a half hour ago over the hospital phone that if I was going to catch her, I'd better dash right over. Otherwise, it promised to be a hectic night, with tomorrow offering to be much worse, she said.

My day had been busy as well. I was still troubled by Bob's encounter with the bones. Then there had been the few minutes I'd spent with Crystal Franklin, the TV reporter. Her troubled gaze, what she had told me, made this whole matter worse, if that was possible.

Instead of announcing my presence, I stepped over the creaking wood floor to a large painting on the wall above the counter.

It showed a woman in flowing robes, a crown of thorns on her head, being born through misty clouds by a pair of healthy-looking gray wolves. Women who ride the friendly skies on the backs of would-be dogs, I thought.

Aurora pushed through a doorway covered with strings of beads to my right. As always, the impression I had of her was of a sturdy, determined person who carried her bulk with passion and dignity. Clad in a billowing flannel dress, her forearms bare, her brown-gray hair pulled black in a plain pony tail, she slung me a withering glance, as if maybe I was death warmed over come to make a house call.

"Hi," I said, meek as a lamb, wishing I wasn't such a wash rag when facing women with larger egos than mine.

"Upstairs," she said. "It started quicker than I thought."

"You're sure?"

"If you want to talk, I am." She turned and trundled on up, making the steps groan as she ascended.

"Should we leave the store open?"

"Connie, the cashier, is at Yesterdog. She'll be back in a flash."

In the second-floor hallway, we paused and faced one another. She had a wide pleasant face, a firm jaw and slender mouth. "We'll have to make this quick. Reverend. I'm busy."

I nodded, looking at the door behind her. I thought I heard a murmur of pain or discomfort. Aurora tilted her head, seemed to detect it too. "Just a second." She slipped in and shut the door. I heard movement below,Connie back with the hotdogs. I figured I'd stop there for dinner when I was done. It had been a long afternoon spent in and around Monica's room. Her father and stepmother made a major fuss over Bob and pumped him with endless and useless questions. Mum was his word, as it always had been. If something or someone had spooked him at the museum or if he just became enamored with the bones, we'll never know, I knew.

As for me, my back ached and shoulder hurt from the tumble off the ledge. Bob seemed no worse for the wear. His dad had taken him back to the home. I had left before dinner to talk to the television reporter, then returned to the hospital just as the phone had rung. It was Aurora. Monica had spoken to her earlier and suggested that she give me a few minutes of her time. Aurora had said she had a baby to deliver and I'd better hightail it over.

She now stepped out of the room, fixing me with a questioning look. "You mind holding this young woman's hand."

Through the partly open door, I glimpsed part of a bed, some feet, flickering shadows, but that was all. "I told her you're a minister. She'd like to pray."

Inside, Aurora positioned me at the head of the bed behind her patient, who stretched out, full belly exposed, under me. "Honey, this is Reverend Turkstra. He's going to marry a very good friend of mine." Aurora had bent, forcing her to gaze at me over the moon slope of pregnant stomach.

The woman, a young Indian with very dark hair, oily skin and firm features, tilted her head back and smiled. "Hi."

"Reverend, this is Penny Blackhawk Cramer. She's from Allegan."

I smiled as she extended a plump, clammy hand.

Penny blinked dreamily in my direction. In her smile were bright white teeth. Monica counseled expectant mothers who came to Aurora for help. Among other things, Aurora was a lay midwife, and she specialized in delivering children of women who otherwise might have sought an abortion and who then decided to have their baby this way. I knew, from Monica and others, that Aurora ran afoul of the law on several matters, but she was very experienced in what she had to offer. I think Monica mentioned meeting with an Indian woman whose boyfriend was in the Army. "Can you say the Our Father with me, Reverend?" asked Penny, still smiling, dabs of sweat on her brow.

She was apparently Catholic, since that's what they called the Lord's Prayer. In fact, that's what my staunchly Catholic mother called it as we knelt every night by the bed in the farmhouse near Zuthpen. "Sure," I told her.

As candles flickered on the dresser and shadows danced on the walls and Aurora did her probing and observations, we prayed and asked for, among other things, our daily bread. Finished, Penny gave my hand a strong squeeze. I pressed hers in return, smelling more incense, this richer, with a hint of charred grass in it, and heard the steady thumping of drums pouring from a boom box on the floor at my feet.

"So, talk, Calvin," said Aurora.

"First, thanks for being there for Monica the other night. If you hadn't, who knows what would have happened."

Head buried down below, Aurora said: "Thank Bob."

I tried not to stare at Penny's ballooning gut. Her chest was covered with a rolled up T-shirt and part of a blanket. Her legs tented up, a cloth draped over the knees. I'd been at births before, once in an alley behind the mission in Chicago, and once in the back seat of a cab, as a minister. Then as a paramedic, I'd even helped deliver a couple and had rushed more than a fair share in for delivery. Even so, the sight of that shiny expanding flesh made me uneasy. There was a perfumed sensuality in the room that made my Dutch flesh prickle. "If I have it right, Tina Martin called you and wanted to talk and you thought Monica should be in on it, too?"

She raised a couple inches, enough to shower me with a glower. Probably thought I was blaming her, which I was to an extent. Although Monica was fully capable of getting into jams all on her own. "Basically." She then dipped back.

I still held Penny's hand. She lay quiet, trying to look down and over the mound of her stomach to the midwife.

"Tina and her boyfriend were trying to blackmail whoever it was that attacked Janet VanTol?"

81

Penny had wide, dark eyes full of liquid curiosity. The drums beat, intermixed with the baleful sound of men chanting. I thought I shouldn't be here, or at least not in the capacity of detective bent on learning about murder. But Penny didn't seem to mind terribly. "Is that your theory?" asked Aurora.

My mind flashed on the pictures Crystal had shown me. Photos sent her in the mail. With a warning. I'd seen her just before the evening news. "It is," I answered.

Aurora did midwifery below for a minute or so. Then said: "Tina was there the night Janet and I were at the bar."

What was she doing down there, I wondered, unable to see anything more than the top of her bobbing head. Penny winced a little, and gripped my hand. I let her do it, flushed from the warmth of the room, this dim, candle-lit chamber.

"But you had to leave the bar," I said when she didn't go on, "and Tina offered to take Janet home?" Monica had told me this.

"Home or to the bridge."

"What was at the bridge?"

"The million-dollar question." Aurora raised, arms held out at her sides, plastic gloves on her hands. She patted Penny's knee. I thought of those photos, porn, women with women, twisted expressions on their faces. Sent to Crystal, she said, by the killer. He'd done it before. Used it to scare her, she said. I had gone to ask her again for her source. Met her in her office. She had just opened the day's mail. The photos, from some rag, were spread out on her desk. She didn't name her source. Even so, I filled her in a little on what I knew. I sensed it was the photos, the naked women, her own kind, that drove her to do the story. I had felt sorry for her, knowing it was men who trafficked in this violence of a different kind. "There's a sicko out there, for sure, Turkstra," she had said.

"You're doing fine, hon," Aurora now told her patient. "It's going to be a little while yet. I think we had a false alarm."

82

Almost immediately, Penny let go of my hand and closed her eyes, deciding to catch a few winks between contractions. "We're going out for a couple minutes," said Aurora, hand on Penny's knee. "If you feel anything or need me, just call. I won't be far."

Penny's face had grown somber, her hands folded over her chest. I wanted to touch her forehead, to give her a little comfort. But she didn't seem to need it. As the voices and drums droned and the light from the scented candles waved on the walls like prairie grass in a gentle wind, I followed Aurora out.

We stood side-by-side at the end of the hallway, next to a room that looked like a small library, and stared out at the falling snow. The streets were blocking up, white caps sat atop parking meters and cushioned the sidewalks.

"Thanks," said Aurora. I turned to her, noticing in the dim light of the hallway the strong planes of her face, the clearness of her eyes, the sturdiness of her shoulders. "Praying with Penny. It calmed her right down."

"The pow-wow music did that to me."

"You like it?"

I did. It made me think of New Mexico, when I worked and lived there. I loved the spectacle and rhythmic reverence of the dancing, the drums, the chants, and the fellowship. I never quite understood why some of the native groups pow-wowed and why others didn't. When they did, and if I had time back then, I was there. Ruth, the married lady who made my life so horrible and so wonderful for so long, was often with me as well. She introduced me to the gatherings. A nagging place in me recalled Monica's comments the night before. About dragon slaying. About Ruth. About my lies.

"What other questions do you have?"

Snow tumbled down in slanting streams, making its way to the ground, where it lay mysteriously quiet. Traffic had slowed. A man walked below, his head uncovered and catching blotchy, dandruffy flakes. "What were you and Janet talking about in the bar that night after class?"

"I think," said Aurora, gazing out, arms folded on her chest, "the part that got her most upset was something a good friend of mine had told me a few days before."

This friend told her about a secret group. A group called Soldiers of the Cross. A group of men in our church, gathered to stop women from being preachers. They'd been together for a few years, and were starting to break up. But they were out there yet. Something about it made Janet look scared. I listened with eagerness, thinking of the Jennings. "I don't know, but Janet had to leave after we were talking. She looked like someone stuck her hand in fire."

Finished, Aurora stepped to the side, ran a hand through her hair and gave me a tired, turned-down frown.

"Did Monica know about this?"

She shook her head. "Thing is, I wasn't supposed to tell anyone about this. I was tipsy that night and it came out. When my friend heard what I told Janet, he got pretty mad."

"Who's this friend?"

She motioned her head behind me. We stepped into the library, where she flicked on a Tiffany lamp that threw spindles of multi-colored light on the slender, stick-legged desk on which it sat. Aurora took a package of Virginia Slims out of a desk drawer and offered me one, which I refused, thinking how much I disliked the product's silly "you've come a long way, baby" commercials. She lit up and took in a deep draught of smoke.

"Have you told the police any of this?" I asked.

She whipped out the match, expelled plumes of smoke and sat wearily on the edge of the desk. I liked being surrounded by all of the books, even if most of them dealt in subjects almost totally related to gender differences. "Now I have. And, of course, I told them every iota about the other night."

"How come you got there after Monica?"

She frowned. "I had another birth." Her firm face sagged in places. Her body, under the tenty dress, looked strong and held solid curves. "To tell the truth, I didn't want to go. I thought Tina was just drunk and wanting a shoulder to cry on again."

"She called before?"

"A couple times."

Standing together in the small room with a sloped and shiny wood floor, the books and the rainbow of light, she looked a little scared.

"What was different about this time?"

"Something frantic in her voice."

"Did you know her boyfriend?"

"He was bad news. He was at the bar that night. I think they drove in his car."

"No idea why they dropped her off at the bridge?"

"None."

I saw a current of kindness, mixed with calculation, shift in the dark shimmer of her eyes. "Reverend, I've got to get back."

"Tell me about Soldiers of the Cross."

Snow pattered the window behind her desk. Yellowish street light made it look snotty as it puffed against the beveled glass. The room smelled musty and sweet.

One hand cupping an elbow, the other holding the cigarette next to her cheek, Aurora answered: "You need to talk to Henderson Portfliet."

"Your friend?" I knew him. Who didn't, in our church. The solid conservative voice and pastor from LaGrave Avenue CRC who fell from grace for obscure reasons a year or so ago. Then it immediately hit me. Maybe the reason was standing in front of me.

"He knows I'm talking to you and that I'm giving you his name."

"He's a chaplain in the jail now?"

She bowed her head in a brief nod. "Exactly how much he'll tell you, I'm not sure."

"How is he connected?"

85

Aurora smoked thoughtfully, her cheeks cupping around the smoke, let it out. "He'll have to tell you that."

Down the hall came a groan, muted, but there. Aurora immediately crushed out the cigarette in a metal tray on the desk by an open Bible. The Book of Ruth, I saw and immediately looked away. I stepped out to let her pass. "Just know, please, how sensitive this is for Henderson." She looked back at me over her shoulder.

Henderson had a wife who had been seriously injured a few years back in a car accident. He had written about her, and preached about her, and spoken often about the tribulations she had faced as someone coping with a closed-head injury. As far as I knew, they were still married. His sudden retreat from the pulpit made more sense now. Before Aurora pushed back through the door, I added: "You know, the police might want to talk to Henderson after I do."

"Take it up with him." With that, she was gone, into a room in which I sensed I was no longer welcome now that the precious moment had grown close.

CHAPTER FOURTEEN

Arms digging into and dragging out of the water in the pool at the downtown YMCA, I moved in what seemed like slow motion. Here it was not long after 6 in the morning and my long and lanky body, knobbed and battered from any number of close and troubling encounters over the years, felt like warm glue. I'd left the hospital as Monica lay sleeping and told the security guard still on duty that her father would be there soon. I headed in the aftermath of last night's snow down Bostwick Avenue Hill, across the campus of Grand Rapids Community College and in the front door of the Y. A quick change of clothes and a dive into the steamy water brought me only half awake. Making it to the far end, I dove, did a twist off with my foot and torpedoed back.

As I swam, I thought about God, submarines, and babies being born. Between phone calls and a conversation in Monica's room last night, Aurora called and said she had helped deliver a boy, to be named Derrick Blackhawk Cramer. After the call, Monica told me the dad was in Germany. She also told me the Lotto tickets had been a bust.

As for submarines, I'd been a cook and part-time librarian on the *U.S.S. Virginia* in the late years of the Vietnam War. We'd patrolled fringes of the Pacific and much of the South China Sea for the eight months that I spent on the boat. I thought about subs often when I did my morning swim.

I had loved floating hundreds of feet below the surface, ensconced in a manufactured atmosphere where silence was regularly demanded. It was sort of a deep sea monastery. It was where I came face-to-face with God again. I'd been hiding from him for quite awhile before then, and ended up running from him for many years after. But in the sub, in the soft light of that small makeshift library, or even when mushing up oatmeal in the morning, I had this inkling, this calling from somewhere outside of me.

It was as if the Lord was tapping on the metal of our ship, trying to get my attention gently but with determination. It was during an especially long and grueling patrol off the China coast that I first seriously read Martin Luther and John Calvin, as well as delved into the New Testament.

Swimming the length of the pool, I retraced myself. My heart had started to catch on that sleep no longer was an option and it was time to get pumping. Water buoying me, my legs kicking, the arms still pumping, I drove myself forward, head awash with the froth of my movement. God, I prayed as I swam, stay with little Derrick in this life that is already playing him a tough hand. Dad's not there; mom, Monica told me, might have a problem with booze. God, I thought as my lungs filled from the effort, keep me in mind, too. Not to mention Monica, Bob, and, what the heck, Rodriguez also.

The detective had stopped by last night about 10 and wanted to chat. We did. I told him what I'd learned. But I left out the part about Henderson Portfliet, who I would meet later today. The detective particularly pumped me about Herb, our friendly construction company owner. On this I could be more forthright, and told him that I was well aware now that he was the guy who leaned on the mayor. I told him there was more in there than met the eye. I also mentioned Crystal and the pictures she got.

Finally, Lord, I prayed, lead me further on, help me get deeper into this, for Monica's sake and for mine and for our church's. On the amen part, I dunked my head under, feeling the rush of water in my ears, and swam that way, blindly on, keeping to my lane for several yards.

Praying finished, I got down to business in the water. Gulping air as I turned my head side-to-side, I stopped filling my head with words. Having checked in with God, I set about not thinking. Just swam. My body plowed through the water, the warm wetness sliding around me. I was a dumb fish, a patrolling submarine, riding the rim of the waves. Full of effort and a burning in my chest, I was able to do three more laps this way. Coming to a stop, no longer heavy from sleep, I stood on the tile in the shallow end. Heard the trickle of water sloughing through a trough to my right, re-draining itself. A couple lanes over came the slap and kick of someone else, forging ahead in bubbling water as the world outside arose to five inches of snow.

"Reverend Turkstra?" I heard above me. My arms were splayed on the cool lip of the pool, my chin resting on cement. Hardly moving, I caught the shiny leather of shoes not 12 inches from my eyes. Without raising my face from its perch, I looked up through faint swirls of steam. At first I saw nothing. But then fog shifted, revealing a face, poking out above. Sharp-featured, with a hacksaw jaw. "Yes?" I said, still catching my breath.

"Can we talk?"

The steam shifted in again, then out. He wore a sharply pressed navy blue suit, starched white shirt, red-and-blue striped tie, wedged triangularly into the button-down collar, and had a sharp, sardonic expression on his face. An overcoat had been draped carefully over his left arm. I addressed the shoes, burgundy wingtips: "What do you need?"

"I think you know."

I shoved up and stood, my chest singing from the effort of two miles in the pool. I wiped a stream of chlorinated pool water from the sides of my face. He was a short, peppery man, a bantamweight with flushed red cheeks. Branson VanTol.

"Can we talk over there?" He turned his rooster's body and stepped to a bench by the wall.

Steam twisted between us again, obscuring him. On my walk to the Y, the three blocks down from the hospital, had been wonderfully quiet in the world of white. I suspected angry

89

cars and people would be out there by now, racing down the salted roads or trudging through the drifts on the way to Tuesday morning. I grabbed my towel from the floor and joined him.

I knew I loomed over him as I dug water from an ear and tilted my head this way and that, hearing a tiny slosh in the drums. He stood, still much smaller than me, and held out a hand. I took it and felt him squeeze. Quick, firm, then gone. His eyes glittered and kept after me. I'd never spoken to him before. In his mid-50s, he had the nervous, energetic demeanor of a man on the run. He'd already made me feel guilty for wasting the time to dry off.

"This won't take long," he informed me.

I looped the towel over my shoulder and sat. Then he stood over me, although in his case it wasn't a loom. He seemed momentarily put off his game. A hint of a smile trickled across his thin mouth and then he took a place on the bench next to me. Rubbing a hand over his close-cropped, fuzzy white hair, he asked: "I've been told you're asking about me?"

"I am?"

"Don't play games."

Three others swam in the pool. I loved the smell of the place, the warmth, the echo of water being slapped by hands and feet. But this man had put a damper on it. I felt him bristle with anger without even looking. "How did you find me here, sir?" I slid my eyes at him. He sat straight and stiff, his hands in his lap, his attention on the swimmers.

"I called the hospital. You're father-in-law, I think it was, told me you had come here."

I leaned against the wall, felt my back stick on the tile, found myself still struggling for breath. "You could have left a message."

"This saves the trouble." He hardly blinked when he looked. His eyes, a strange color of blue, didn't leave me. "Your wife," he went on, "I trust she's getting on."

I didn't correct him. "She'll be out soon." I closed my eyes, saw fingers of steam float from sewer grates, opened them, fingered at the slight burn from chemicals in the water. I tugged on the edges of my towel, heard the splash of someone else diving in.

"Herb Wierenga says you have questions?"

"Did he mention what they are?"

VanTol had the poise of someone comfortable in many situations. I knew his family had worked hard and fought when necessary, especially during the Great Furniture Strike in the 1920s, to maintain their business on the West Side. He turned to me, slowly, a thin hard line making his mouth almost disappear. "Reverend, I didn't come here at dawn to parry."

"Do you mind if I stretch?"

He shrugged as I stood, stuck my palms on the walls and worked to draw kinks from my calves. "Herb says he asked the police to shut the book on your daughter's death."

No answer.

"Why is that?" I asked.

VanTol had turned his attention to the pool again. "I'll get right to it, Turkstra. Are you accusing either he or me of wrong-doing?"

"No, sir."

"Then what?"

I leaned into my arms, pushed up on my legs. The warmth of the pool kept water fresh on my back. "I don't understand why the pressure on the police if this was an accidental drowning?"

"Exactly what are you aiming at?"

I shoved hard into the wall, keeping my legs stationary, feeling the blessed tug in the hamstrings. "Is it your theory she slipped and fell in?"

"As you may know, the medical examiner found high levels of drugs and alcohol in her system."

He spoke very clinically about his daughter, I thought. "So you're convinced it was suicide or an accident?"

He blink-stared at me, hands still in his lap. The mouth moved, as if to readjust itself, curling at the side in a half sneer. "Quite possible."

"Do you know. Was she meeting someone at the bridge?"

"Where is this leading?"

I turned and windmilled my arms, toe to toe, releasing knots in my lower back.

"Those are your questions?" he asked.

"I still don't understand why you asked Wierenga to intercede with the mayor."

"Blatantly untrue."

Oh?"

"Herb is a good friend. He took it on himself." He slid a finger over a suit cuff, inched up fabric and checked his watch.

"Because your wife, I understand, was taking it pretty hard," I said.

He edged the cuff of suit exact with the cuff of his shirt. Preparing to leave. Then he stood, puffed out his chest, gave me a banty rooster's glare, a fine flush blooming on his face. "Leave my wife out of this, please."

I stopped stretching, felt the heat evaporate and the chill of the place rub against me. I used my towel as a cape. "Mr. VanTol, it looks very much like what happened to your daughter is connected to what happened to Monica and to the others."

"Which others?"

"Have you been watching the news, sir?"

He glared at me with a hard flinty expression, his chin extended, his fists at his sides. Like Herb, he wanted to mix it up. He bounced twice on the balls of his feet. I could see anger swell in his body, ballooning it up and out. I once read a story about a fistfight he had gotten into on the floor of his factory with a man who was trying to unionize the place. "Why are you sticking your nose in this anyhow, Turkstra?"

I rubbed my nose, patted it into place, let my gaze drift beyond him to the churn of water in the pool.

"What right have you to be probing into my personal business?" He edged closer, his aftershave lotion wafting up at me. I noticed his skin was so closely shaved it shone. His scalp, pink in places, poked through the bristly white hair.

"Either you are a very private man, Mr. VanTol, or you have something to hide."

"I have nothing to hide, Turkstra. Take it from there."

I stepped around him to the edge of the pool, where I knelt and cupped water in my hand. I dumped some over my head, a gesture that reminded me I was supposed to baptize an infant at Sunday's service. I reminded myself to give the family a call. I figured, if Monica came home, I could get back to some of my duties at the church. As it was, work was piling up. I spoke to water that glistened and rolled before me, "Have you heard of a group called the Soldiers of the Cross?"

Nothing.

I looked over my shoulder at him. "No?"

"That's my answer."

I stood. "I'm sorry, sir, if I'm getting you mad," I said, well aware it was a blatant lie.

"You're too young to get my goat." I doubted that. "Do you have anything else?" he asked.

"The Promise Keepers you have heard of."

"Of course."

"They might be involved in this somehow, too."

He mouth continued its curl. "Reverend, someone has been reading too many spy novels."

"Why's that?"

"Our church is having problems, but I sincerely doubt anyone has turned some secret organization loose."

"Even if your daughter was killed by it?"

The color heightened in his face. He seemed to swell even more, his upper body boosting up toward me. "My daughter was a troubled girl. If you can prove this terrible accusation, please, I want to be the first to know. Otherwise, Pastor, go

93

back to your pulpit and leave this work to people who are trained for it."

"I suppose, then, that you won't want to tell me what things were troubling Janet?"

"My daughter is dead, Turkstra. Leave it alone." His voice rose and cracked with emotion.

We faced off another few seconds. As we did, I noticed his eyes change. They grew colder, less clear. He struck me as a very hard man. Fit and full of rage ready to blow at any second. Yet, he'd kept his business afloat all of these years. "Anything else?" he then asked.

"No, sir, nothing."

Still, he didn't leave. Those eyes, they changed again. Pain leaked into them. A primal hurt. Grief over a daughter? I wondered. But then they changed once more. Grew brighter, more animated. He nearly smiled. "Do you really think you know?" he asked.

"Know what?"

"What it's like to lose a daughter?"

"I don't. But I can sympathize."

The smile turned into a sick smirk. He rubbed a thumb and forefinger together. "They teach you that in seminary?"

"Pardon?"

"How to act like you understand someone's pain when you don't?"

Mostly, they taught us about God and grace, which was about suffering, I thought, but didn't reply.

VanTol shook his head, as if I was a kid who misspelled his own name. "I have to get to work." He turned on his heels, stepped over and retrieved his overcoat, folded neatly on the corner of the bench. "Mr. VanTol?"

He paused, not turning, his stiff back bristling.

"Do you still attend West Leonard?"

"I do," he replied, and let his head twist partly back in my direction.

94

"Are you a member of the PKs?"

He faced me fully before answering, a natty man whose suit held its sharp creases even in the humidity of the pool. "Is the pope a queer?" He watched my reaction, which I kept poker-faced, or so I hoped, just wanting him to further explain. "My opinion, they are momma's boys, crying in spilled milk," he added.

"You've told Herb this?"

"He knows what I think." Tough old buzzard, I thought, as he turned and disappeared through the steam.

CHAPTER FIFTEEN

Waves of stale heat beat my face from the dashboard vent. A minor cloud of bluish cigar smoke settled between us, infecting the air with a rancid, dirty socks stink. I waved a hand at it, returning it an inch or so to its source. Manny Rodriguez gave me a one-eyed glance and cracked his window a milli-inch. "Don't smoke, Reverend?" He twirled the stogie, thick as a blood-filled slug, and let watery-looking smoke leak from his mouth.

"Where'd you buy it, the dump?"

He snorted and leaned back in his seat, letting the tube tilt up, the flaring tip fuming toward his eyes, which were brimmed with a wide white straw hat with a black band. In it, he looked like a middle-aged Jimmy Buffett who planned to crash a winter beach party.

"You guys have some law against smoking? You figure it's a sin or something?" His dark humorless eyes slid toward me. We were parked on Bridge Street, by a meter next to the First Step House, a storefront AA meeting place, and across the way from Kale's Bar, our destination. I wasn't sure why we were shooting the stinky breeze when what he wanted was inside the beer joint.

"To be technical, it is in Paul's tenth letter to the Romans. Anyone who smokes cigars fat as yours comes down with terminal hives."

He nodded, the inch-long ash dropping onto the chest of his leather coat. He shoved it off. "Never read that."

I suspected we could go on, trading ill-humored barbs for awhile, but I was a little like stiff-lipped VanTol. I had business to take care of today, if nothing else than to answer the calls

96

piling up in my office and to make arrangements for Sunday's service. But this could be important, too. "You know Branson VanTol?"

He turned to me, no hint of a smile on the mouth, from which he yanked the smoldering cigar and held between two fingers about chin-high. "He's a hemorrhoid."

"You're best pals then?"

"Ha ha."

I sank back in my seat, crossed arms over my chest and gazed at the snowy road, down which cars and trucks spattered salt. Their headlights were dim in the gray morning light that obscured the fronts of stores that comprised this seedy near downtown business district.

"Why do you ask?" wondered the cop.

"He paid me a visit this morning."

"You're a popular guy."

I filled him in, briefly.

Rodriguez rolled the cigar thoughtfully. I wondered what possessed him to stick a summer hat on his head in the dead dregs of winter. "Sounds like you sent a few bees buzzing up his ass."

"Right around his hemorrhoids."

This drew a quick smile, which the detective put away almost as soon as it showed up. "Maybe I need to pay him a visit."

"Bring the Preparation H?"

"Something like that," he grumbled, probably wondering why he ever brought up the topic.

"Tell me again why you think Preacher is going to talk to me?" I asked.

Crunched between us on the console of his Buick Electra was a bag of donuts. He had set a jumbo cup of coffee on the top of the dash. When he picked me up outside the church, he'd asked me to jump in. He offered a donut, which I declined. He had then munched away without asking me again.

97

I stared at the bag now, my stomach rolling with hunger, my pulse just starting to quiet from the swim. I picked up and rooted through the bag, dug out a chocolate with sprinkles, and stuck a bite in my mouth. He watched me with a frown. "Help yourself."

Sprinkles dribbled onto my chin. Rodriguez looked disgusted as he scooped a wadded napkin from the floor by his feet and handed it to me. "You wipe your nose on this?" I wondered.

"My butt."

I let it drop, swiped the donut debris with a wrist and waited for him to answer my previous question. But he hunched back, squinting over his steering wheel, cigar unsmoked in his hand. He wore jeans and those snakeskin boots. Wiping his face with his free hand, he said: "You like this city?"

"Why?"

"There's hardly anything to do on weekends."

"Try church."

He straightened and gave me a withering glance, making his mustache move as he did. "You on a recruiting binge?"

I thought of several nice things to say. Instead, I did a frontal look out the windshield, watching traffic, then turned to my right to the AA place, where a picture of praying hands hung in the window. Under it was a sign: "One Day at a Time." "Are we waiting for him to come out?"

Rodriguez took up his cup of coffee and slugged it down with a scowl. It had to be cold. "That's what I'd been hoping. But looks like we have to go in after him."

"First?"

He paused, crouched halfway out the door, and turned to me with one eye wider than the other, which made him look expectant. "Why am I here?" I asked.

"I might need your help." With that, he climbed out and headed across the street, moving fast, dodging a diaper van and a rusty Escort belching smoke and thumping with hugely amplified rap music. On the way here, I again mentioned the dirty pictures sent to the TV woman. I wondered if he might want to check them out for prints. He'd said he was way ahead of me. Crystal had called, as she had in the past. Before, they had ignored her. This time, they decided to give them a powder.

Instead of following him, I waited a second, drawn back to those folded hands. I didn't know much about AA, except that it seemed to be the only thing that really worked with dyed-in-the-liver drunks. No one seemed to be inside. I pressed my hands together a second and made a quick prayer. This one for Monica. Somehow her presence had been with me all morning, the sound of her breathing last night, the soft glow from the window on her face. It enraged me to think of what happened to her. More than that, it scared the daylights out of me to realize another couple bumps in the wrong places on those stairs and I could have lost her for good.

Preacher was holding court in a corner booth behind the pool table and just below a Budweiser poster showing a bevy of buxom women in pink swimsuits. Waves hung above them, about to crash down and drench their hairdos. Rodriguez had pulled up a backwards chair and was sipping some sort of drink out of a glass. Two others, a man and a women, sat next to Preacher. His mouth made a rodent-like nibble as I approached across the dark room. Some sort of whiny you-left-me-high-and-dry song was warbling from a jukebox. "Look what the cat drug in," said Preacher. "Buy the man a double."

No one moved to buy me anything, which was fine. Two drinks of any kind turned me into a simpleton. Some folks would say that's no change, but it's a turn in the old inner landscape that I can always feel. I leaned on the edge of the pool table, looking down. Rodriguez, on my left, swirled the ice in his glass. I could tell his anger, always present, had shifted into gear. His eyes smoldered in Preacher's direction. "Sit, Turkstra," Preacher said, flopping a hand at an empty spot across from him in the booth.

"No, thanks."

Preacher had three beer bottles in front of him. The woman on his right was skinny and had a nose that took up three-quarters of her face. Her tiny mouth, outlined in red, was filled with a cigarette. The guy was dumpy, fat and acned. Quite a pleasant trio, just passing the time of day in a dive that smelled like lighter fluid and burned popcorn. "C'mon, guys," Preacher said to the both of us. "Join the party."

On the way over, Rodriguez said a patrol officer had spotted Preacher rolling down the shoveled sidewalk on Bridge about 7:30 in his wheelchair. The cop stopped to have a word with him, since he knew that the detectives were hoping to ask him again what he'd seen around the dumpster the other night. The fact that he was so far from home, at least a mile and across the river from Heartside, had apparently got the policeman curious. In their talk, Preacher said he was going for a morning pick-me-up at Kale's. He told the cop if Rodriguez wanted him to stop by, fine, but to bring me along, too. Exactly why I got the invite was still unclear.

"No party, Darrell. We want to ask some questions," said Rodriguez, tipping back the brim of his Jimmy Buffett hat.

Preacher didn't like his Christian name. So he pouted. Slouched over his beer, sucked on the top, ignoring us.

"Why don't you two go make a novena or something," Rodriguez said to Preacher's companions.

The woman smiled, as if she had been complimented. The fat one got the picture and hoisted himself to his feet, bumping the table with his belly in the process. "Let's go, Cam."

Cam smiled some more, her nose dipping toward her mouth, about to go in, it seemed to me. The big guy leaned over, across Preacher, who was still in never-never land, and jerked her arm. This got her attention. She wheeled back, as if trying to balance her head on her shoulders. "Let's hit it." He started dragging her, shoving into Preacher, who sat up and pushed back.

100

I stepped in. "Slide out this way," I said, nodding at my end of the horseshoe- shaped booth. She tried to focus on me. "She don't need your help, mister," said the pudgy slob, weaving toward me.

Rodriguez bullied him back and away. The guy didn't resist. He stared over the detective's shoulder at me. "You want to boogie?" he said.

Rodriguez kept him in fast transit all the way to the end of the bar, where they had a brief discussion, during which the cop stuck a finger a few times in the man's chest.

Cam came meekly out, smiling with dog's eyes. "Hey, what's your name?" she slurred, touching my jacket with a hand whose fingers were filled with silvery rings.

"He's a minister, Camile," said Preacher.

"I like men of the cloth," Cam said.

"He's already got a woman."

"Oh? Is she sexy like me?"

I stepped away from the blast of her breath. She wore a purple-and-white striped blouse, cut low to reveal a wrinkled neck. Her hips hugged the jeans she'd somehow climbed into. "No, ma'am, she's not like you at all," I replied.

Preacher started to cackle, which turned into a cough. Cam looked hurt, her eyes filming, her mouth trembling. I touched her shoulder. "She's older, a minister, too. We're getting married."

The eyes clicked into clarity. "Isn't that nice." She turned to Preacher. "Did you know he's getting hitched?" Saying that, she hiccoughed.

Preacher slapped the table with a palm. "Damned straight. Soon as he gets the guts to walk the plank. Right, Turkstra?"

"Hey, that's no way to talk to a minister," whined Cam.

Preacher shook his head. "Turkstra ain't no regular churchman."

Rodriguez returned. "Blimpface needs you to take him to pee," he said to Cam, who didn't quite get it.

101

"Later, Cam" said Preacher.

Still, she stood there. Fatso started our way. I touched her bony shoulder. "You better let us alone awhile. We need to talk." She smiled, trying to flirt, but stumbled instead. Even so, she got her bearings and wobbled toward her man. The two of them took seats at the bar, a couple of lovebird beer guzzlers.

I slipped in one side of the booth. Rodriguez took the other. Between us, Preacher was back to lipping his bottle, pretending we weren't there.

"Where's your wheelchair, Darrell?" asked the detective.

"Cut with the Darrell business, OK?"

Rodriguez slumped in his seat, hands folded in front of him on the table. He shrugged and smiled at me, as if I was in on a joke.

"I checked it at the door," Preacher replied.

"How do you get to the bathroom to whiz then?"

Preacher shook his head heavily. He had long brown stringy hair, a pinched face with features that seemed sliced carefully out of his flesh. It was nonetheless a handsome face, presenting a strong chin and firm bones. "You have a toilet fetish, Detective?"

Rodriguez straightened up and leaned forward, over his hands, ready to talk turkey. He twisted his face, heavy with a shadow of beard, at Preacher. "Where'd you get the hat, by the way?" Preacher wondered.

The detective's eyes rolled up, as if to check it out.

"I mean, it's a little out of season." Preacher really liked this and chuckled, making watery sounds in his chest. He smelled like charcoal and wet wool.

"What'd you see the other night, Darrell?" the cop asked.

Preacher idly tilted his beer bottle back and forth. The lovebirds, I noticed, were smooching. There was nothing dainty about it. Oddly, I wondered where did they go to church, if anywhere. They'd fit right in at my place. All the while I'd been watching them kiss, Preacher had kept his trap shut. Rodriguez started jiggling his hands on the table; he looked nervous and ready for some sort of action. "You're planning to waste my time again?" asked the cop.

"I didn't ask you here."

"Jerry said you did."

"Who's Jerry?"

"Dick who stopped you coming over here, which makes me wonder. Why'd you travel across town to get drunk today?"

Preacher swung back his hair. His wore a baggy turtleneck sweater, probably mission issued. Under the table were his twisted legs, the victims of a land mine in Vietnam, he always told everyone. But he was only in his early 30s, too young for Vietnam. The mayor told me he broke his back in a fall a few years back when he lived in Texas. He didn't answer Rodriguez.

"Why'd you want me here?" I asked.

Preacher came to my church sometimes. Once in awhile, he'd argue during the sermon. The first time it flustered me. After that, I realized I just had to shoot a few theological barbs his way to shut him up. "I don't think you're out to fuck me," he said seriously.

Rodriguez looked at me, as if wondering why anyone would put their faith in me. "I'm hurt, Darrell," he said.

Preacher clammed up again.

"I mean, why don't you trust me?"

"Wild guess." Preacher shook his head in disgust.

"You know," I said, "if you have something important to say, I'd have to tell the police anyhow."

Preacher sat up, looped his arms on the back of the booth. "I need another Bud."

Rodriguez smoldered me a glance, his mouth tight under the mustache, and got up. "You mind if I piss in it first?" he asked.

"There you go again."

The cop sauntered off and leaned on the bar by the lovers, who were now drinking from one another's glasses. How tender, I thought, feeling a strange pang to think of Monica confined to that bed, her body still recovering from the violence. I leaned across to Preacher. "What'd you see?"

He closed his eyes, as if he'd filed it away and had to roll it up on the back of his lids. He placed his palms flat down on the table, mixing in with a puddle of beer. His head nodded. I recalled how he had come to me a month before, distraught about the cancer his sister in Ohio had come down with. He wanted money to take the bus to see her. When I asked for the number to her home or to the hospital, he called me cheap and left. But that's when he said maybe he'd try our AA meeting again. Which he did, at least until lately.

"Preacher," I said.

Summertime often found him, when he was in town and wasn't in some jitter joint or traveling, on the corner near Division and Weston, sermonizing to beat the band. I'd heard him a couple times and had actually been impressed. The mayor told me Preacher did attend a Methodist seminary in Florida for awhile. "Brown van," he said softly.

Rodriguez had twisted around, beer and glass of something in his hands, staring darkly at us from his spot at the bar. Waiting, giving me some slack.

"When was this?"

"Not too long before the bag lady opened it up for dinner."

"Where were you?"

"Me and the little woman was popping a few in the weeds by the old depot."

"You saw someone dumping things?"

"Truly."

"Can you identify him?" It was Rodriguez, our swarthy guardian angel, in for the kill. Preacher frowned as he stuck the beer in front of him. "Huh, Darrell?"

"I forget."

I breathed deep. "We were talking here," I told the detective.

104

Rodriguez plopped down and slid close to Preacher. "I felt left out."

"Why don't you play pool," I suggested.

"Can't. I'm on company time."

"But you can drink?" I said, eyeing his glass.

He took a sip. "Iced tea."

Preacher sat there, as if dazed, arms at his side, facing his untouched beer. "Drink up, Darrell."

"Why don't you eat a straight razor?"

Rodriguez leaned in to him. "I'm not screwing around anymore. You have something to say. Say it. Who was driving this van. Or is this just another figment of your squirrely head?"

"You're a real charmer, Manny."

He turned to me, his eyes flashing. "Put a lid on it, Reverend." Rodriguez made chewing gum motions with his mouth, swilled back a slug of his black tea, and then wiped his mouth with the sleeve of his leather jacket. He still wore the silly white Panama hat. But there was nothing else silly about him. He addressed Preacher in a low voice: "Why don't we drive you home. On the way, we'll stop at my office."

"I got a doctor's appointment."

"Then what are you doing here?"

"We're going to meet. He'll do surgery in the back. Penile implant." For some reason, Preacher thought that was funny as all get out. He flung back his head and began to laugh. At first, I thought Rodriguez was going to reach out with one of those hams he used as hands and squeeze Preacher around the voice box. But Manny surprised me. He started laughing, too. For the better part of 30 seconds, the pair of them yukked it up like a couple of old-time pals.

CHAPTER SIXTEEN

Usually I loved the silence of the library, especially the richly wood-paneled Michigan Room, where high ceilings and tall windows encouraged deep thoughts. But not today. Spread out before me in news clippings and slick copy machine reproductions was the disturbing story of Rene Wierenga.

Included were photos, mostly accompanying the articles. Here she was stretching on a balance beam, her back straight and chin pointed forward, knees properly bent. There, in a *Grand Rapids Press* Sunday magazine piece, she stood with a few other Olympic hopefuls, smiling in a group, a championship medal slipped over her head. She had strong, attractive features, chestnut hair, a lithe, muscular body, a lively and yet strangely distracting mouth. I ran a hand over the surface of one story, the obit, a powerfully written, insightful and thoroughly compelling look at her life, and death. It also came out of the *Press*, written by a man named Jim Mencarelli.

I looked up when a stocky woman in glasses and a baggy wool sweater took the seat across the table. She smiled sadly, her eyes obscured behind glasses. She wore her hair brushed back with a couple waves riding the crest of her forehead. "Find what you're looking for?"

"There's a lot here."

The librarian who had helped me find this file nodded, making no attempt to hide her mood. Her somber expression, however, fit my own feelings.

"Mind if I make copies?"

"Certainly not."

My hand continued to rub across the pages, as if I was trying to divine more than the words and pictures could tell.

After our little sit-down at the bar with Preacher, Rodriguez had dropped me off at the church, where I spent a couple hours catching up and trying to dodge the questions brought by street people who drifted in from outside, with good intentions. But I just didn't have time for much dilly-dallying.

Then, about one, I'd called Monica and told her I'd be right up. Which is when she mentioned she'd had a visit from Missy DeGraaf, a student and roommate of Janet VanTol. Missy came by to tell her something that may or may not be important. Janet VanTol had talked often, Missy said, about Rene Wierenga, who was older and yet was a guiding light in her life. Missy told Monica she somehow felt there was a strong connection, maybe even to what happened to Janet. She also said there was lots of information on Rene at the library. Janet had told her that. Janet, in fact, had insisted if anything ever happened to her to make sure people knew about this. Exactly why Missy decided to spill the info on this now, who knows. "I think maybe learning about what happened to me and then hearing again about Janet got her thinking," Monica had said.

Monica had wondered what I thought. Since I didn't know much about Rene, but had a hunch Missy was on to something, given the tie to Herb, I decided to stop at the library, a three-block walk from my church, to see what was there. I wasn't sure why I had the feeling this might help, but I was glad I'd acted on it.

As soon as I mentioned what I wanted, the librarian directed me to a special card catalogue filled with biographical information about local people. The card in the file pointed me to a mother lode of a folder filled with clips and stories about Rene.

Rene, I read, had been a gymnastic star in high school at East Grand Rapids and then again at Western Michigan University. Somewhere in there she'd almost made the Olympic team. In her junior year in college her life fell apart. She had gotten pregnant, quit school, moved back to Grand Rapids, had the baby and then in the winter of 1986 had been standing on the pier at the lighthouse in Grand Haven, her infant in her arms, in a storm. More than a few people had seen her go out there. Two men, fishermen riding in on choppy water, watched a huge wave wash in and carry mother and child away. This last part was written powerfully in the *Press* article about her death. The reporter had gone the extra mile on that one.

Still touching the pile of paper, I had no idea how significant any of it was. But I felt a strong link.

"Do you remember any of that?" asked the librarian.

Only a few patrons sat at the long tables in the Michigan Room, hunched over books and magazines. Sickly yellow light stuck to the windows, trying to get in. Paintings of local and state political luminaries lined one wall. "No, I wasn't living here then," I answered.

"It was sad."

It sounded so. But there was something else. Two yellowed news articles in the folder. These described the death of Rene's mother, Ann Wierenga, in 1973. The woman passed away suddenly at her cottage near Saugatuck, apparently when she accidentally fell and hit her head on the side of a table. Not much there, just enough to raise a bunch of questions. "You know, I'm surprised to find so much," I told the librarian.

"Well, there's a reason for that," she said.

Contained in the pile were small clippings of Rene's many accomplishments on the balance beam, from grade school on. There were several about her run for the chance to grab the gold. She'd been one of the finalists in competitions in Florida and Colorado before bowing out. In an obit on her mom, it was mentioned that she, too, had been an athlete. A crack golfer.

"I called the police about this once, but they didn't think it was too important," she said.

I glanced down to find Rene smiling at me, dressed in a gym uniform, sweat on her brow. Next to that photo was a stormy-looking picture of the wave-tossed pier at Grand Haven, with the lighthouse barely visible through the angry roll of weather.

"Someone brought it in, last year, and left it," the librarian told me.

"Janet VanTol?"

"How did you know?"

I gave her a quick rundown. As I did, I felt my attention quicken, my pulse jump. Knowing in my bones things were brewing.

The librarian sighed. She reached over and lightly touched a corner of the pile. "You see, she'd come in to research, on this possibly, but I'm not sure. I had seen here a few times. I'd helped her find a few things. Then one day, she showed up with the whole mess and asked if we would mind starting a special folio on her friend." The librarian watched me carefully, the eyes moving behind the glasses. "I told her it wouldn't be a problem. This is a local history room. The more we have on Grand Rapids people and their accomplishments the better. My boss agreed."

Again, I looked down. In one photo, Rene stood atop the balance beam, arms extended, a huge smile on her face, the bodysuit stretched to the hilt. In the story on her death, there had been no mention of the father of her child. Nor was there solid speculation on whether it had been an accident or suicide. More or less, it had been treated like an accident. Friends said Rene loved the pier. Why she went out there then, and with her baby, no one could, or wanted, to say. The reporter mostly wrote about her accomplishments. "What we've got here is Janet's personal collection?"

The librarian gave me a quick "you-hit-the-jackpot" nod. "I think so."

"But why leave it here when she did, and why keep it anyway?"

"Good questions." She turned to the left. A couple customers stood expectantly at her research desk. She gave me a shrug and got up.

"The copy machine . . . ?"

She crooked a finger, indicating a spot behind the catalogue containing information on all sorts of West Michigan lore, some of it funny, some of it silly, some of it downright tragic.

CHAPTER SEVENTEEN

Wearing her pink-tinted glasses, Monica sat up in bed and read through the copies I had made. She was so intent that I stepped over and stood at the window, from which I could see a wide vista heading due south out of town. Heartside Ministry Center, my modest place of business, was out there somewhere. From this perch in the DeVos Women's and Children wing of the hospital, the stark picture was of snow, the soaring spires of the mainline downtown churches, the minor sprawl of downtown and in the far, far distance the rolling hills around 92nd Street, which marked the southern edge of the county. It was a bright day, full of sharp sunshine and clouds clear as the mind of God, or so one of my former Sunday schoolers would have said.

"So, Turkstra, what do you make of this?" she said.

"Strange isn't the right word," I said, "but it's what comes to mind."

She slid the glasses down and peered at me over the wide lenses. The swelling was gone on her face, the bruises muted. Her full shy beauty was back. Earlier, her stepmom, now down eating a late lunch with her husband, had done Monica's blonde hair in a series of soft puffs and swirls. My fiancée, with makeup on and liveliness back in her face, looked striking. Maybe it was the sun; probably it was a healthy dose of middle-aged lust. The both of us were in our thirties, never married, but certainly not celibate, which was or wasn't sinful depending on your reading of your own conscience. It was the body part, the touching and the joy, that was forcing us to make a decision about marriage. A decision turning into roadblocks because of a past I couldn't quite digest. "I mean," I said, "there's some-

111

thing going on here that ties in with Rene and her death, I just have to think."

"Why?"

"A feeling I have. Plus, the tender care Janet took to assure this information had a safe place. Finally, because she was a Wierenga."

Monica gave me a skeptical look, pushed her glasses back up and read on, setting the pages to her side.

I sat on the window ledge as a nurse came in and fussed and checked things, gave me a smile and left. Monica's broken leg no longer was elevated. It was in a cast, but she had been up, hobbling the hall earlier. "Thing I'm wondering," I said, "is about the water."

She set the stack of papers in her lap and folded her hands on them, giving me her full attention. She wore her own pink nightgown, silky and frilled at the collar, a gift from yours truly at Christmas. Pink lipstick shone on her mouth.

"First, Rene is swept up in the lake, and then Janet supposedly falls in the river. Both die. In both cases there's a question of suicide."

"Either could have been an accident."

"Or worse."

"Or worse," she agreed. Monica lapsed into thoughtful silence for a minute. I took the opportunity to just look at her. The skin, the curves of her face, her body. No, she was not like skinny, hook-nosed Cam at all. When we had left the bar, Cam and her blubbering buddy were arguing about how much snow we had gotten last night.

"What?" said Monica, gazing over, as if just becoming aware of my tender gawking.

"I'm glad you're doing OK."

"Is that all?"

I bit. "Plus, I love you."

Pleased, she smiled, but then her expression grew dark. "I wish I knew what to make of Rene and Janet and . . . what happened to me and the others." She stared hard at me, pain spreading like a stain, the memory of her fall down the stairs and the hooded man no doubt stabbing into her again.

I stepped over, sat in the chair and took her hand through the siderail. It swarmed with heat. I pressed and held it tight. Monica turned her face to the ceiling, the eyes closed, breath coming fast. She squeezed me back, as if the mere touch gave substance she needed.

"You know," she said after awhile, "Janet was in therapy pretty heavily when she was in my class, and probably after."

Besides working on her doctorate in psychology at Michigan State University and teaching courses at local colleges, Monica was a counselor herself. An overachiever well beyond my belief, she had a Master's in Divinity from the University of Chicago and a Master's in Social Work from Central Michigan. "You're thinking that's important?" I said, no doubt giving her a glimpse of my acute powers of investigation.

"I just wonder," said Monica, addressing the ceiling, "if something happened in there to get her going? Compiling the folder on Rene and then handing it off to the library makes me think." She turned back to me, a hopeful, probing look on her face.

"You think she was getting her affairs in order?"

"I don't know."

"You're wondering if something in therapy got stirred, made her look back at Rene, and then drown herself, too?"

Monica frowned. "I don't know about the drowning part."

"Hard to argue that both of these don't have some elements of suicide in them."

"True."

My eyes drifted to the harsh sunlight at the window. "You know who her therapist was?"

"Aurora might."

Black dots bounced before my eyes as I kept them locked on the sun, as if staring through it would give us answers. "But

113

if there was something, wouldn't it have come out by now. No therapist is going to keep confidential information that could clear up a death."

"Probably not," she said.

I closed my eyes, the events of the day tumbling through my mind: the steamy pool, the stinky bar, the quiet buzz in the library. A brown van. Two women who met their deaths in water. But if they killed themselves, what about Tina and her chopped-up boyfriend, and Monica? Maybe, it struck me, they weren't connected.

"Turk?"

I looked back at her, focusing on her face, washed in sun, the bruises faint on one cheek, the other round and pink as a baby's behind. Why that image came to mind, I can't say. Maybe our upcoming nuptials, the discussions we'd had on becoming doting middle-aged parents. Or the midwife's room, the Indian mother praying with me.

"I love you, too, by the way," she said.

"Good."

Our hands, still linked, flirted around, sliding and slipping against one another. The relief I felt that she was OK was enormous. As I looked at her with what had to be adoring eyes, another image shouldered its way in to my mind: Ruth. Dark-haired, tawny-skinned, full-lipped, an adulteress. Me the other half of that very painful and obsessive equation. I blinked my eyes, forcing it away.

"But one other thing?" said Monica. As if sensing that Ruth's memory had intruded again, her hand ceased its action, got a little limp, ready to pull away. "Charley Scholten was in here earlier."

Scholten served as senior pastor of Eastern Avenue CRC, a fairly progressive congregation on the Southeast Side. It sat next to railroad tracks near which there had once been a riot when Dutch immigrants tried to stop the streetcar from running through during Sunday worship. Bashing heads to keep the

Lord's Day sacred was about our speed. As for Charley, he was a burr in my side, given his intentions for Monica. Not romantic notions, I mean. His desires were entirely professional. "Just paying a pastoral visit?"

"Sort of." Monica was a member of his congregation, and had been since before I took over at Heartside. She'd been dividing her time between the places.

"There's more?"

She gave a quick, serious nod, our hands returned to their respective owners. "He's still after you?" She pursed her mouth, not pleased with my choice of words. I pretended I was aboveboard and thoroughly ministerial. I wondered if she chose to bring this up now to punish me for Ruth. Women, I often believed, had a second sight when it came to matters such as this.

"He told me they're going to issue me a call, if I'm interested, for the church they're starting in Forest Hills."

They'd been threatening to formally ask Monica to agree to become pastor of the small suburban sister congregation, now meeting out of a motel room on 28th Street near Woodland Mall. If it came to be, and our summer Synod signed off to let women preach, she could end up being one of the first female pastors in our denomination. Quite a feat, but scary and probably full of dangers. "Why now?" I asked.

"Why not now? I'm not crippled. I'll be home soon."

We'd been over this many times. I'd had mixed feelings and thoughts on the whole business. On a broad level, I struggled over whether the Bible lets woman assume preacherly roles. Mostly, I think it makes room for them to be ordained. But more personally and selfishly, I'd wanted to be the pastor in our upcoming union, not the both of us. Thinking that in the hospital room, I realized again it was a power struggle, and not theology, that had kept us apart on this. But there was another thing: the viciousness of the attack on her, maybe connected to our theology. "What're you thinking you'll do?" I asked.

Her head lolled back, eyes on the ceiling again. "I don't know." She read the ceiling tiles awhile, then added: "Probably accept."

"Even after what happened the other night?"

She looked at me, a firm expression turning her lips into a thin line and her eyes into determined slits. This is particularly where she was different from Ruth. Monica was more than able to make up her mind. "Especially now!"

What happened next surprised the daylights out of me. But there you are. You bumble along, waffling this way and that on matters of weighty importance, and suddenly clear emotion overwhelms thought and you know where you stand. My reservations seemed to pop like balloons. Not sure why. I leaned forward in the chair, dropped my elbows over the bed rail. "Good!"

She blinked, twice, as if getting me lined up in her eyes. "Really?"

Monica had been a minister in a non-denominational church a couple years before. It turned out that her boss, the senior pastor, Richard Rhodes, was a crook, and she left, vowing never to assume an ordained leadership role in a church ever again. When she returned to the CRC, the faith of her youth, she said to me that she wouldn't involve herself in the boiling women's issue. But slowly she had, particularly through the course she taught at the seminary. Now, she'd taken the wagon train farther. "If you're up for it, I am," I said.

"It may be rough."

I shrugged and touched her hands, folded on her stomach. Her leg, covered by the cast, sat below. "Seems to me, it already has been."

CHAPTER EIGHTEEN

Shouts, screams, laughs, and loud conversations mixed with the slam of cellblock doors, the thump of music and squawk of TVs as I followed Reverend Henderson Portfliet along the hallway in the Kent County Jail. A few years back taxpayers forked over millions to build a huge, new, state-of-the-art addition to the lockup. I'd been in that part a few times to visit church members, or would-be church members, but I'd never had the dismal pleasure of walking through the old section, as we were now. It was much darker and cramped.

I looked in the cells and noticed men in drab green jail uniforms lounging on their bunks, sitting at tables, playing cards, or standing blank-eyed by the bars. A couple of them gave a hard-guy glower, one showed a gang sign, but most ignored us.

At the end of a hall that seemed more a dungeon-like tunnel than anything else, Portfliet indicated a large cell on our left, stepped back to let me go first. I hesitated a moment, detecting the distinct odor of urine, before entering. Once I was inside, Portfliet waved down the hall at the glassed-in guard booth. As soon as he joined me, the heavy metal door slid shut, moving from its place in the wall and locking us in with a sturdy clang. It sounded so final, like the rock rolled in front of Christ's burial cave. Although he sprang free. Which gave me hope. "So," said Portfliet, turning to me.

"Thanks for making time," I said.

The jail chaplain nodded quickly, checking me out with nervous eyes, and wandered over to the window. It was painted yellow, covered with chain-link fencing and closed. There was nothing to see, but he went there anyway. I'd tracked him down

117

from Monica's room. He told me he was visiting inmates in the county jail all day. Then he left tomorrow for something or another. If I wanted to talk, today was it. Except, he said, he couldn't leave the joint.

I told him my ID would get me in. So he met me downstairs and waited on the other side of the revolving, thick-paned doors that led in and out of the jail.

"We could have met in my office, but that's way over in the new part, and I've got a Bible study in here in a half-hour," he said.

Translated: Get a move on Turkstra. I sat at a thickly painted brown picnic table. To the left was an open toilet, the source of the not-so-jazzy smell. A pile of tracts and prayer booklets, and a Revised Standard Version of the Bible, sat on the table. The walls were slime-green cinder blocks, the ceiling a harsh yellow. "I've never been in this older part before."

Leaned against the window, his hands behind him, Portfliet nodded. He was a chubby man with receding black hair, dressed in dark slacks, a black sweater vest, open-necked pink shirt. I didn't know him very well, but every time we'd met I'd sensed he considered himself a hotshot. He had a smug smile and kept adjusting his neck, as if making room for an ascot. Sorry, Lord, for the judgment, but, hey, there you are. The guy hit me as a prig. The fall from grace at his church and the job in the jail hadn't seemed to have brought him down any rungs. "Turkstra, I have to make this quick," he said.

"Aurora says you told her about a group of men in our church, a break-off from the Promise Keepers, who are working behind the scenes to keep women out of the pulpit. She says it was probably some of them who got you canned."

He blinked, as if I'd thrown sand at his face. But soon enough, he was back at it, facing me with that snaky smile. He was the sort of fella you have to figure was constantly telling himself jokes, which he didn't like to share. I don't think it bothered him too much that I had embellished on what his true love divulged. "She did, did she?"

"I might be stretching it a little," I answered, feeling oddly pleased with myself as wind rattled the windows behind him.

He rolled his eyes from my head to my feet. I suspected he knew I was out on a limb here. "I wasn't, as you put it, canned, by the way," he commented.

I didn't fight him on it, aware I was at the mercy of his goodwill, thinking maybe I should have been a little more forthright with him and just thrown myself on his graces to start. But, then again, nope. This guy gave me the heebie-jeebies. "You like the work here?" I wondered, trying to suck up.

"It's where God wants me to be right now."

Cop out, I thought, but didn't say. In my opinion, God wanted me to follow his ten commandments. If so, I was assured at least a passable chance of a decent life. But as for where he wanted me to be, that I never knew. Sometimes I had to fake that one. A few of the powerhouses in our church were big on God's will. "Is there anything you can tell me about this group," I said, cutting to the chase.

Portfliet sighed and started to pace the gray-painted floor. "How much do you know about Aurora and me?" His eyes rolled like marbles in their sockets, wandering everywhere but at me.

"Whatever is between you is your business."

He paused in midstride and let those eyes settle somewhere in the vicinity of my face. It struck me: he's not smug, he's scared of people. A self-esteem problem, I thought. How about that? Even so, I didn't like him. "You mean that don't you, Turkstra?" he asked.

I shrugged, picking up and rifling the pages of a booklet on whose cover was a frozen pond, circled by snow and illuminated by a full-faced moon. "I'm no saint," I said.

I heard his feet scrape the cement floor as he continued to walk. Looking up, I noticed him massaging the back of his neck. "Can we get one thing straight," he said.

"Sure."

"I love my wife very much," he said.

"I'm not here to get into that."

He nodded over his shoulder, still squeezing the muscles above his shoulders. "But, I love Aurora, too." There was something plaintive in his voice, bordering on self-pity. I sure hoped he didn't start confessing to me. As for extramarital affairs, who was I to talk, at least for the end that I held up all those years with Ruth. Thinking of her, even now, made my stomach queasy. I had to shove through her memory, I knew.

Henderson continued pacing for a few more moments and then joined me, taking a spot across the table. His bushy eyebrows squirmed, the smile turned smug again. "If I can help, I'd like to try, as long as this is off the record."

"The group, is there really something to it?"

The smile wiggled into a straight-edged frown. He gave me a very business-like nod. "The part about the PKs, no way."

"You're sure?"

"There might be a tie in, but not because the Promise Keepers in any way sanctioned it."

"Tie in how?"

He shrugged, opening his palms to me.

"You don't know?"

"About that I can only speculate." He examined his hands, folded on the table, as if looking for smudges of dirt. He did it for longer than I was comfortable. I thought he had a Bible study to hold.

"What can you tell me for sure?"

"Only what one of my church members, a man of some standing the community, told me." His face no longer looked smug. Real pain, as if someone was slowing burning his foot with a match, showed there. "I only agreed to meet because Aurora insisted," he said.

"I know you're in a precarious position," I replied.

"For one thing, I've gotten a call to Third CRC in Toronto. I don't want to jeopardize that with more controversy."

120

I wondered: Was he taking Aurora with him? I figured not. He'd probably stick with his wife, as much out of appearance as guilt, with a little compassion for his spouse's handicap thrown in. I could envision him telling the search committee that his sinfulness with the other woman was over. He would repent in a vast and disgusting way. He'd put on his best face. Still, I thought, he agreed to see me. Possibly that was out of guilt as well, as a final gesture to Aurora. Either way he cut it, I knew from personal experience, he was going to suffer. "Henderson," I said, sliding a finger over my mouth, "just give me something I can work with."

He rubbed his face, heaved a sigh, checked his watch. He had a few minutes before the Bible study. As I leaned back in my chair, aware of how claustrophobic the room made me feel, he told me what he could.

CHAPTER NINETEEN

I sat in a folding chair in the back of my church, hardly a church, really a refurbished storefront, and tried to relax, to rid my mind of what Henderson had said and what else the day had brought. This space, the simple room that served as a sanctuary and all-purpose meeting hall, had grown on me, especially when I was alone at night.

I'd come to love almost everything about it in the time I'd been stationed here. The picture window on my right gave a wide view of South Division Avenue. Dark buildings, several boarded-up, stood across the way. A couple folks, possibly streetwalkers, huddled in a doorway. Closer in, cars moved past on the wet, salty street. Closer still, a hump of snow, shoveled from the sidewalk by one of the three court-ordered kids who did maintenance around the church, had been stacked ledge-high to the window. In my chair, in the dark, I turned my eyes from the pale headlight beams sweeping the street and gazed at the pulpit up front.

Now hidden in shadow, the streamlined, movable lectern was the sign and symbol of my job. A slender object, yet, important enough, since from behind it issued the words that connected the faithful to Christ. Until now, women had been barred from assuming a role from behind the pulpit, be it a highly placed hand-carved one in a fancy church or a rickety wooden one, such as mine, in a church that met in a former shoe store. I wondered again if the violence we'd been encountering was really tied to that change. Were there men out there who were so scared of having women in charge that they would resort to drowning, strangling and, the image of that head still stuck to me, decapitation?

I slumped in the chair and linked my hands behind my head. In the quiet, I heard skittering in the walls, the scrabbling of rodents. Downstairs in the dank basement, the furnace roared with its usual hellish fury. The sanctuary in which I sat nonetheless held a fine and hard-to-place holiness. I breathed deep, trying to let the spirit of the room, the aftermath perhaps of words spoken from behind the pulpit, seep into me. For a minute or so, I got some comfort, almost felt as if a soothing hand, from someplace other than from in me, reached down and smoothed my weary noggin. It didn't take long, however, for Henderson Portfliet's story to return like a whiff of poison and to bring me back to reality, a place we in the church often vastly overrated.

In a moment of pain or guilt or maybe Christian kindness, a man in Portfliet's church met him one morning at Mr. Fables on Michigan Street to dump a load of smelly church business. This was a year or so ago, before Henderson got the boot from his richly polished pulpit. The guy wanted his pastor to know about this group of which he had been a member. The group met irregularly. Mostly it decided on its dirty deeds via the phone, quick gatherings of one or two. The snitch was vague on details.

Portfliet figured the man's daughter, after the death of his wife, had twisted his arm to talk. In any case, the well-intentioned tattletale told his story, which was fairly boring. The guy was low on the totem pole in the group and hadn't done much. He simply wanted his pastor to know about these men who were in the background, playing dirty tricks such as buying off votes from a few delegates who were assigned to make church policy at the last couple Synods.

Portfliet said his deep throat source told him caging votes was mostly what the group was about. But it also funded a couple staunchly conservative newspapers, published regularly and filled with angry words about the liberal stink in our church, or so they said. The group also funded, in various ways, spies

123

in our seminary and college, asking like-minded souls to come up with goods on some of the professors. The plan here was to uncover left-wing ideas in academia, and then to blast these ideas in the raunchy broadsheets or to make an issue of them when Synod rolled around. One professor, a vastly decent and devout physicist, had nearly lost his job a couple years before because he had written that he wasn't so sure that man just showed up, fresh from the Garden of Eden, a couple thousand years ago.

But, I thought in my dark church, all of this was well and good. There was this group. Sure, it certainly lacked a Christian spirit. But the truth was, the women were pushing forward, even the physics professor had kept his job, and as for the conservative rags, who read them? Yet, again, I told myself, the whole matter of women being preachers has caused 20,000 or so church members to ditch our denomination and to either start their own or join others. Good riddance, I sometimes thought. Even so, I wondered how many of them made their decision in part because of ferment brought about by these angry men in smoky back rooms.

Of more importance, I knew, was that Portfliet's lowdown didn't help me much. As far as he knew, they weren't in any way violent; nor, he insisted, were they connected to the PKs. As for Branson VanTol or Herb Wierenga, the jail chaplain had no idea if they were hooked into this secret group or not.

Old Henderson did have a suggestion. He gave me the name of a veterinarian up in Apple Country north of town who probably knew things. I asked if this was the guy who met him at Mr. Fables. He hemmed and hawed and said I would have to ask him. Upon entering church awhile before, I'd called the vet's home and got an answering machine.

For several minutes, I tried to pray on it. But, try as I might, prayer seemed only to make matters worse this night. Images and thoughts and vague ideas raced through my brain as I knocked on God's door and asked him for a moment of his time. I couldn't quite get anything straight. If he was talking back at me, I couldn't hear through the racket in my own head. But then, and maybe it was divine intervention anyhow, I detected a commotion outside.

First, a couple beeps sounded from a car horn, which I ignored and continued trying to dial in to God. But another insistent toot or two, followed by some shouts, dragged me out of my restless prayerful state. I glanced through the picture window and saw three men, guys from the neighborhood, gathered around a white Cadillac Seville.

It must be a pimp or drug dealer, honking at the others for some reason. As one of the men stepped over, leaned on the hood and began bouncing it up and down, I caught a better look at the driver. It was a woman, no hooker for sure, huddled behind the wheel, fearfully gazing out, her hand now heavy on the horn. The sounded wailed and bellowed. One of the other guys leaned in and slapped palms on the passenger's window. The third guy stood to the side, hands in his pockets, weaving side-to-side, drunk. The woman seemed vaguely familiar. She also looked desperately out of place in my neck of the woods.

I felt my side pocket, where there was a bulge. I was embarrassed to admit that, however much I enjoyed the solitude of my empty church at night, I carried protection. A pastor thus armed for trouble, I stood and went to the door, unlocked it and feeling the sharp nip of icy wind on my hands and face, tried to make better sense of the scene. In that moment, framed in the windshield, I figured out part of it: I recognized the woman. "Hey," I said, stepping onto the sidewalk.

The guy bumping on the hood stopped and craned his head at me. His eyes looked bloody and blistered. He wore a long black jacket with the patch of a cutlass-toting pirate displayed on the chest. The horn continued to whoop and rage. I waved at the woman, asking her to stop. She let up.

I also recognized the guy by the driver's door. "Ramon, what are you doing?" I said.

He straightened and gave me a nonchalant "what-of-it" stare. He had a mean slice of face. The hair, combed straight back, shone dully in the light. "Do I need to call the police?"

The guy by the hood sat where he'd just been pushing, arms over his the chest, making the pirate disappear.

"Time the cops get here, we'd be long gone," Ramon said, turning his gaunt face angrily in my direction. I wondered what was making him so surly and figured it was the need for money for dope. Normally, I can handle street people, as long as they aren't too hungry for a high.

I stepped out further and pulled the small caliber handgun from my pocket. A .38, unloaded, but a necessary tool whenever I was at the church alone at night. Jesus, I knew, wouldn't need it. But they didn't have crack cocaine in Nazareth either.

Ramon's eyes widened. He sawed a finger under his nose. The guy on the hood slipped to a standstill, his feet in a mush of snow, the pirate back in view. The third man had started to wander off.

"Hey, Rev, we were just giving this lady directions," said Ramon, his eyes goggling everywhere but at me.

"Take off," I said to Ramon, who checked the guy in the front of the car for his reaction. He shrugged inside his pirate jacket and started around the other way. By the driver's window, Ramon slapped glass and grumbled something, but kept going. The woman looked horror-stricken.

"Talk down here is you're piece ain't loaded," said Ramon, stopping and shivering inside his long wedge of a coat.

"You want to push me a little harder and see?"

He held up his hands. "Man, you Jackie Chan or what?"

"Head home."

"Where's your Christian love, padre?"

I dropped the weapon to my side, but kept him in my sights. Cars whooshed along on South Division. A couple men had gathered across the way, wondering what was up. Wind cut through my pullover sweater and flannel shirt. "Ramon, I tell

126

you what. Leave peacefully and I'll make sure to pray for you on Easter."

He shook his head, scratched his chin. "I'll be dead by then."

"Stop using."

He shrugged. Stood there, looking helpless. The woman didn't seem much better.

"You need money for food or a place to stay?"

"Might help."

"Come back in the morning. Ask Florence. I'll leave her a note."

He moved his shoulders inside his thin coat. "Need help tonight."

The woman was shivering. Dwarfed by the wheel, she looked severely in my direction. I wondered why in the world she'd braved her way down here tonight. "The mission's got beds."

He took a hard look at me, probably realizing he wasn't getting a handout. He shook his greased-up head. "You got a better coat in there I can borrow?"

"Take off."

Ramon turned and juice-walked away, his arms swaying at his sides, hips jiggling. Sick as he was, he still did the motions, not wanting anyone to get it wrong and think he wasn't on top of his game. His friends had long since disappeared.

I walked to the driver's side, face tingling with chilly numbness. The woman looked up at me and punched down the window. "Reverend Turkstra?" When I nodded, she added: "I'm Audrey VanTol, Janet's mother."

CHAPTER TWENTY

Across from me, Audrey VanTol took up little space in my used, gunboat of an office chair. She was wiping her face with a tissue she'd snatched out of the box by a stack of magazines and books perched on the corner of my desk. I'd decided earlier I'd handle the Sunday sermon and planned to do some research on a passage in Daniel about fear. "I've never met a minister who carried a gun," she said, finished with the brief clean-up job on her face.

I'd slipped it in a bottom desk drawer. Locked it in, stuck the key under the desk blotter. "It's not loaded." A box of bullets, however, were with it.

She had bright white hair, cut close to her head and stylishly brushed back. A silver stone studded each earlobe. Her face was taut and tanned and had clear blue eyes that had regained their luster once she'd plopped herself down in my study. "What kind is it?" she wondered.

I told her, trying to take a measure of her. "I'd never really use it," I assured her, thinking how it had been turned against me nearly two years before at a cottage near Lake Michigan. My shoulder still bore the scar. Occasional pain served as a reminder as well.

"In any case, thanks." She stuffed the tissue in the pockets of her woolen coat, woven with a colorful Southwest design with a hood in the back, and zipped to her chin. The dumpy, dilapidated woman I remembered from Janet's funeral, fresh out of the mental hospital, lived only in my memory.

"You were just in the neighborhood and thought you'd make a visit?"

128

She shook her head, just barely, and gave me a small smile. The woman had fine features, fairly well-preserved, some of it possibly face-lifted. "I wanted to talk to you. I stopped, thinking it was you inside."

My office wasn't more than a cubicle, but it was about all I needed. I also had a larger place to ponder theology and get away from the rat race in my upstairs apartment in Heritage Hill, a mile or so away. Audrey VanTol sat beneath a blown-up photograph I had of the Catholic monk Thomas Merton who was dressed in his Trappist robes and smiling impishly for the camera.

Next to that was a poster showing a nuclear submarine diving for the deeps. And next to that a painting one of the street guys did of Christ walking along this very avenue. In it, Christ looked a little like the mayor. He wore jeans, T-shirt, sandals and sported biblically long hair. A bag lady walked on his right, a couple gay guys on the left. A row of boozers leaned in a doorway in the background, a few kids in rags played in the near foreground. The street scene itself was realistic and held a special sort of grace. Pete Hathaway had been given it as a present. I asked him if it could stay put.

"I saw your husband this morning," I said.

She frowned, hardly moving in the chair. "He mentioned that."

I rubbed my face, aware what a terribly long day it had been. It had started with her spouse in the steamy poolroom at the Y. I wanted to rest. "That's why I'm here," she said softly.

Again, I wondered about the difference. Given the tan and the weight loss and even the vitality in the eyes, I wondered if she'd been to some expensive spa. At the risk of coming on too familiar, I remarked: "You look different than when I saw you before."

Her face registered this as a compliment. "Have you heard of the Woman Warrior's Institute?" she asked, hot on the heels on my spa rumination.

"In Arizona?"

Her face didn't move, but something shifted underneath it, a hint of displeasure or distaste, as if she picked up on the haughty tone in my voice. Monica had told me about the institute. Stuck in the middle of mesa country, it was run by a couple women, now lovers, who once belonged to our church. They offered courses in many things, including self-defense in which they taught students how to kick mean old men in the family jewels. But not all of it was flaky. They also worked hard to help women start to like and treasure themselves and learn to get what they wanted from a world run by the boys. "I've been there three months. I only returned yesterday, and that was because I heard what had happened to your fiancée and the others," she explained in a firm voice, giving me a steady, probing glance.

"It made the paper in the desert?"

"I got a couple calls, from friends." Chin held high, she dared me to go on in this direction. I didn't. I gave her credit for trying to change, even if it meant going to war with those of us of the bearded gender. For that matter, if it gave a woman courage and kept her out of the psychiatric hospital, the place deserved high praise. "I came here, Reverend, because I have some questions."

I flopped my hands on the desk, giving her the green flag. She crossed and uncrossed her legs, covered by the tight tan fabric of expensive looking ski pants. She arranged herself in stages, as if getting ready to get down to business. "Do you truly think my daughter's drowning was an accident?" she finally asked.

"Do you?"

"I'm asking you, Pastor."

I linked hands behind my head and looked at Merton, the mad Catholic monk, grinning down at me from the wall. "Have you had your doubts, Mrs. VanTol?"

She frowned, pinching thin pink lips, wrinkled around the

edges. "Please, Reverend Turkstra, I want to know what you think."

I sat straight, leaning forward, hands on my desk. "Why come to me, ma'am?"

I could sense I was rattling her. The strength, although there, was a veneer. "Others have told me you are a man who can help."

I wondered who they were. Rodriguez? I doubted it. Her husband? No way. But it hardly mattered. I decided to hand her the truth as I was starting to see it. "I'm thinking there's probably something here."

"Why?"

There were many reasons. I looked back at her, trying to get a better idea of her mood and state of mind. I decided to keep with the honesty ploy. "A gut feeling mostly."

"That's all?"

"I've come across things that make me think there's somebody or some group out there stirring up a load of trouble."

"I'd say murder is more than trouble."

"True." She had a nervous shimmer to her, even in the midst of her new warriorized self. I suspected she was forcing herself to push ahead with this. "Why are you asking, Mrs. VanTol?"

"Because," she answered, staring at her hands, whose fingers wormed in and out. "Because I've been wondering about it ever since that night. In Arizona, I couldn't get it off my mind. Then, when I heard what happened, I knew I had to come back. I had to find out why."

"What night?" I wondered.

She looked back, the eyes losing their clear luster and starting to swim a little in a film of milky emotion. "When my daughter drowned."

"Have you asked your husband?"

"Pardon?"

"He seems to have some theories, mostly that it's all a quirk of fate."

She shook her head, eyes shut. "No, he's worried, too."

"Worried?"

"He told me he thinks these things are connected." The eyes opened and bored into me.

"How so?"

"He says he thinks that group of men, the ones who were at the Silverdome, are responsible for it all."

"What makes him think that?"

"My husband has his sources."

Merton was watching me warily from the wall. I wondered if Branson had put her up to this. "What do you think, ma'am?"

A wrinkled hand, tipped by pink manicured nails, touched her chin. I gave her credit for driving down here in her Caddie and then braving the advances of Ramon and his degenerate pals. But I wondered how deep did her curiosity go. "I don't know," she said.

"What can you tell me about Rene Wierenga and your daughter."

She hadn't expected that question, but I sensed a click of recognition in her. Even so, it was replaced almost immediately by a blank, almost stunned expression. "They were friends, of course. Why?"

"Good friends?"

Audrey VanTol looked in her lap, wiped there with her hands. Her coat was decorated with a rendering of desert plants. For a moment, fire flashed, engulfing, demanding, bursting from a car. Skin dripped. I shoved it away.

"Yes, Pastor, very close. Rene was older, but they were like sisters. Janet was totally devastated, as were we all, when that happened to Rene."

"What happened?" I asked.

She paused, eyeing me. "The accident on the pier."

I stared at her, hard. I wondered what she really thought about that. I thought of Ann Wierenga, the dead mother. "Did you know Rene's mom?"

"Of course."

Here she was, sitting in front of me, a target for my questions. I shoved on. "Can you tell me about her?"

"Why are you asking?"

I gave her some of my theory, just pieces, but enough to let her know that I strongly suspected Rene was on Janet's mind in the days before, if not on the very night, she died. I told her about the folder in the library.

Audrey VanTol didn't react to the last chunk of information for several seconds. Then, as if rousing herself from a dream, she said: "Impossible. There is absolutely no tie in here. At all!" A hardness had edged into her voice and her mouth had become rigid, her body a compact package on the chair.

"So you think Rene's death was an accident, too?"

"Of course! Don't you?" she said.

"Or a suicide?"

"With her own baby in her arms? My God, Reverend, what kind of woman do you think she was?"

Another thought struck me. "Did Janet have a boyfriend?"

She blinked as if I'd puffed air in her direction. "Janet didn't like boys it turns out."

I was going to ask more when I heard tapping on the door to the church, just outside my office. I ignored it a moment, then went to check it out, aware that my newly empowered warrior guest was starting to unravel.

It was Ramon at the window, nose crushed to the glass, eyes peering in. I held up a finger. Looking like a fish in a tank, he put hands on either side of his face. Back in the cubicle, I said: "It's Ramon."

She looked at me with cold, distant eyes. Audrey VanTol had seemed to drop through a trap door. "Did you have any more questions?" I asked.

She stared in her lap, a beaten, distressed expression having seeped into her face. "Do you think my husband is right? That it was those promise maker people who did this to our daughter?"

133

"I doubt it"

She gazed at me with a far off expression. "But why are you bringing Rene and her mother into this?"

"To tell the truth, because someone nearly killed my fiancée and I want to know who."

"So you will stop at nothing to find out?" She said it without much punch. More resigned. Distracted.

I didn't think she expected an answer. "I'm starting to believe what happened here is more personal. That it doesn't have much to do with groups."

She nodded, her attention off in that other world. I wondered if she got the import of what I'd just said. Didn't seem like it. "Ma'am," I said after a bit. She glanced up, as if I had shaken her from a dark daydream. "Is there anything else?"

"Is that man still out there?"

"I'll walk out with you."

Slowly, she stood and gave me a quick, uncertain smile. "I wish you knew more, Pastor."

"So do I."

She nodded. "But why would Janet leave all of that material in the library?" she asked, as if hurt.

"To keep it protected."

"From whom?"

I shrugged. She held out a hand. I took it and felt brittle bones and rawhide skin. She didn't clasp me back.

CHAPTER TWENTY-ONE

Dirk VanderGoote strained over the prostrate horse. Wearing a floppy trout fishing hat and blue, zip-up coveralls, the vet grunted, hands buried deep in the animal's gaping mouth. He glanced at me standing in the doorway to the pole barn. I'd knocked on the door to the home and been directed here by his middle-aged daughter, the one I talked to on the phone last night. "Turkstra?"

"Take your time," I said, freezing my fingers.

Doubling as a garage for a shiny black Bronco, the one-story barn housed only the one stall in which the family pet, Midnight, was kept. Carol, the daughter, told me her dad had decided to yank a bad tooth from the animal while waiting for me. She also mentioned, with a wary tone in her voice, that dear old dad was having second thoughts about having this little interview with me. But there he was, doing his dental work.

"Can you give me a hand?" He peered over the horse's head, which had been propped at a slant inside a cloth gizmo attached to metal pole stuck in the ground.

Rubbing my hands together, I stepped inside. "Shut the door," he barked, which I did before approaching.

"Hold the jaw up," he ordered as I slipped through a small gate leading into the stall.

I felt tall and clumsy.

"Just takes a pair of hands." I inched closer, noticing a rim of filmy eye under the horse's downed lid. The vet held a pair of silver pliers in one gloved hand; he pointed with the other. "Angle her at me."

The odor of hay, sweat and manure stunk up the place. I wasn't so sure about this and hung back, staring at the doped animal. "Get down and tilt her up," he said, exasperated.

I knelt on the cold dirt floor. Guy reminded me of my dad. He had that mean Dutchman's streak that expected the world to do as it was told.

I reached on over, lifted my arms under the jaw and jerked up. The vet stuck his skinny, deeply lined face close to Midnight's open mouth. I noticed, stenciled on the right breast pocket of his work outfit, the words "The Horse Doctor." He shoved on the jaw with one hand and went tooth hunting with the other. He shook his head, ducking even closer, his face a couple inches from the gaping maw. "Jiminy Cricket," he said.

Disney bugs inside the mouth? I asked: "Bad?"

"Got to come out."

I'd spent another night at the hospital, this time on an oversized cot they wheeled in. Monica had been asleep when I got there and had hardly awakened when I took off for this early sit-down in Apple Country. My arms clasping the inert horse, I detected another smell: bushels of apples stored on rafters. "What happened to her?" I asked, feeling the strain in my shoulders.

"Chipped it on her feed. Pus pockets, sure enough."

Very nice, I thought, twisting my head away.

The vet chuckled. "Won't get any on you."

Midnight snuffled, stirred. I eased back. The vet shook his head. "Don't let it go!" He dropped the pliers in a pile of tools, picked up a large black file and started sawing. I winced. "Why's it you want to talk?" He scowled with a small, weathered face that reminded me of a walnut. The eyes were sharp and blue, the skin ruddy, the fleshy slash of mouth made smooth by a wispy gray mustache.

I gave him the short version, starting with Janet VanTol in the river, moving on to Tina on the bed, Monica in the basement, Johnny Keester in the dumpster, and all of the rumors connecting the mayhem to a maverick group of PKs. When I finished, he picked up a ball-peen hammer. With it, he started whacking a chisel he'd stuck by the molars. As far as I could tell, he had no response to my story. He beat away, biting his lip, wheezing slightly. "Bugger," he observed at one point.

I let go for a few seconds while he searched for more tools. This time he came up with a long knife. As I took up the jaw, he stabbed in and made what looked like a circular cut. Blood geysered out, dotting his chin, which he wiped on his shoulder. "Why're you coming here and bothering me?" he asked.

"I thought Reverend Portfliet gave you a call?"

"We talked." The vet took the file and went back to sawing. I looked down and noticed the animal's right eye loll open, revealing a liquid, egg-yolk pupil, large as a quarter. The horse's brown coat shone dully in the dim light. On her side, Midnight's belly ballooned and collapsed and bellowed out again.

I thought of Bob. There was a struck-dumb strength about him. Monica had said earlier that he was getting restless at the home, apparently still cranked up from whatever happened at the museum, and she wondered if I minded picking him up later today. Her dad and stepmom had taken him to dinner the night before and he'd been next to out-of-control. For some reason, they figured I could calm him.

So I had to get him at some point. The other thing Monica said, this morning as I prepared to leave, had to do with Janet's therapist. With help from Aurora, Monica had tracked her down to, of all places, Bosnia, where she had gone many months before as a missionary. Monica hoped to get her on the phone this afternoon.

"What's it you want to know?" the vet wondered, shining a small flashlight into the cavern.

"Is there a break-off group of PKs who could be responsible for this?"

The vet glanced at me and wiped the back of an arm over a cheek. "Do you believe that rot?"

"I believe there is a group, not with that name." I watched him carefully, hoping he went on. I felt he was opening a box that contained answers. When he didn't respond, I asked: "Is there?"

The vet dropped on his haunches, picked up a cloth, reached over and stuffed it in the horse's mouth, wiped it around, kept it there. Hand holding the cloth in place, stopping the blood, he sighed. "God help me, Pastor. Could we pray a minute."

So we did, heads bowed, silently. In the space between us, over the horse, I asked for the Lord's presence to descend. To smooth the way, make this guy feel the need to blab.

"The one I know is Soldiers of the Cross," he said finally.

"Why did you quit?"

His eyes dug into mine; his face was a pinched mask, protected by obvious anger. I had checkmated him without him looking. "You can't know everything."

"Tell me what you can."

"I've already confirmed a group."

"Are Branson VanTol and Max Wierenga members?"

He took a deep breath, and so did I. His eyes did a little dance, from the horse to me to the ceiling and back to the horse. "I will not talk to the police or anyone about this, Reverend Turkstra. On a stack of bibles, I swear I won't. Ever."

"It's between us." Open the lid, let me look in and see the putrid mulch heaped inside.

He yanked the cloth out of the horse's mouth, glommed with blood, and shone light on the target. I'd let go of the jaw, my hands resting on the sides of Midnight's neck, my legs cramped and cold. Somehow the discomfort seemed to bond us. The vet stuck a finger in, tickled it around, made a face and shook his head. "Still in there."

I heaved up and grabbed the jaw as he used some sort of spoon-tipped instrument. His features, pinched and narrow, focused on the mouth in front of him. A rope of vein twisted at a temple under his fishing hat as he reamed the poor animal's mouth.

Starting to rock back and forth, he corkscrewed the instrument. After a moment, he pulled it, reached for the pliers again and dove back. He strained, jerked, shoved, and tugged. Fi-

138

nally, the vet slumped, the pliers in front of him. Blood and tissue dripped from a stony lump, the buried chunk of tooth. A faint, satisfied grin crinkled his mouth. As he examined his prize, I let go and sat on the ground. The vet watched me, the hard, angry mask of his face giving way, for a second, to mild humor. "You could make a good horse doctor."

"Too much work."

He reached out a hand and patted Midnight's broad brow. "I didn't know you hurt so bad, lady."

I stretched my arms above my head, edged over and leaned against a post, noticing hay and dirt mashed into the knees of my jeans. I unsnapped my Bulls coat, feeling heat rise. "You need more help?"

He shook his head, fiddling in his tool sack. I closed my eyes, hands in my lap, seeing Monica behind my lids, asleep last night. As my mind played over that image, she seemed too still, hardly breathing, as on the lip of death, but my attention brought her back in a quick explosion of fire. I felt myself moving in quicksand, working to reach her. I saw her eyes open and a smile bloom, just as it had in real life, glad that I was there.

"I'll tell you a story, Turkstra, but that's all I'm going to do." I looked to see him stitching. The needle in his hand, as it emerged, was curved at the tip. The material was reddish.

"Two years ago January, my missus died of cancer. She passed away at home, in the front room, with hospice." I made sure he knew he had my total attention when he glanced my way.

"Emma wasn't one who makes waves, Turkstra. We never talked politics, for sure nothing about women ministers." The hand pistoned in and out, looping and weaving, the horse in slumberville.

"But my wife surprised me. The day before she died, Pastor Portfliet was there. It was him and me in the room when she told me she wanted me to quit that terrible group as she called

139

it." He worked a moment or two in silence, checking his handi-work with the flashlight. He continued on, tightening the stitches before needling back in. "I never knew it was on her mind so deep."

The barn was very chilly. A heater, raised on the wall, blew out warmth in a far corner, above the parked Bronco. Midnight's tail swept twice near my feet.

"I didn't argue. But I knew it was very important. She said to talk to Pastor Portfliet about it. Then she let it go and started to sleep. She never woke up." The vet stared at me, his mouth drooping open, grief in his eyes.

"So, you . . ."

He held up the hand holding the stitches. "Did nothing, at first. But I knew Emma knew me. I'd been bothered by it for maybe a long time. They had been getting too serious."

"Meaning violent?"

He gave me a "shut-up-I'm-not-finished" glare. "I don't know, Turkstra, if I would have honored her wishes. But then I got sick. My heart." He tapped his chest, right by "The Horse Doctor" stencil. "They took me in. I had four bypasses and a valve replacement."

As if to prove it, he unzipped the coveralls, revealing a v-neck T-shirt. He used a couple fingers to drag it open, showing me the shiny scar rivering down the sternum. I nodded. He went back into the mouth, feeling around, done stitching.

I wondered if he'd finished his story. But then he sat back, grabbed a towel, ran it over his face and looking at Midnight, clued me in on the finale. "Carol is my only daughter. She stayed with me through the whole thing. Right by my side. I had an infection that lasted two weeks after surgery." His hand idly poked inside the T-shirt. "When I was out of it, I learned I had been talking to Emma about what she wanted. Telling her I didn't know. These were my friends. Somewhere in there I became conscious and there was my daughter and Portfliet. They were smiling and said I'd made the right decision."

We watched each other over the horse. Sunlight crawled through a window above him, slanting over his shoulder. A weak smile washed over his mouth. "I must've been talking. I must've told them I'd honor her wishes. I remember my daughter was holding my hand and crying."

I had the sense he was testing me, carefully gauging my reaction, wondering if I thought he'd turned over too easily on his buddies. I kept to myself everything but a quick sniff of my chilly nose.

"When I came home here in August, I called Branson and told him it was quits for me. I was no longer in it."

My heart made a funny leap in my chest. "Branson?"

He nodded.

"Branson VanTol?"

"My story is finished, Pastor. I have nothing more to say."

"What about Max Wierenga. Is he in the group, too?"

The vet pushed himself to his feet, glancing down at Midnight. "She'll be awake soon."

"This is important."

The vet gazed at me, infinitely sad. "You mentioned Promise Keepers, ask Herb Wierenga about that."

"Why?"

He shook his head. No more.

I unfolded myself from the floor with effort. "Please then, just one more thing."

His eyes left the horse and locked onto mine before drifting back down to the animal.

"Are these Soldiers of the Cross tied in with the Promise Keepers?"

"Quite the opposite."

I wasn't sure what that meant, but another thought crowded in. "Did you quit because VanTol's group got violent?"

The vet zipped his coveralls and bent to pick up instruments. He dropped them into a large black bag. Dust motes floated in the air around his head. Midnight snuffled. Her tail

141

swept the floor. A hoof jerked, as if testing the air in the day-time world. Finished packing, he turned to me. "I'm done, Turkstra. Don't ask me to repeat it again ever, to anyone."

"But, the violence?"

He straightened, hands on the crook of his back. His face had frozen, its features harsh and ungiving. "I told you, Pastor, why I quit. It was my wife's final wish. Please, leave it at that."

Outside awhile later, I stood on the driveway as the vet bounced off in his black van, headed north to Sparta for more horse doctoring. He turned right at the end of the sloped, shoveled drive and gunned the engine east to Baumhoff. Watching him, my hands buried in the deep pockets of my coat, I felt the clear, crisp chill in the air and had to squint to keep the bright sun, gold and buttery, from making my eyes hurt.

"Great place you've got out here," I said to Carol, who had come out just as her dad was wrapping up in the barn and Midnight was waking up. Typical for a horse, they told me, the animal seemed to burst out of the stupor. Her head popped up as soon as I helped the vet unsling it from the gizmo. Then, Midnight climbed to her feet and started shifting around in her stall. Already, she was loping in a corralled area behind the barn.

"I grew up here," said Carol.

Apple trees, bare-branched and aligned in perfect rows up and down the sides of snowy hills, stretched to our right and ran into the distance across the street. Located north of town on a ridge of elevated land that made it good for growing, Apple Country was a wonderful counterpoint to the sooty smoldering city not three miles to the south. There were fruit farms in all directions.

"I grew up in Overisel in the muck lands," I said. Instead of apples, we grew onions and celery. At least when I was a kid, before my dad took a job as a pipefitter at a GM plant in Wyoming.

142

Carol turned to me, wrapped in a bulky plaid coat, her stumpy brown hair swirling in the breeze rolling our way from the hills. "Did my father tell you what you wanted?"

"Some."

She had a square face, worn hard around the edges. Monica said she had heard Carol's former husband had left her two years before for a waitress at a Red Lobster on 28th Street in Grand Rapids. They had two children, both of whom had been climbing onto the bus for Kenowa Hills Elementary School when I'd pulled in. "He's been through the wringer," Carol said, as if apologizing for whatever it was he didn't tell me.

"It sounds like you really hung in there," I said.

She brushed hair from her brow with a cupped hand. "He's a good man, whatever you might think. He's just from the old school."

I let the wind smack the sides of my face, aware of clouds massing in the west, threatening more snow. "I liked your father. I think he told me absolutely as much as his conscience would allow." Watching her carefully, I asked: "Do you know anything you could tell me?"

She turned and gazed at the area behind the barn where Midnight paced. "Perhaps."

We faced each other, a couple feet apart on the driveway. Although she was much stockier, she reminded me of her dad. Among other things, I saw the look of determination in her eyes, the jutting chin, the rigid mouth. "I really don't have anything, but my boyfriend who works at the incinerator in town, the place where they burn the garbage, might."

Over her shoulder, I spotted a plastic-covered temperature dish hooked to the trunk of an elm. The needle pointed to 30 degrees. When I looked back, she tried to smile. "His name's Dick Woudstra. He's a nice guy."

I smiled, hoping he was nice, since it seemed she and her two tykes deserved someone who loved them back.

143

"Anyhow," she said, "he works with Janet VanTol's former boyfriend, whose name's Larry something or another."

"You think he knows anything?"

She shrugged. "Dick says he does. I talked to him this morning and mentioned you were coming by."

Around us the apple trees, moving off in all directions, looked tortured, their limbs bent and knobby. Even so, they gave off a sturdy strength. Sunlight still shone harsh and hearty on the snow, although clouds had started to act as a filter. "Would it make sense for me to stop by there?"

"It might."

"Has this Larry talked to the police?"

Carol pushed out her lips and raised up her eyebrows. "You'd best be asking him."

CHAPTER TWENTY-TWO

The huge teeth sprang open as they sank hungrily into a mass of crud. I watched as the monster-like mouth of the machine bobbed around a few seconds, scrounging for a good gobble of garbage. Having found some tasty morsels, the drag chain drew tight as the mechanical jaws took a munch.

"It's something, isn't it?" asked Dick Woudstra, who stood next to me on the lip of the huge cement cavern in which bulging bags of debris had been dumped.

I shook my head, awestruck by the mounds of junk that had been probably sitting on curbs this morning. "How much you run through here a day?"

Woudstra shrugged. "Few thousand tons," he replied over the din of trucks backing in and dumping their loads, the crane feeding and other gears and belts and bearings grinding.

I had decided to stop by the Kent County Steam Generation Plant, actually a big incinerator for garbage, before picking up Bob. It didn't take long for me to find Dick, a wide, friendly man in jeans, work boots and hooded sweatshirt. He had been in the front office, chatting with a couple other guys, apparently on break, when I walked in. He had someone radio Larry, the one I really wanted, and got the go-ahead to run me back. "What part do you do?" I asked.

"Haul ash," he shouted.

Done dipping and scavenging, the head of the crane popped free of the moving morass of garbage and rose, trash trapped in the teeth, to a height of about 50 feet. The jaws opened, dropping the junk on a conveyor belt rolling to a furnace, out of sight behind a thick bricked wall. That done, Dick grinned and led me up a metal walkway to our left. Two flights up, we reached

145

a closed metal door, on which he pounded his gloved fist. As he did, he peered over his shoulder, looking at me with humor in his eyes. "Larry's a case. He loves working the pulpit."

"Pulpit?"

"What we call it." He pounded again, stuck an ear to the door, nodded and twisted the handle. He shoved open the door, then stood aside to let me step up and into an circular, glass-encased room, in the front of which was a large padded swivel chair, a bank of levers and dials and the bouncing, ponytailed man who had to be Larry Sanders. Woudstra waved a hand. "He's all yours, Reverend."

I waited for Dick to slip out before turning back to Sanders, who was jerking on a lever, a wild grin on his face, shaking back his ponytail, eyes intent on the sea of plastic bags sprawled in the vast room in, which trucks continued to spill their guts. He looked like he sat in the cockpit of the Starship Enterprise, a universe of junk before him.

Looking down, I saw I stood on thick glass or clear plastic, which allowed for a view of the trash below.

"Just a sec," said Sanders. Groaning motor sounds were muffled by the window. Otherwise, the room, shaped like a large covered bowl, was fairly quiet. I waited it out, feeling a rumble in my stomach, the eggs and toast and sausage I'd eaten at the hospital making room for lunch.

"You can talk," he said, swinging my way in his Star Trek chair, his arms wrestling the levers.

"Quite an operation."

He nodded and smiled some more.

I watched as the crane's mouth rose, chock full of bags, a mattress and what looked like the ribbed tank tire. It swung to the far side and spewed the debris onto the merrily rolling belt. "Thing is though," said Sanders, "I sort a got to keep my mind on buttons, so you probably ought to make it quick."

"Dick's girlfriend, Carol, told me you'd been talking around here about Janet VanTol. She said you were Janet's boyfriend."

He gave me a narrow-eyed glance, took me in for the first time, went back to work. He fiddled with the knobs and lever a bit. "Three years ago. I'm hitched now, I'm happy to tell ya." As Sanders jounced in his chair, he took one hand off a knob, dug cigarettes out of the pocket of his green flannel shirt. Shook one up and pointed it my way.

From behind my halting hand, I shook my head.

"Hey, I hear ya," said Sanders, lipping it out and letting it roll to one side of his mouth. He patted his chest, then dug in the pocket for a Zippo. Flashed a light and sucked. "I'm planning on quitting soon." His attention was locked on the pit below. The neck of the crane, bent and probing without his assistance, seemed to lock on to something inside the muck. Sanders scooted forward in his command chair, raised and gazed down. He stared for a good ten seconds, hands pushing at the glass in front of him.

"Whoo-ee," he said, plopping down and yanking on the middle lever. "Check it out, Jack."

Slowly rising, caught in the metal teeth, limp and lumpy, was a bag of logs. No, on second glance, it was a cow. Its black eyes, frozen open, gawked at us through the window. Its legs looked stiff, its belly swollen, its hide fuzzy and slick with some sort of snotty sheen. He glided it over, high across the cavern and onto the belt, where it thudded and began to move with all the other crap. "Here to tell you, son, the things I see could make a movie."

"You dig out many cows?" I couldn't believe my day. First an inert horse in a strange sling, now a cow with rigor mortis.

"You'd be surprised," said the crane operator.

"Where'd that come from?"

"Farm. Maybe slaughterhouse."

"They put it in a trash bag and stick it at the curb?"

Sanders laughed. He liked that.

I shook my head. It was a like a primordial ooze, full of the stuff of life and death. Maybe a sermon there. "What else do you haul out?"

"Got a body once."

"You're kidding!"

"Well, yeah. Actually, it was a dummy, but sure looked real at the time. But, hey, time's wasting."

Leaned against the wall, I sketched the short version of why I was here and what I wanted. He smoked without taking the cigarette out of his mouth. A large coffee mug, decorated with stock cars, sat on a ledge by the dials and gauges. He jammed levers, jiggled in his seat, happy as a race car driver on his victory lap at the Indy. "Bottom line, you probably want to talk to Charley Robbins."

"Who?"

"Catbird Robbins. The guy does the weather on the radio."

The name, Charley, that is, rang a distant bell. "Why do I want to talk to him?"

"He knows the whole deal."

Wondering what his crane would pull up next, maybe a dog or a cat or rusty Polaris warhead, I waited for him to go on.

"This is the short version," said Sanders, when he'd turned completely away from me. "Charlie's probably not gonna be too keen on my talking, but, screw him, here it is." He twirled back, the crane dragging the deep for more prizes. "I was in one of his flying classes last year. Learning to work the twin engines." He looked at me. I shrugged, hands in the pockets of my coat.

"Well," he said, "we had this party, like, the week of our final exam. It was in Brann's on Division, the night after Thanksgiving."

They were drinking and watching a football game on the big screen TV about 11 p.m. when a news flash appeared. None other than Crystal Franklin, the TV-8 reporter, came on to inform the audience that a fisherman had just pulled a body out of the river. She said police believed it was Janet VanTol. The TV even flashed a photo, gotten from somewhere, probably from the series Crystal had done on would-be women ministers, on the screen. She'd hardly gotten the name of Janet

VanTol out of her mouth when Catbird, sitting next to Sanders, gasped, got real pale.

Sanders was pretty upset, too. Even though he and Janet hadn't been an item for awhile and even then they had only dated for a few months, he still liked her. Surprised and shocked, he tried to talk to Catbird about it. Asked the flight instructor if he knew Janet. He mumbled something and shook him off. The instructor didn't want to talk about it. Soon after, Catbird swallowed his brew, glared for a few moments at the TV, which was then back to the game, paid his check, said good-bye to his would-be pilots and left.

For Sanders, it wasn't over, his training, that is. He was supposed to make a final flight to do an instrument landing two weeks later. "So," Sanders said, leaning hard into the middle joystick, the engine rattling the window, "I went up with him that day. We got to talking, which is when he told it to me." I waited, suspecting Sanders was toying with me a tad. He apparently liked having a story to tell and me acting the part of careful listener. Thing is, I didn't have to act.

"Weather that day was pretty bad. He ran me through my paces. Anyhow, I'm not sure how long we'd been up when he mentioned Janet's funeral. He asks if I went. I told him I didn't. So he tells me he didn't think so because he went, couldn't stay away. I asks him, did he go out with her, too, but he says no way. She was like a little sister once, when he was going out with this chick named Rene."

Sanders leaned back, taking a break, hands cupped over the top of the middle lever, staring at his domain. I tried to be patient. "I wonder as we're flying along, who's Rene? He tells me she and him were thinking about getting married once, a long time back. Figuring he's getting chummy, I make some wisecrack about it not working out, huh? But he says, nope, she died. Sort of like Janet. She drowned."

I checked my watch. It was moving fast toward 11 o'clock. It seemed as if the case was moving even quicker. I was getting lucky. Sounded like I was going to have to hunt up Catbird. "Did he say anything about a baby being with her when she went in the water?"

Sanders' small dark eyes widened. He swung his ponytail side to side. "You got to be kidding."

"He didn't?"

"Nothing like that."

A horn blared below, the racket echoing, making Sanders return to his crane, whose bent tower showed out the window like the neck of a dinosaur. "Man, you think someone killed this babe?"

I didn't know. Could it have been Catbird? But, if so, would he have talked so freely about his former love? I thought of Bennie Plasterman, an elder at the church I'd served before coming to Heartside. He was an Ottawa County Sheriff's detective. I could ask him for the report on Rene. I should have thought about that before. It could explain a lot.

"Any of this help?" asked Sanders.

"It might." I recalled what Audrey VanTol had told me about her daughter. About boys. Going out with Larry didn't fit. Or maybe it did.

One arm looped atop the huge joystick, his face went slack, as if suddenly zapped with numbing medicine. "You think someone deep-sixed Janet, too?"

I shrugged. "Did she ever say anything to you about problems with her dad?"

"That little dipshit?"

I smiled, curious.

"Not much. Except he didn't like me. About ran me off a couple times with a shotgun."

I wanted to know more. But he got busy, checking gears, distracted. So I thanked him for his help. He nodded, dragging back on stick, raising a twisted mass of rope, metal and plastic sheeting from the swamp of garbage. "If you don't mind, don't tell Catbird where you heard all this. I mean, I still log hours out there and I'd rather he wasn't on my case."

150

I didn't see any reason to drag him in and told him so.

"Thanks," he said, nodding and flipping me a dull grin.

I started to go, but he held me there a second, his face clouding, the eyes growing serious. He yanked on the back of his head, tugging at the ponytail. "Janet, man, she was a serious chick. I always remember it was like she had lots on her mind. She was a Bible-thumper. Always talking about God."

I figured that was true. Getting a sense of an ugly oily thing twisting in the litter below my feet, I thought of the hell of flames, but also of families and their own sort of hell. "Anything else?" I asked.

Sanders shook his head.

"Why do they call this the pulpit?"

When he laughed, his whole mouth moved as if pulled by strings and his body shook. His bad memories, I suspected, had been quickly processed and discarded. "Because I'm on top of everything, probably like you are on Sundays."

"Some Sundays," I told him, "but not all, by a longshot."

He gave me an odd glance, then turned back to his job.

CHAPTER TWENTY-THREE

Behind the dinky steering wheel of his Piper Cub four-seater, Catbird Robbins took us straight up off the tarmac at Kent County International Airport. Bob sat quietly in the back. Strapped in the front, I barely recognized the sharp profile next to me. As the plane droned upwards a steep trajectory toward a swirl of grayish clouds, I repeated the old axiom to myself: "It isn't what you know, it's who you know." Simple as that. Even if it was a kindergarten playmate.

Way back in my fuzzy memory, I did recall Charley Robbinette, as he was known then, as one of the kids whose mothers dropped them off at our farm for day care. My mother did that for as far back as I could remember. Mostly, I didn't mind. I enjoyed having so many kids to play with. What I could drag back from down there in the sloppy brain matter about Charley is that I stole his rosary.

A half hour earlier when I'd bushwhacked him in his office, just showing up out of the blue, he'd recognized me right off. I'd heard him on the radio a few times, but with the stage name and years putting a whiskey edge to the voice, I'd never made the connection. In fact, I had a hard time doing it as I stood in his office. It took a few seconds, and then faint recognition dawned.

But it didn't much matter. Catbird knew me and seemed darned glad, at first, that I stopped by. He smiled as I introduced Bob and had us sit. After the "so-what-brings-you-here" expression bloomed on his face, I gave him the lowdown. Needless to say, his smile dropped clean away, replaced by a grim line.

Us two pre-school era buddies fenced back and forth a bit then. But we negotiated around to an agreement, which took us out to the plane and up in the air so he could whiz over town and check out traffic for the midday news.

As the boiling tuffs of cumulus moved our way, I felt funny in the stomach. I turned around to see Bob grinning like a Halloween pumpkin. I'd picked him up on the way to the airport. I had debated both bringing him as well as just showing up on Catbird's doorstep. I opted to drag along Monica's brother partly as an icebreaker and partly because I knew how much he loved the airport. Sometimes his sister and I would drive here with him and park in a lot on the far rural end of the place and watch the jets roar in and out. As for letting my legs do the walking with Catbird, I figured a personal visit would be best.

"Might be a little rough up here today," said Catbird over a headset he had had me slip on over my ears. Billows of white, looking like driving snow, slid past my window. The plane shook, buffeted by clouds. "Ever see downtown from 4,000 feet?"

I shook my head, swallowing back my hasty late morning lunch of a sausage from 7-11, the plump greasy wieners that twirl under electric lights.

Catbird dipped the plane to the left. More than a dozen dials and gauges, none of which meant a thing to me, faced him on the dashboard. Seemed to be a morning for moving machines and men operating them, I thought. "There she blows," said Catbird as we dashed through a tunnel of clouds into the open.

Buildings spread every which way, boldly thrusting themselves toward us. I recognized the dark towers of the Amway Grand Plaza, a hotel; the glittering glass of Riverfront Place; blocks of offices and the gutted pink tombstone shape of the Eastbank Towers. Gazing out my window, I saw the clogged, icy curl of the Grand River and the rusty red span of the Sixth Street Bridge, the spot from which Janet fell, jumped, slipped or was pushed, who knew.

153

I returned to Bob. His Halloween smile remained. He gave me a thumbs up. I patted one of his knees. "Awesome, Bugs," he said, or so I lip-read.

"How's your mother by the way?" asked Catbird.

"She's in Rest Haven in Holland."

"Still have her marbles."

"Well, she hasn't lost any."

Catbird bent his head and laughed. He had fluffy red hair, cut closely around the ears. Thick lines furrowed his forehead, the corner of his eyes and the sides of his mouth. He had a deep, scratchy voice I recognized from the radio, not the kid's throaty sound from days on the farm. "My mom's remarried in Florida, to a plastic surgeon who specializes in lipo-sucking fat," he offered.

"Your dad's dead?"

He gave me a somber nod. We'd slipped into clouds again. The belly of the plane rattled under me. Bob seemed to be having the time of his life, looking this way and that, blowing out his lips. Snow-driven wind whipped at us, slamming the window.

To get my mind off the weather, I paid closer attention to music from his radio station, WGRD, humming faintly in my ears. It was some sort of rap song about dirty sex and underwear. As a pastor, I tried to be open-minded on contemporary beats and lyrics, except when it came to rap. I was convinced it was so bad not even Satan would tune it in. The plane bounced awhile. Finally, Catbird asked: "What about Rene?"

We flew into the open. Through patches of clouds, I spotted neighborhoods, fields of snow, moving cars, bare trees. We had established his relationship with her earlier, more or less. Now was brass tacks time. "Tell me about her," I said.

"A big question."

"Start with her relationship to Janet. What you know of it," I said.

He stared grimly out the window. Lousy weather swirled ahead. My stomach continued flip-flopping. "Janet was like her kid sister."

"You knew her well?"

"Where we went, so did Janet."

"When she died, did you suspect anything?"

"Janet?"

I gave him a quick nod, still aware of the wash of animal body parts bubbling in my throat. I had washed the greasy sandwich down with a Mountain Dew, a full 20 ounces of sugar and caffeine. Folks around my church often asked why I ate so bad. I could only be honest: Because I'm a sap for lousy food and sweet fizzy drinks.

"Larry Sanders sent you here, right?"

Earlier, I'd told him it was rumors that led me to his office at the airport. I didn't answer. But I didn't deny it either.

We flew on, west toward Lake Michigan, the plane jerking, the snow flaring in gusts before us. I wondered how he was going to give an accurate traffic report with the blanket of clouds blurring the roads. On the radio came a song that sounded like tin cans exploding in an oven. I closed my eyes.

"To be honest, it struck me as strange, them both dying the way they did," Catbird said.

"How about Rene? You figure that as an accident?"

He shrugged, his face looking ashen. "It's hard to think she'd let it happen with the baby," he said over the mike. "But she was in a bad way." Catbird glanced over, his expression hooded.

I suddenly made a leap of logic. "Were you the father?"

His hands squeezed the wheel. He pulled back and the plane began to climb and strain its way through the layers of clouds. Leaned into my seat, I waited for God to punish me for the sausage. But blessedly the quick upward jerk seemed to shove down the swirl of food and Dew. I breathed gratefully again, immediately aware the pilot was staring my way with streams of tears on his face. "Christ, Turkstra," he said over his mouthpiece.

155

I twisted in his direction, feeling guilty for tapping so quickly and cruelly into his past. "Man, I'm sorry."

He shook his head violently, smudged away the salt and water and set about the serious business of leveling us off and pointing us in the right direction, or so I assumed. In the back, Bob was swaying slightly, no doubt enthralled by the rap song, this one about an uncle who liked to eat police badges and burn telephone poles.

Catbird didn't say anything for a full fifteen minutes, except to chatter to base about his location, the 10-50, he called it. As his silence grew and the plane moved through soupy weather, I waited, pretending to be cool and calm. But I worried all the way that he'd do something drastic, like drop us nose first into the slushy drink of Lake Michigan, which finally appeared about ten minutes into his self-imposed silence far below through a large parting of clouds. I wondered if he had talked about Rene or the child much before this.

Bob was peering out a window and Catbird still wasn't talking as the plane swept over the water. A little more than a year before I'd been involved in a deal in which a seminary professor supposedly went missing down there. Eventually the police found his body, not in Davy Jones's back pocket or washed up on shore, but buried in a shallow grave with his lover. Straining to catch a view of the lake, I saw tiny bergs of ice, a choppy flow of waves, and an endless metallic blue-green that made my eyes hurt trying to take it all in.

My shoulder jammed the door as the plane swung hard right, buzzing north, cutting through clouds. Not too long into the move back toward shore, Catbird dipped through the muck, making the Piper swoop and forcing my stomach toward my throat again, but opening a better view of the lake. "There," he said, nodding.

Behind me Bob looked happy as a cat who had just swallowed a bird.

156

"Where? What?"

"The lighthouse."

Sure enough straight ahead, cutting through the outskirts of Grand Haven, was the Grand River, hardly moving, petering out into the lake whose shore was chunked and cratered with hills of icy snow. At the far edge of the river, at the end of a thin boardwalk, stood the tiny red tower of the Coast Guard lighthouse. Where Rene had been when the waves crashed in and took her and the child. From this perch, the lighthouse looked tiny. It rose 50 or so feet, thrusting up and over its station at the mouth of the river that flowed in from Grand Rapids and beyond.

"I was at college, at Notre Dame, when it happened," said Catbird, skirting the shore and heading back south, toward Holland. The strip of beach bordering the state park in Grand Haven looked lonely and frigid. Clouds packed us in again.

"I'd as soon not get into this, Calvin. But I will." He spoke over the headphones; his voice distant and scratchy. This wasn't the best way for a conversation of this type. Then again, maybe it made it easier for him. I gave him a "have-at-it" nod.

"I loved her. I was in high school, a senior. She was in her second year at Western. But our families had always been tight, my dad worked for hers, as a foreman."

Once again, the shore showed up, lined here by handsome, turreted homes placed proudly atop cliffs of wind-hardened sand. By the grim look on his face, I assumed he was going to spit this out for me, get it out and over with.

"We got involved that year, at Christmas. We found out she was pregnant just after Easter." He glanced over, his face stiff and expression free. "One thing led to another, but mostly I panicked. I took it to my dad, who went nuts. I had been accepted to Notre Dame, something he'd wanted for me forever. He told me I had a choice, convince Rene to have an abortion or forget about him paying my way in South Bend. Here he was Catholic to beat the band and he wanted that."

Catbird seemed to want my approval now, or at least for me to acknowledge the painful dilemma. I couldn't find it in my bag of ministerial tricks to give him anymore than my attention.

"So," he said, switching us through fingers of clouds hanging thick and ugly over the outskirts of Holland, "I talked to her. She wouldn't hear of an abortion. She just left town, for up north someplace. I didn't see her again."

"At all?"

He shook his head, face a stone.

I wanted to ask him more questions, but didn't have the chance. As the plane motored over Holland, he flicked on his mike and assumed his radio voice. All the way back, he bantered about what he saw on the roads underneath us, which was mostly nothing.

Traffic was sparse to say the least. As we rode, the clouds breaking up again and pale sun dripping through the windshield, I tried to imagine the horror and pain that would drive a woman, and a young mother at that, to go on the cement walkway to the lighthouse in weather like that. Especially a woman who had a world to live for, an athletic skill she could pass on to her child, or even teach.

I had to think Rene's despair ran from a deeper source than rejection from a Fighting Irishman. Or, who knows? Love will do twisted things to you—like crashing your car in a desert. I did wonder again if someone didn't give her a push, just as I suspected had happened to Janet. Or did it? Maybe she, too, had felt inner torment beyond all reckoning. For some reason, I thought of that cow being torn out of the sea of garbage. Somehow it seemed to fit. Somehow it was an image, pulled from a deep place, that made sense.

At that point, I turned to Bob and saw that he had taken a ski mask out of his pocket. He was stretching on it, sticking fingers through the eye slots. I wondered why he wanted to play with it now. He tugged on it, making himself look like a commando at Entebbe.

In quick order, Catbird brought us back to Grand Rapids and took us down onto the runway. Taxiing toward the hanger, he remained silent, until he slowed to a stop and flicked off the engine, which made the props spin to a jittery halt. "You know, Calvin," he said, turning to me, "I just related to you the absolute worst thing that ever happened to me."

I suspected he had. "I mean," he went on, tilting his head and gazing at dials on the ceiling, "my boy would have been 11 last month."

"Did you know she never got the abortion?"

"I didn't know what to think. I made the football team. Joined a fraternity. Put it out of my mind. Figured she was older, she'd handle it." He spoke to the window in front of him. "Which, goddammit, she did."

Bob leaned forward. "Give peace a chance."

"Just a second, sport." I took a leap of faith and tried to break through his grief. "Do you have any idea, other than just downright black depression, what would have driven her to do that?"

Catbird shook his head sadly as he faced me with eyes blurred by the bad memories. "You got me. All she ever said, once when we were at her house watching TV late at night, is that she wished she knew her own mother. Plus, she wished she really knew her dad. I wondered then if she was adopted, but she said that wasn't it at all. When I tried to get in it some more, she shut up."

As he spoke, his eyes grew wide, as if a ghost had flitted between us. When he didn't say anything, I pressed: "What?"

"It just hit me. That was the night that, you know, I think she got pregnant with our baby."

Watching him, the pain on his face, I wished there was some way I could help. I thought, oddly, that I wished I had the old rosary to give him. His sorrow, I knew, was the kind that only God, or maybe the Blessed Mother, could take away.

CHAPTER TWENTY-FOUR

Across from me, Bob munched popcorn in his peculiar one-kernel-at-a-time fashion. Not that he wasn't consuming a large amount of Orville Redenbacher's finest. It's just Monica's brother did it slowly, fingers dipping lazily in and out of the blue bowl on his lap.

I sat in my sagging Lazy Boy, feet propped up, glass of Irish coffee in hand. I'd just consumed the better part of a platter of microwaved spaghetti. The tomato-stained plate sat at my side on the carpet. Racing on the tube, the sound muted, were the white and black and red flashes of hockey players. The Detroit Red Wings, on a roll this year, were playing the Chicago Blackhawks. While I believed the Bulls were a basketball team designed by the Lord as an instrument of everyone else's destruction, the Blackhawks I could take or leave. The Red Wings, I liked. But Bob was obsessed with them. He'd been the one who stood when we'd come in an hour or so before, hands hooked at his sides, staring at the blank screen until I punched it on. He watched a real-life cop show until the game started.

Comfortable in my living room in my upstairs Heritage Hill apartment, I had the phone on the table at my side. I'd just made the call to my former elder and continuing friend, Benny Plasterman. He was showering and would, his daughter said, call me right back. Monica had two friends, one of them Aurora Benchley, tending to her tonight. I'd been with her for a few hours this afternoon, mostly as she slept, which gave me time to ponder this case and, just as important, sketch out Sunday's sermon, answer some correspondence and make a couple calls to keep things from tumbling too far off the tracks. For now, I wanted to relax.

160

"You know, Bob, hockey's a funny game," I said.

He paused, one piece of popcorn pinched between thumb and forefinger, and gazed at me, mouth hanging open. He wore baggy jeans, a long-sleeved black polo shirt, and wool socks, inside of which his toes kept moving, like fat fingers playing a pretend piano.

"It's fast, faster than any sport. It takes great skills, especially making the passes inside the blue line. But it's so violent. It's almost like these kids have to keep whopping one another to prove a point."

The popcorn slid in his mouth and the fingers returned to the bowl. Bob blinked and turned back to the game, where a flurry of players were wrestling, smacking each other with gloved fists and generally playing it like a barroom brawl in some old western. I sipped my coffee. On the cop show, the police had spent the hour chasing drunks of one sort or another. When they caught one, he bashed in a cruiser window with his foot. "Why do you like hockey so much?" I asked Bob.

"Silly rabbit," he retorted seriously.

I nodded, considering his point. Then I changed the subject, not that he would mind. "I hope your sister and her friends make progress."

Monica and Aurora and a woman named Connie DeKorne were trying to get through to Bosnia. They'd tracked down a phone number for Janet's former therapist, at work at some camp in the northern part of the country, and had a tentative interview scheduled at 10 o'clock our time. It was morning back there.

DeKorne was apparently a good friend of the psychologist. Aurora was there to lend moral support. When I had left, Monica and her pals had a quiet, no-nonsense cut to their jibs. They were going after this one and, no, they didn't need me around. Stay by the phone; they'd get back to me, or so I took from the quick kiss and hug Monica offered as I headed out with Bob for the pasta and popcorn banquet at my house.

The phone rang. I picked it up and punched the button. "What'a you think about Jimmy Swaggart?"

"Is this multiple choice?"

"I'm serious," said Manny Rodriguez. "How's he stack up in your book?"

Actually, I had tapes of swaggering Swaggart that I liked to turn on full blast so he could rage about a bloody, world-redeeming Jesus. I had to admit Swaggart, egomaniac showman that he was, could breathe real life into the man from Galilee. Bottom line, when all was said and done, we needed Christ if we weren't going to wash fast and furiously down the tubes. Swaggart knew that, even as he slid into his own private swamp.

"I like his suits," I replied.

The cop snorted and sucked, likely on one of his stinkpot stogies. "Otherwise he's too crude for you, right?"

"He's got a great haircut."

Not much response. "Is he still preaching, by the way?"

"Last I heard, he was, at some church in Tulsa or somewhere. Why, are you thinking of joining his fan club?"

Bob munched and picked, munched and picked, as the hockey players took a break from fighting to knock the puck around.

"No," replied Rodriguez, "I'm already spoken for. Fact is, I'm secretary of the Mother Theresa auxiliary, Grand Rapids chapter."

"I didn't know you were Catholic."

"Mother Theresa doesn't care."

A black guy strumming a guitar in front of a bricked building appeared on TV. Bob grinned and pointed. It was a Pepsi commercial. I figured he was thirsty. I waved at him, hoping he'd divine my gesture to mean what it meant, which was cool your jets. "So, you called for spiritual advice?" I asked.

"Hardly."

"Then what?"

"I was hoping for an update on your secret movements."

"No secrets. I'm just doing your job for you."

His chilly response spewed like freezer smoke over the phone. "You got anything new?" he asked without humor.

I said: "A couple things."

"Spill them."

I did. As I finished, I heard a call-waiting beep on my line. I told him to hang on. It was Ben. I told him I'd get right back to him. "You really think this old family business means anything today Turkstra?" Rodriguez asked.

"It could."

"I mean, shrinks in Bosnia, crybaby pilots, nut-brain garbage men, a horse doctor."

"You've come across something better?"

He didn't answer my question. "You talk to Preacher?"

"Actually, someone mentioned he wanted to tell me something about that brown van." That had been Ramon, after he banged on the door as I led Audrey VanTol out to her car.

"What did he want to say?"

"I don't know." At the bar the other morning, Preacher said he'd keep an eye out for the van. Maybe he'd seen it around before, he had said. "Why don't you give him a call?" I asked.

"I stopped by today. He wasn't in."

Bob held an open hand over his mouth. His eyes looked devilish.

"By the way, were you bullshitting me about that cow?" asked Rodriguez.

"Honest. It was a cow if I ever saw one."

He coughed into the phone, as if trying to get bacteria on my words. "Turkstra, give me a call if you have something important to say."

"Where are you at?"

"Doing some real work." Click.

Then there was Ben, fresh from his shower, happy to hear from me by the sound of it. I asked him if he knew Rodriguez.

"Sure, a good cop, probably a little too cynical for my liking. Has a son who has cerebral palsy."

"He's married?"

"He was. From what I hear, he's a single parent these days."

"That's got to be hard, with the job he has."

"I think he lives with his mother."

I took this in, let it settle, thought about the cop. This added some human dimension to him. A kid with a bad brain, like Bob. Ben and I continued to make small talk as the hockey players returned, waving sticks, throwing gloves, working hard to whale on one another. Bob watched it with fierce anticipation, fingers still picking popcorn.

"So, what's it I can help you with, Pastor?" Ben finally asked. One player had a bloody eye; another was shouting at the camera. A couple others were boxing on skates.

I gave him the lowdown on my recent activities. He interrupted at one point to say how sorry he was at what happened to Monica. I thanked him and talked on. I knew he was listening with all of his might. Ben Plasterman was like that.

"You know," he said as I wound down and the players took yet another break from the brawl to resume the game, "you're in luck."

Bob turned the bowl in my direction. It showed empty. His expression blamed me. I jerked my head at the TV. "Don't mess with Bess," Bob said. I shook my head. "How is that?" I asked Ben.

"Works this way. I was one of the guys called out that day. It was a Sunday, in January or February, I think it was, when she and her baby drowned."

"You were?" I sat up, reaching for a notepad on the floor by my dinner plate.

"As I remember, it was cold as all get out. But it had been pretty warm that year and the lake didn't freeze. The waves were rolling in like Jehovah's wrath."

I imagined huge foaming breakers, crashing over the board-walk. "What's it you remember, Ben?"

"We were there all day. But it was a devil of a search. Boats wouldn't work in that mess. Helicopter couldn't see anything. If we hadn't had a couple good eyewitnesses, we might have let it be and hoped it was a mirage."

"Did these eyewitnesses see anyone else out there?"

"Someone who could have pushed her?"

"It's a theory."

"They didn't. Plus, back home, she left a pretty detailed note. I was the one, actually, who found it, right on her pillow, by a teddy bear of all things."

Bob had slumped back on the couch, lips puffed out, surly, wanting something to drink and probably more of the same from Orville. The players were circling, ready to duke it out.

"Do you remember the note?"

"How could I forget?"

"You mind sharing it with me, Ben?"

A brief silence, during which one player blindsided another, which made them both fall in a tumble. I was amazed at what happened next. They got up and skated after the puck, without as much as an elbow, fist or kick exchanged. "I don't suppose after all of these years it would hurt."

It was my turn to listen now. I took a few notes as he talked. If the hockey players started to mix it up again, I didn't see, because I didn't care. I scratched away, taking it all down, my mind racing ahead to the next move. I'm not sure how long I'd been talking to Ben when I realized there was a problem with Bob. When I looked over, he was gazing at a spreading stain in his lap. If I wasn't mistaken, the expression on his face was one of mild delight.

I grabbed the phone and grunted into it before becoming aware anything had been ringing. The voice sounded gruff and muffled. Far away. I suddenly thought of Monica. Had something happened to her? "What?" I said, checking the clock to see it was almost 3 a.m. Snow dropped past my window that looked out on the alley. The streetlight out there made the flakes look tarnished.

"Herb Wierenga," the voice said.

"What about him?"

"I'm him."

I scooted forward in the bed, dragging the phone cord across the covers. My feet touched the cold wood floor, making my calve muscles tingle. "What's up?" I asked.

Nothing for a few seconds. I dragged fingers through my hair, rubbed the back of my neck. Heard Bob's snores in the next-door bedroom. Throaty snuffles that sometimes kept me up. But not this time. After making a series of calls and setting a meeting with Rodriguez for 6 a.m., I'd dropped in here and tumbled into sleep. That, of course, was after cleaning Bob, getting him in some other pants and squirting disinfectant on the couch.

"Look, you have to ease up."

My senses were finally alert. The snow, damn, we had a long drive to make. I didn't like seeing it out there. "On what?"

"Let sleeping dogs lie."

"In their own mess?" I asked.

Again, nothing.

"Why're you calling me?"

"I never did a thing."

At first, I'd sensed this was a threatening, "lay-off-me," phone call. But there seemed to be something else going on. "Then why call in the middle of the night?" I asked.

I thought I heard heavy, painful breathing. Not Bob's snores, rather Wierenga's overactive lungs. Beyond that, it sounded like metal scraping, a grinding in the distance. "Are you at home?" I asked.

"Why?" The word sounded like a moan.

"Are you all right?"

"Who're you to ask?" I detected a slur in his voice.

166

"I've got to get up in two hours," I told him. "Is there something you really wanted?"

"I told you."

I stood at the side of my bed. Shadows filled the room, swarming in all corners and slithering across the bed. The high ceiling loomed overhead. I lived in an upstairs apartment in an old restored lumberman's home. "What is it that you never did?" I asked.

Nothing.

"Look, Herb, you're the one who called."

"Killed Janet," he said.

"What about the others?"

"Who?"

I wondered if I should pursue this or find out exactly where he was and send Rodriguez. Who was already pleased as punch with me. He'd love getting roused to go wild goose chasing a drunk construction boss. "Your wife, your daughter, Tina Martin. Johnny Keester," I rolled out at him.

I heard a soft gurgle, as if he was gulping a drink. The background noise continued: bumps, clanks, chugs. "Herb?" I asked.

Nothing.

"I was wondering something," I then tried. When there was no response, I asked: "Did you break away from the Soldiers of the Cross and join the Promise Keepers? Is that what bothered Branson so much?"

"You're an idiot, Turkstra."

"Flattery doesn't become you, Herb."

He swore, mean and angry, into the phone.

I stretched the cord to the window. Parked cars were covered with snow. The large houses across the alley stood silent and dark. The sky looked endlessly gray, lit by the stark underglow of the city. "How about we talk about this later, after I get back from Petoskey?"

"Huh?"

I suppose it was the idiot remark that spurred me to be indiscreet. Or maybe it had to do with some buried urge to hurt a man who hurt others. In any case, I blurted: "Manny Rodriguez and I are going to talk to your daughter's real mother."

A strangled groan burst from the phone. I knew I'd hit pay dirt. I also realized I had said too much. Before I could talk to him again, he was gone. The connection remained for a half minute or so. But then it broke, shattering the line with the sound of a train roaring through an endless tunnel.

CHAPTER TWENTY-FIVE

Just south of Big Rapids, snow started dropping in great windy slaps, quickly turning the northbound lanes of U.S. 131 into a pair of two-tracks. Here it was not too long past dawn and the pale light that had started to light our way toward Petoskey was shuttered by clouds and snow. Darkness, which had just moved onto the sidelines, slipped back in. This made Manny Rodriguez grouse, jerk on his wipers and punch up the high beams. "This keeps up, we're turning back."

Cup of fast food coffee cradled in my lap, I could hear background voices on the radio. Some talk show out of New York. They were telling jokes about a high-profile murder trial. A famous football star had been acquitted of killing his wife and her boyfriend. The smartalecks on the radio were wondering if the guy was going to open his own domestic assault center.

The sick humor made me think of Monica, whom I had briefly visited before meeting the grumpy cop. She'd been asleep, her face less puffy, but her leg still stiff in its cast. What had happened to her wasn't the least bit funny. Hers hadn't been a deal of domestic violence, but I was beginning to strongly suspect that that was at the root of some of this—that is violence that occurred inside and then spilled out of a family. I hoped we'd find out if my theory held water later this morning.

"It's a blizzard," the detective observed, wiping a palm on the window in front of him.

"I thought cops handle bad weather on the road," I responded.

Headlights cutting through the small hunks of snow, the city-issue Corsica seemed to be swallowed up in the curtain of falling white. "You want to drive, be my guest," he snapped.

I had dialed Rodriguez, still at his office, after the second call-back the night before from Ben Plasterman and after making a call, with the number Ben provided, to the home in northern Michigan.

I told the Grand Rapids cop what his counterpart in Ottawa County had told me. I also mentioned that the woman, who lived in Harbor Springs outside Petoskey, agreed to see us, reluctantly. Right off, he wasn't hot on a road trip. But I pressed him. He said he'd check to see what his boss thought. Ten minutes later, by the time I'd helped Bob get cleaned and plopped back in front of the Wings, Rodriguez informed me that, yeah, he'd go. But was I sure this woman wanted to talk? I assured him that that's what she had said. Rodriguez wanted to call her himself, but I explained that she had told me she was going out and wouldn't be back until after midnight. She'd pretty much kept her mouth shut this long. It wouldn't take a lot to keep it that way, especially if he bugged her.

"Turkstra, I sure keep thinking this better be good," he now complained, cracking his window and blowing smoke from his Imperial out the inch-size vent.

I sipped cold coffee. At my feet sat the bag that had contained four egg muffins. We'd split them in silence not long after motoring north out of town.

I'd dropped Bob off with his dad and checked on Monica just after 6 a.m. Before meeting Rodriguez in the Butterworth emergency room parking lot, Monica's father told me he was cooking up a surprise for his little girl. It was sounding like she could go home anytime. Monica's dad had an in with the folks at the Amway Grand Plaza, a four-star hotel in town, and was thinking of putting her up there for a few days. He told me there was a special wing in the hotel devoted to the recovery of persons who quietly came to town to have plastic surgery by a bunch of doctors whose swanky offices, replete with operating rooms, were in a building next to the Amway. He wondered what I thought.

I'd said it sounded OK. Monica would probably like recuperating in those surroundings. He said they had nurses on duty around the clock. His buddy, one of the plastic surgeons, assured him that his daughter would be cared for better than if she stayed at the hospital.

"We're driving four hours north in a snowstorm to talk to a woman who may or may not have anything to say," said Rodriguez. His face swiveled my way, the black hair combed back and wavy in the back. He wore the bomber coat with the fleece collar. An insignia of a snake strangling a rat was on one shoulder. No silly hat today.

"So, I'm to assume this trip takes you way from the key interview?"

He sucked hard on the smoke. This time he didn't spit it out the crack. It rolled toward me in a smelly plume. I waved a hand and cranked down my window, more than an inch. As snow slipped in and splashed my face, I turned it back up, leaving room for his stink to escape. "You want to know what grinds me about this deal?" he asked.

"Being with me?"

"Besides the obvious."

"Going to Petoskey?"

"No, the whole shit bucket."

Red lights from the back of a truck suddenly appeared in front of us. We bore down fast, but Rodriguez swerved into the left lane at the last second. The tires skidded, bit and kept rolling. The cop's eyes barely left my face. "What?" I asked, my heart dropping out of my throat.

"It's complicated and fruity."

"How's that?"

The speedometer registering close to 75, he pushed us down the road, straight into the snow. Fat flakes skidded across the windows. "I like my murders clean," he said. "Give me greed, lust, drunken rage, that I can understand."

"I've never been much for murder myself."

He gave me a glare, making the tip of his cigar flare and spark. He pulled it out and blew smoke against the ceiling. "Thing is, you religious types can't just kill somebody without mucking it up with all sorts of weird reasons."

"I'm missing your point, Manny."

Rodriguez shook his head and looped an arm over the top of the steering wheel, guiding it with ease, as if we were on a pleasant Sunday drive. We roared along, oblivious to the weather. "You got a girl falls in the river. Maybe somebody pushed her. Maybe not. Maybe it involves some stupid group, and maybe not."

I swirled the rest of my coffee in the bottom on my cup, took a gulp, and shoved it down my throat. I tried to see if anymore trucks were about to appear in the storm.

"Then," said Rodriguez, powering us back into the right lane, itself covered with white, no tracks visible, "you have this other broad calls your girlfriend up. She's going to give her the poop, but then she's killed in bed. Monica's shoved down the stairs, Big Bob chases whoever did this away, and then we get chunks of Keester showing up in the dumpster in the T-shirt."

I was nodding, waiting for the punch line.

"So, I look into all this. I talk to people. I check some things out. Everywhere I go I got people telling me this thing's about men hating women. It has to do with woman being preachers, or whatever. I hear these Promise Keepers might be involved, now there's this other bunch of sickos."

"You sound frustrated."

He jammed the cigar back in the corner of his mouth, jumped in the left lane to pass a Toyota going turtle speed, and thumbed up the heater. "No, pissed. Because now I'm hearing it might go back to another woman falling in the lake with her kid." He looked over at me, as if to make sure I wasn't asleep. I wasn't. "But, top it off, we get to go even farther back in time, boys and girls, to yet another woman, this one a lesbian living in Petoskey."

"Who says she's a lesbian?"

He shoved a hand at the window, dismissing me. He jammed the pedal even harder as we raced into the right lane to pass another truck. "Let me finish."

"Don't kill us in the process."

His face jerked my way, as if I'd just asked him if he wanted to dance. But he let up a little, letting the car drop to a cruising speed of 60.

"Anyway, everyone keeps trying to feed me the idea that there are high-minded reasons why these women are all getting whacked, or killing themselves, or whatever."

"There's Keester, too."

"He's a crook. I'm not counting him."

"Blackmailing makes sense."

"Damned straight."

"So what's your point?" I was irritable and scared. His driving made me wish I was anywhere but there.

His cigar, now a stump, rolled in the corner of his mouth. His jaw worked; his hands circled the steering wheel. "Chief said I had to check this out. He didn't say anything about having to take any guff from you. Or having to take you along for that matter."

"Drop me off. I'll walk home."

"That has a nice ring to it." But Rodriguez didn't stop. We drove on in silence awhile, passing Big Rapids, nearing the Reed City exit. Up here, the snow started to let up. Even so, it still slopped up the road. As we blasted back to 75 and did a little tailgating of a salt truck, I shifted toward my exceptionally upbeat sidekick and asked: "So, what's it you're trying to say?"

Rolling his neck, the cop said: "Explain to me, if you would be so kind, what this is all about, theology-wise. Then give me the details again of your late-night call from Wierenga."

I stared down the road, through the dancing snow, trying to find a true break in the weather. Weak, milky sunlight up

173

ahead perhaps a sign, but otherwise things remained dead-of-winter dreary. "The theology is quite simple."

Rodriguez didn't react, his attention finally snagged by the job of driving.

"It boils down to who's got the upper hand, which has mostly been the men."

"That's your motivation?"

"Like I said, the PKs aren't involved in this in any real way,"I said. "They're thrown out as a convenient smokescreen, although there is the other group."

"Don't give me gobbledygook. Who's doing it and why?"

I leaned back in the seat, arms over my chest and watched snow-laden trees whip past. In a break through the pines, I spotted huge metal phone line towers marching into the distance.

Last night, Monica had gotten through many miles of phone lines and microwave dishes to the therapist in Bosnia. The gist of the story was that the psychologist had left town right at the time Janet VanTol was dipping into some dicey personal stuff. Seemed Janet, for whatever reason, didn't bring up the bubbling brew of bad experiences until just before the therapist said bon voyage.

What Monica got out of the static-filled conversation was that Janet had put off dealing with things, knowing her psychologist was leaving, but had ended up getting sideswiped by a raft of emotions. Instead of getting the help she needed, she pulled up just enough baggage to make herself miserable and have no one to share it with. Apparently, the therapist recommended someone else, but Janet never lived to connect with that person. Sounded like all-around bad timing. Poor Janet's psyche had played a dirty trick on her.

Monica had pressed the therapist on exactly what Janet was confronting. The psychologist said she wasn't sure, but strongly figured it had to do with her family. Some awful things from the past were trying to get out of her.

"I'm thinking this whole thing boils down to Max Wierenga and Branson VanTol. They are our bad guys. They are the Soldiers of the Cross," I said to the blobs of snow kissing the windshield.

"Our killers?"

"Could be."

"Together, they've wiped out their daughters, a grandkid, and Tina on the bed and Keester in the garbage?"

"It does sound extensive."

Rodriguez shook his head. "My experience, lots of men hate women, and vice versa, and do pretty bad things to each other, but dads don't commonly do that to their girls."

"You've never come across it?"

"I didn't say that. I'm just saying you people in your church are so damned flaky. You've got reasons for everything."

Four hours of sleep had left me more than normally dulled in the brain. Three days of lousy, get-it-on-the-run grub had left my gut in a mild uproar. But even deeper, I was feeling out of sorts with God, or maybe it was with my denomination. Rodriguez was right: We thought too much and that thinking occasionally made us lethal. "I know it does sound a little funny," I said to Rodriguez.

"I'm busting a gut."

I decided to try it another way. "Sure, our church is fighting it out over whether women can be preachers. But the tea leaves say it's going to happen. Monica, in fact, is apt to be one of the first."

Rodriguez gave me a sidelong glance, almost as if he was impressed, or maybe he was thinking Monica was nuts, given what had happened.

"I just don't think we've got the violence because of some change in church policy." I could tell he wasn't exactly thrilled with my take on the matter. But I pushed to the end. "What I'm thinking we have is dirty family linen."

175

The detective notched his window another half-inch, shoved the remains of cigar out, the litter bug, then gunned us around a pickup. We quickly rolled up a hill and curved out on a vista across snowy fields, a stark red barn and sun. "Let me get this straight, professor." Rodriguez used the corner of his eye to make sure I hung on his every word. "We're driving all the way to Petoskey in a snowstorm to poke through smelly underwear?"

"I'm hoping it fills in the picture."

The cop shook his head. "Ask me, we'll be lucky if this broad tells us anything we don't already know."

"Maybe she'll tell us if you're right."

"How's that?"

"It's possible, when all is said and done, that what we are dealing with is greed, lust, and drunken rages."

He motored on in silence a minute. Then, pressing again on the pedal, asked: "Herb called, then, to confess?"

Hunched in my seat, the sun peaking through clouds, a county road commission snowplow scraping sparks from the road ahead, I tried to put my finger on it. "No," I said, "more like he was falling apart. Like he didn't want his secrets to keep getting him sick any longer."

Rodriguez laughed. "Turkstra, you're in the wrong line of work. You should be writing self-help books."

CHAPTER TWENTY-SIX

Harbor Springs, our ultimate destination, is an ultra-ritzy, mostly vacation spot on the tip of the finger of land jutting into Little Traverse Bay from Bay View, a small community just north of Petoskey. We had to negotiate our way through a guard shack, where Rodriguez chatted for a couple minutes with a chunky rent-a-cop. Then we wound along narrow streets, past huge hulking mansions, to a road marked Cherry Lane that led up a winding drive to the place we were looking for.

Parking in a shoveled area outside the garage, itself bigger than most homes, Rodriguez squinted and craned his head to have a look at the massive yellow structure. All turrets and painted wood siding, with curved windows, hand-crafted dormers and a couple wrap-around porches, it could have been a turn-of-the-century rest home, hospital or spook house. "Some digs," he observed.

To the right, between other monstrous, Victorian-style homes, shone the cold, choppy waters of the bay.

"You say this lady's going to tell us all about her shady past, just out of high-minded civic duty?" He turned to me, an arm resting on the steering wheel. His face, touched by pinkish sunlight, reflected hard crevices, bumps, and nicks and a mild case of envy. Harbor Springs, once home to one-fifth of the nation's wealth, or representatives thereof, could spark wishful thinking in the best of us, even crusty Hispanic cops. As a preacher, I was beyond such crass consumerism. Except, I wondered if folks nearby needed a pastor. Someone to whom they could offer an expansive parsonage. Certainly such a place would be conducive to the Lord's work.

"My sense, Manny, is your silver tongue will do the trick."

He gave me a cynical twist of the head, cracked open his door. "Let's get it over with."

Up the circular bricked steps we went, our shoes crunching salt crystals, to the front door, thick with leaded glass windows. Rodriguez punched the bell button, then turned, rubbing his hands, to idly examine the neighborhood whose homes stood around us, half-hidden among bare trees, their peaked roofs and well-painted fronts reflecting the money spent to put them here. "Who you have to rob to live out here, huh?" he asked.

The door opened with a scrape and a woman appeared in a billowy blue smock, her black-gray hair arranged carefully around her head, bright red lipstick forming her mouth, and a pair of pruning shears in her hand. "Mrs. Klock?" asked the cop.

"I was hoping," Dorie Klock said to the both of us, "you had changed your minds."

"No, ma'am," replied Rodriguez, bouncing on the balls of his feet, which were as usual stuck in the snakeskin, stiletto-toed cowboy boots.

The woman frowned and stared at him as if he had leprosy. He gave her a sly trick-or-treater grin.

I introduced myself as the friend of Bennie Plasterman. The expression on her face turned mildly curious. "You're the pastor?"

"That's right."

She nodded, pale sun dabbing her face. "Come in," she said, and left the doorway. My leather-jacketed companion followed, leaving the door-closing part for me.

One inside, we entered a large, formal room, filled with furniture, wooden tables topped by fresh flowers, colorful paintings on the walls. To our left, in a doorway, appeared a grizzled, angry-looking cuss in a wheelchair. "Who's here?" he snarled.

"Company, Lou."

"Whose company?"

"They're for me, dear."

His face went almost immediately blank, as if a magical potion had stripped it of emotion.

"This is Lou Klock, my husband," she said. "Lou has Alzheimer's."

A slender, short-haired woman appeared behind Lou, her features bird-sharp and focused. I immediately made her as a health food eater. She had that gaunt, clear-eyed demeanor. "This is Mim Hathaway."

Mim gave us a brief, thin-lipped smile. She wore a turtleneck sweater. Her hands, on the back of the wheelchair, showed bulging blue veins, the hands of a worker.

Dorie Klock seemed to suddenly notice the pruning sheers in her hands. "I was in the greenhouse, cutting back the glads," she explained.

Rodriguez, hands in his back pockets, nodded at Lou, who came quickly back to life. "I hate flowers!" he said vehemently.

His wife gave him a tender look and shook her head. "Mim, could you see if Lou wants to watch his shows?"

Mim seemed to consider this a moment, her small oval of face serenely alert as it watched the three of us standing in the middle of the shiny wood floor in a room that could have been used for a dancing competition. "Sure," she said, pulling back the wheelchair, dragging Lou with her. "Who are they?" he demanded of Mim.

"They're here to talk about Rene."

"Rene who?"

There was a garbled answer.

"Shall we," said Dorie, sweeping out a different door in the middle of the room between a pair of overstuffed, probably antique couches. She led us along a wooden hallway that creaked as we walked, its planks bowed and valleyed. "How old is this house, Mrs. Klock?" I asked.

"Dorie," she replied. "My husband's grandfather had it built in the late 1800s."

"Quite the neighborhood," said Rodriguez.

"We like it."

I could smell the greenhouse before we got to it. As she guided us through a huge kitchen with pots and pans hanging from hooks in the drop ceiling and a silver refrigerator the size of an upended gas guzzler, my nose caught a mixture of sweet scents. A doorway led from the kitchen through an enclosed porch to another short hall and then into a bright, dome-topped indoor garden.

Rows of flowers, banked in rich black dirt, spread before us. Intermixed with the colorful display of various kinds of flowers were plants of different sizes. A skin of snow covered the highest windows above us. In here, the temperature was a good 15 degrees warmer than the rest of the house. Along with the flowers, I smelled manure, dirt and a tangy odor of chemical cleanser.

"This is great!"

I had to give him a second look. But, if I wasn't mistaken, Rodriguez meant it. His sardonic mask of a face, with its mean mouth and twisted nose, had been transformed, if only for a few seconds. I saw softness there, a quick pleasant coloring along the rough edges of his cheeks. He held out his arms, the joyful gesture of the fiddler on the roof. "My mom would've loved this."

Dorie Klock noticed it, too. She watched him with interest, the pruning shears at her side. "She was a gardener?"

"Green thumbs galore."

She smiled and shook her head. Manny, you've got a way with words, I thought. His face shifted from her to me and back, as if he'd suddenly realized he'd become the butt of a joke, or that he'd given us an unwarranted glimpse into himself. In a flash, I saw a schoolboy's hurt in his features as they closed in, grew hard and prickly again.

But Dorie Klock reached out to him, touched the sleeve of his jacket. She was in her fifties. Her body, under the smock, had a pillowy softness, full in places that hinted at a not-so-hidden sensuality. The word that came to mind as I looked at her was fragrant. Keeping her hand on his arm, she said: "Do you garden?"

"Some." He shuffled away from her down a bermed row of plants whose leaves and fronds looked rich and healthy. Pausing in front of a group of upside-down flowers, he looked at her over his shoulder. He touched a few large, slender leaves and cupped one of the bulbs yet to open. "Passionflower?" he asked.

"That's right." She joined him and they strolled the row, stopping here and there in an area that I gathered contained the bulk of her herb garden. Old Manny knew the names of many of them. "Where are you from, detective?" she asked as we neared the end.

"Grew up in Miami."

"How'd you end up in Michigan?"

"A long story."

If I wasn't mistaken, Rodriguez had turned on a few volts of charm I hadn't known was there. Dorie Klock stood next to him, her round, creamy face giving him her full attention. "I thought we'd talk upstairs," she said to him.

He bobbed his shoulders, a sign that was OK with him. I thought of clearing my throat, to remind them I was there, but just kept up as she stepped through another door and took us up a spiral staircase into a room filled with the sort of light I hoped to see in heaven.

The stairs dumped into the middle of a room with large windows looking straight out on the rolling blue waters of the bay. Yellow walls, where there wasn't glass, added to the bright, sun-washed effect. The sky out there ballooned far into the open expanse of Lake Michigan. Directly across from the house, about three miles from where we stood, spread the hazy shore of what had to be Petoskey.

"Please, sit." She indicated padded wicker chairs aligned with a perfect view of the rocking water through the gleaming squares of glass. As we chose our seats, she drifted over to a counter. "Coffee?"

"Sounds good," said Rodriguez, rubbing his hands together after having unzipped his jacket.

I wondered if being perky was a police ploy. Maybe he was going to soft soap her story out of her. "Reverend?" she asked.

"Sure."

Side by side, we took in the sights. Sun rode the sky to the east. The bay, in the last days of winter, showed a powerful, self-absorbed beauty. I could feel it calm me. Dorie Klock set a pot, cups and other coffee-drinking accessories on a table in front of us. She disappeared a moment and returned with a plate of Oreos. Rodriguez waved them away. I took four.

"So," she said, arranging herself on a wide-backed chair to our left, leaving her a place from which to gaze at the landscape if she wanted. "You want to know about Rene?" She nibbled an Oreo, her coffee cup in the lap of her smock. She wore belted sandals on her feet.

Rodriguez sat up straight. "Before you begin, ma'am, you do know this is an official investigation."

She separated her cookie, examined the side with the filling, took a tentative lick. She's toying with us, Manny, I thought. "I'm not sure I follow."

"We're dealing with a couple a murders, Mrs. Klock, so I want you to know this is serious."

"The phone calls I got last night told me as much."

"Calls?" I chimed in.

Her color dimmed as she looked in her lap. "Herb called after you."

"Wierenga?"

She nodded, her face serious.

"What'd he want?" asked Rodriguez.

Dorie Klock shook her head. "I suppose for me to keep quiet." She looked at both of us with expectant, probing eyes.

"Which," she added, "I have no intention of doing anymore. Especially after his terrible intrusion."

"Did he threaten you?" I asked.

She held up a limp hand. "I hung up before he could even try."

Watching her, I felt a bubbling of anger, this growing sense of the rotten bastards who had been ramming their ways into and out of the lives of women who were likely much stronger than them to begin with.

Dorie Klock stuck a cookie half in her mouth and chewed thoughtfully, staring hard at me, a hint of cruelty, or perhaps buried rage, in her eyes. "Where should I start?"

Rodriguez had pulled a small notebook out of his jacket pocket and was scratching something with the nub of a pencil, maybe a grocery list. He didn't seem interested in starting, so I gave it a whirl. "Which one was Rene's father, Wierenga or VanTol?"

It was as if a light went off inside her skin. Storm clouds rolled into her eyes. Rodriguez stopped scribbling long enough to give me quizzical look. Dorie Klock had been about to twist off another Oreo lid, but put the cookie back. Settled her hands gently on her knees. "We'll never know," she replied simply.

"Both of them?"

"Does that bother you, Reverend?" She showed me her chin, a delicate shape jutting under powdered skin.

Last night Benny had told me that he had learned that Branson VanTol was sent up here in the mid 1960s by his father to start an office chair manufacturing plant south of Petoskey. He brought his buddy, Max Wierenga, along to help with construction plans. The two of them ended up living up here and working for the better part of a year. "No, Mrs. Klock, it doesn't," I answered, trying not to sound prim.

Her eyes turned to Rodriguez, daring him to disagree with me.

"Sort of turns me on, Doris," he told her.

183

"Dorie," she shot back.

Rodriguez narrowed a predatory cop's gaze on her and said nothing.

She seemed to take his measure a moment, a band of tension between them, then turned and faced the window, a hand to her throat, the years dragging back at her. "All of that was such a long time ago."

"Do you have any reason to believe, ma'am, that either of these two men was involved with your daughter's death?" asked the cop.

She turned slowly back to him, hand still at her throat. "You mean did either of them kill her?"

He shrugged, doodling on his pad, which he'd propped on his knee.

"Truthfully, I think we all had a hand in that."

From my perch, I saw currents of emotion working under her skin. She combed a hand through her black hair, so black it had to be dyed, but full and curly and shoulder-length. "But did someone actually do it?" I asked.

"I can't speak for them."

"Any speculations?" I asked.

Her forehead wrinkled as her mouth edged into a frown. "Is one of them under suspicion for Rene's death?"

I thought of the suicide note and wondered if Ben had ever shared it with her.

Rodriguez checked his watch. The sun did dirty tricks on his face. It lit on bumps and left shadows in crannies under the eyes. Mostly, it made him look blotchy and brutish. "How about tell the story," he said. "That's why we're here."

Both of them turned to me, as if seeking confirmation. "Maybe this whole thing started up here," I said. Last night, I'd filled her in on Janet, Monica and the others.

She blinked and made for the window again with her eyes, this time leaving her hands still as drugged birds in her lap. "If

I didn't think there was some truth in that, I wouldn't have agreed to this interrogation."

She shot Rodriguez an angry look, then returned her attention to the lake whose waters in the last couple minutes had begun to sparkle in the deeper spots with a metallic blue. Closer to shore, ice chunks bunched shoulder to shoulder. I thought of the lighthouse at Grand Haven over which we'd flown yesterday.

"I was working at the South Shore Inn," she said, letting one hand flutter up and indicate some place across the heaving water. "Max and Branson stopped in quite a bit for dinner and drinks. I got to know them there. After I got off, I drank along with them." She stared outside for awhile in silence. The room seemed to float around us, the yellowish light dizzy with dust motes. "That was before I got sober. Long before it, in fact."

I now noticed a couple needlepoint plaques placed on the wall to my right. "A Day at a Time," said one. The other the famous Serenity Prayer. She's in AA, I assumed.

Dorie Klock sighed, rubbing a spot in the back of her neck. "Do you want all the dirty details?"

"I do, but I suppose you better give us the PG version for the pastor here," said the cop, smirking.

Still facing the bank of windows, she took a little digression. "Can you see the huge homes going up along the shore, way to the right, south of Petoskey?"

Just barely, I told her.

"That's where Lou owned his cement factory. I met him in AA, eight years ago this Christmas. He'd been sober a dozen years, but it was a tough time for him. His wife and three kids died in a car accident in Escanaba. Me, I was just getting straightened out. He took me under his wing. Obviously, we got married."

With that little background under her belt, and without mentioning Mim's role in this upscale, teetotaling household, she wandered back to the topic at hand. In a somber voice, she talked about a night in 1986. She'd just returned at that time

185

from many years trying to get the geographical cure, she said. Back in Petoskey, she returned to barmaiding, this time at a bowling alley. One night, it had to have been this lousy time of year, the off-season, someone said a young woman with a baby was there, sitting in a corner of the lounge, wanting to talk.

It being about closing time, Dorie was hot to trot out of there. She had a friend she wanted to smoke dope with in Traverse City. So when she went over to see who wanted her, and with a baby nonetheless, she was definitely in no mood for a hearts-and-flowers confrontation with her past. Fact was, she was pretty looped, having slugged on brandy most of the night as she filled booze orders for the bowlers. Almost as soon as she spotted the young woman, Dorie had an idea what she had on her hands. Reluctantly, she sat, looking across the table for the first time since birth at her only child and grandchild.

Thing is, when Rene was born, she explained, she started bleeding badly and had to have an emergency hysterectomy. She ended up in ICU, in fact. When she came to, the child was gone and so were Max and Branson, both of whom helped to arrange the birth in a small community hospital outside Flint. They had told her they were going to put the kid up for adoption. She didn't care, or pretended not to. Almost as soon as she got out of the hospital, she hopped a Greyhound and went to live with a cousin on an Air Force base in California. That started her cross-country journey, most of it spent deep in the bag, that eventually brought her home and to the bowling alley.

Anyhow, she said, there was her girl and her grandchild. She had seen pictures of Rene but never met her in person. Until then. You would think, even with her head rattled by more than two decades of hard chugging that she would have felt at least a few whiffs of parental affection. But, not her. She hardly heard the first words out of Rene's mouth, when she told her she couldn't talk. She had to be somewhere.

186

Rene wanted to know if they could meet the next day. Dorie said, sure, no problem, got up and didn't return to the bowling alley for the better part of two weeks. When she did, the boss said, here, read this. It was a newspaper article describing the death of a Rene Wierenga in Grand Haven, and of the infant. Then the boss said, "You're fired, honey." The boss also said: "The girl a couple weeks back who was here, the one who died, she left a letter for you. She came back for you four times. When you never showed, she gave me this."

Rodriguez listened carefully, watching her every move and gesture. As she talked, I was moved by the way she told her truth: Straight, clear, with no hint of self-pity.

"I took the letter, drank the better part of a fifth of vodka and opened it up, back in my crummy apartment. Even though I was polluted, I got the gist."

The letter, she said, told her that Rene's stepmother had apparently served as a punching bag for dear old Max. Sometime, somewhere in there, apparently the stepmom gave Rene the scoop on Dorie.

"Well, who knows why, but it sounds like the stepmom got drunk one too many times, cracked her head and died."

Dorie Klock's voice had taken on new meaning. I heard passion, anger, and deep sorrow in it. But she kept addressing the window. Sunlight had dimmed a bit, as if someone had twisted down an adjustable switch in the sky. The water out there looked terribly cold and lonely. "Isn't it funny, Max's wife had a drinking problem, too."

Rodriguez flipped his notebook shut on a finger. "She died at their cottage in Saugatuck. Police wrote it up as an accident. No one had any other reason to think different," he told her.

She shrugged. Her eyes filled, the hand went to the side of her face again. She seemed to sink into herself.

"This letter," said Rodriguez, "you still have it?"

"It burned that night, along with my bed, my clothes, my legs and the better part of my apartment."

187

"In a fire?"

"I went to bed smoking."

I shifted forward in my seat, leaning toward her, still aware of the dark beauty in her face. Thinking of fire. "That's when you got sober?"

"When they let me out of the burn ward, they put me in treatment in Traverse City." Her gaze shifted between us. "It didn't take, but I finally got clean."

Rodriguez snapped a finger at the face of his scrawny notebook. "What's the bottom line? You think Max killed VanTol's daughter, or your daughter for that matter?"

She flinched and flushed and pursed her mouth. She didn't reply.

"Or VanTol, you think he did it?"

Dorie Klock remained still, her face draining now of its quick flash of color. She shook her head. I suspected the memories were flooding in too fast and hard.

"I mean, it sounds like these guys have got a lot to hide," the cop prodded. I wondered why Max got Rene and not VanTol.

"I've told you everything I can," she said.

"In that letter," I tried, "did Rene mention why she had sought you out?"

Now the tears spilled, just rolled right out and down the cheeks. There were no sobs, no shakes of the shoulders, no gulps for air. The water poured, as if a spigot had been turned. "Because, Reverend, she said God wanted her to. Because, she wrote, she and her daughter had no one else in the world and all of the men had abandoned her. Because she thought me, as her blood mother, might be able to help."

I saw the pain there and wanted to reach out to her. Rodriguez edged forward in his seat, giving her an intense lookover. "Mrs. Klock?" he said softly.

She wiped her eyes with the back of her hands. Her age was in her face now, deep in the lines around the mouth. She glanced at him expectantly. I gazed around for some tissue for her.

188

"Which one did your daughter look like?" he asked.

She shook her head, not quite getting it.

"VanTol or Wierenga? Which one was the father?"

Again, color rose in her face. You can't keep her down long. She seemed to straighten in her seat. "This does turn you on, doesn't it?"

"Please."

She sighed and returned her attention to the water. As if addressing the lake, she answered, with lots of remorse mixed with a hint of pride: "The both of them. I saw each of them in her. They helped create her, and all of us destroyed her."

CHAPTER TWENTY-SEVEN

Mid-afternoon at the former topless bar in Kalkaska was slow pickings, at least on this late February day. Smoke clung to the air like mold in a dirty basement and dim light ran all through the place, making me feel like I was in a cave. As Rodriguez ambled toward our table with plates of high-fat food, I noticed the stage to his right, crammed with instruments for some country band that apparently played nights in this rambling log cabin on the outskirts of town. The cop dished me up the huge hamburger and order of fries, dropped his plate on the other side of the table and started back, this time for drinks. He paused after a couple feet, turned. "You sure you want milk?"

"Builds strong bones."

"Instead of minds?"

I'm not sure who was more glib, he or me, but I let it go.

The bartender, when we showed up, made it clear he could fix us up some lunch. We'd just have to do the toting from the grill and back. Rodriguez offered to serve as waiter, this stop being his idea.

Only a couple others sat at the tables in this part of the Country Crossing Inn. The bar itself was half-packed with daytime boozers. The atmosphere of the joint, with its lazy liquored seediness, wasn't what I needed. Not after the session with Dorie Klock. Her story had really dug into me, making me remember a few things, and stirring a kind of primal shame at what men have been doing for centuries to women. Images of Ruth, that awful crash in the desert, the flames rifling from her Jeep, and of my father crying that one time he shoved my mother after an argument over religion in the kitchen of our farmhouse rolled through me. Beyond that was a powerful feeling about

190

woman-hating done under the guise of God. The Catholics didn't let women rule the roost, but they were upfront about it. Not so in parts of our church, where much of the hating happened in backrooms. Or so I was thinking. I dug my thumbs into my temples and pressed hard, trying to shove out the tension.

"Chocolate's all she wrote, Ace." Rodriguez pushed a tall glass across the table, then sat with his plate of food and a longneck Bud, capped by a glass, which he quickly removed and filled with foaming brew.

I sipped the milk. It was good and cold. "You've been in this supper club before?" I asked.

Rodriguez chomped into his burger, his cheeks puffed out with meat and bun. He nodded, chewing, and swilled some beer. "Used to stop and catch the show on our way deer hunting."

I nodded.

"Which I got to figure, you Christians oppose," he added, hamburger held even with his mouth.

"Topless bars or killing deer?"

"Both."

I shrugged, staring at my burger, feeling anger swell. "You know I'm getting sick of you lambasting my faith."

When I looked back, he replied: "Sorry." I suspected he was. Which made me feel testy and a little guilty. Still, this was the thing that ruled my life. Down below my own cynicism, and questions, lurked a hunger to stay connected to my maker. I did that through my church. Through Christ.

The cop continued the attack on his burger. I hefted mine, gobbled a corner, set it down. He eyed it. "Not hungry?"

I shook my head.

He bit and chewed, licked mayo from a forefinger, slugged down more beer. Wiping mustard from his mouth with a wadded napkin, he gave me the evil eye, maybe trying to read my mind. After he'd gone back to his burger, he stopped his munching long enough to say: "Woman was a trip."

191

"You don't believe her?"

"What's not to believe. She led a hard life before hopping on the gravy train."

I grabbed a fry, swirled it into a tiny cup of ketchup, slithered it over my tongue, let my teeth gnaw a second. "Where'd you get the lesbian thing from?"

"Police work, Turkstra." His incisors mangled the last chunks of his burger, his jaw on overtime.

I drank more chocolate milk. Let my eyes wander the darkish bar, the buckled wood floor, the tawdry beer company gimmicks hanging from the ceiling—twirling pictures of women in swimming suits, a team of horses hauling a sleigh, another group of women in bulky fur coats, all of them fondling beer bottles.

In an odd way, I felt as if the ghost of the bare-breasted dancers hovered in the air, the cheap entertainment provided to middle-aged drunks and horny kids barely 21. I'd been in a couple topless bars during leaves in the Navy. What always bothered me about them is that a desperate part of me liked them, while still another part was well aware the women were making fools of us as they twisted and jerked and pumped vacant-eyed from elevated stages.

"This place make you nervous?" Rodriguez asked, digging a finger back by the wisdom teeth, finding a prize and wiping it on the napkin by his Bud.

"Whole day's got me out of sorts."

He nodded, pouring beer into the glass, which he tilted just right to minimize the foam. He'd left most of his potatoes. He wore a blue button-down collar shirt, starched and form-fitted, showing the bulk of his shoulders and arms and the hard iron of his slightly mounded gut.

"Was it a waste of time?" I asked.

He leaned back, stuck an arm over his chair and lowered his chin to his chest. "She didn't give me anything I can use."

"Nothing?"

"Zip." He drank beer, watching me close. "Might've filled in a couple blanks, but I already figured those two yahoos were dirty."

"So arrest them."

"Not that simple."

"Have you even interviewed them yet?" I knew I sounded peeved.

Rodriguez settled forward on cupped fists. "You got a way of getting under my skin, Reverend." His expression inched from indifferent to threatening, the mustache coming alive over the mouth.

"I've got a personal investment in this," I returned.

"So far, you've been lucky. "

"Because Monica wasn't cut up and put in a dumpster?"

"Or you."

I sucked in a swallow of air. I adjusted myself on the chair. I poked around in my potatoes. I took another bite of burger. I knew he watched me as I wasted time, trying to cool down. I wasn't sure if I was scared, angry or just disgusted. When I spoke, I said: "If you've talked to them, what'd you learn?"

"Told you, zilch." He stared at his hands, actually seeming to think a couple seconds and not just bluster ahead with words. "I suppose it wouldn't hurt for you to know what we got on them in the files." His greenish eyes, clear and precise even in the dusky light of the bar, turned up at me.

I waited, munching more burger, suddenly hungry, wanting fuel.

"Wierenga used to like hookers."

"Used to?"

"Either that or he's being more discreet, last few years."

"Before that?"

"Picked him up three times soliciting on Division."

My neck of the woods, but before my time. "Was he violent with them?"

Rodriguez wiped the sides of his mustache with a thumb and forefinger. Opened his hands and gazed somewhere over my shoulder. "Nothing to pin him on."

"VanTol?"

"Mean little prick."

"Besides his personality flaws?"

His eyes shifted back to me as he leaned in his chair and dug around in an ear. "We're working on him. Nothing kinky so far."

I examined my mostly uneaten burger, set it down, turned it over on the flat side of the bun, as if trying to get a better view of things. "Where's that leave us?"

"Us?"

"You."

He sat there, immobile, lazy-eyed now, his chin drooping. "Could use a nap."

I tried to quickly calculate it. The two of them up north, getting Dorie pregnant, dumping her, taking the infant. Giving her to Herb. Rene learning of her heritage, desperately seeking help, getting rejected, taking a dive off the pier, with her own kid. Then Janet. Somehow she figured it out, or part of it. Somehow Monica's class stirred things up, as did sessions with the counselor. Keester and Tina Martin enter at this point as the blackmailers. Both lose out big time. Working into all of this, maybe not so important anymore, were the Promise Keepers and the dirty offshoot. What I had originally thought was tied closer to our church now seemed like a much bigger and far uglier problem.

At root was rage at women, I was starting to think. Not two years ago, I had helped my church write a document decrying domestic abuse. But when working on that, I had not had such a terrible taste of what it truly meant in my mouth. I knew, but I didn't know. And moving through it was my own remorse. I ran some of this by Rodriguez, sketching the connections. If I wasn't mistaken, he actually listened to what I said with a level of interest, even as he continued to scratch and dig and let his eyes wander.

"So," he said when I finished, "who exactly did what to whom?" He leaned his chin on an upended palm.

"I'm not sure, but I believe the two of them are our villains," I answered.

"Dastardly," he said.

"What have you got that's better?"

Poker-faced, Rodriguez slumped in his chair, idly reached over and tipped the empty beer bottle toward him, keeping it on the table. "How about these church groups, just smoke?"

"More or less they've been used to throw us off track."

"There you go including yourself again."

"Look," I said, "you have to stop these guys."

The cop twisted around and peered at the empty stage, maybe drawn by the ghosts, too, although I doubted it. "We haven't got a thing tying either of them to any of the deaths."

"So, where's that leave things?"

He showed me empty hands. "Lean on them some more, hope something turns up."

"What about the story Dorie Klock just told us."

"It's going to keep me up nights," he replied, a sardonic glint in his eyes.

I shoved back from the table, ready to get up. "So, going up there was a waste of time?"

He scraped his chair back as well and pushed up from the table. "Her tale of woe tells me shit."

"You're just going to let them be?" I felt my hands clench around the empty milk glass. I stared up at him, feeling fire in my face.

"Look, Reverend. As far as I can read it from here, both of these girls could have dumped themselves into the water."

"Monica," I said in a loud voice. "What about her? She just threw herself down the stairs and Tina Martin choked on a chicken bone and Keester cut himself shaving!"

195

A calmly lethal look formed slowly on his face. He picked up and slung his arms into his jacket. Yanking up the zipper, he said: "Keep it down, would you?"

I stood. "No! I have to know that these maniacs aren't going to hurt anyone else."

The few heads in the bar turned. Other conversations had stopped. The stage remained empty, heavy with shadows.

"Sorry, folks," said Rodriguez, raising a hand, "our friend is having bad day." On that point, he was right.

CHAPTER TWENTY-EIGHT

We drove back in a funky silence. The freeway was clear; snow had been shoveled into small hills on the shoulder. Sun had followed us down from Petoskey, filling the sky and the large white fields with deceptively warm-looking light. Pleasant as it was outside, my mood was grim and dark. I slumped in the seat, letting Rodriguez motor us south to Grand Rapids. At one point, he said: "How's Bob?"

"Why?"

"If he could talk, maybe we'd be in business."

"What do you think he saw?"

"Who knows? He was in the house."

"So was Monica."

"But, he tussled with our guy. Maybe . . . I don't know."

I heard frustration in his voice. It made him a little more human, but it also reminded me that he probably had no rabbits up his sleeve. "Do you think both of them were there that night?" I asked.

"Turkstra, I'm still not convinced both of them are involved or either of them."

"What about the blackmail?"

"Maybe Keester and the girl saw someone else."

"Such as?"

Eyes locked on the road, hands at ten and two on the wheel, the cop shrugged. "Try Mr. Mayor on for size."

The Corsica hummed along, dropping down U.S. 131 just north of Pierson, our destination within dinner range. I didn't respond for a second, just letting his speculation dip into me. I wanted to know how it felt, if it fit in any way, if it had been hovering on the edges and would now came crashing in with dread reality. But it didn't make sense. I told him so.

Another shrug. "Then try Aurora, what's-her-name, the new age midwife."

"Why her?"

"Women have their reasons."

"How about me, or Monica, or maybe Bob?"

"Well, we still have those Promise Keepers, and from what I gather there's a lot of them out there. So who knows."

"We, again?"

"Look, Turkstra, you know as well as me you're into this up to your ears. I'm saying keep an open mind. But," he said, easing up on the gas as he spoke, "any more great ideas like Petoskey, keep them to yourself."

We didn't speak the rest of the way into town. As he exited on Leonard Street on the edge of downtown, I asked him to drop me at the Sixth Street Bridge. Riding along the service drive to the expressway, he shot me a curious glance. "Why?"

"You have to know everything?"

He shut up, looped along Sixth Street under the freeway and pulled to the curb at the start of the bricked road leading onto the turn-of-the-century, rust-painted structure. "You going after a brainstorm?" he asked.

I sat there, noticing chunks of salt and slick water covering the wrought-iron bridge leading across the Grand River. Along the river, from here south through downtown, several bridges spanned the water. Many of them were lit at night. Downriver a few lights flickered. The Sixth Street Bridge remained dark, its thin, riveted girders linked in rectangles and squares above the place in which Janet VanTol had dropped. I looked on either side of us, shook my head and got out.

I knew Rodriguez sat in his car, watching. I ignored him and stepped onto the wooden walkway, now covered by a mashed path of snow, and stepped halfway across. At the rail, with a dark sky rolling in overhead, I gazed toward downtown. Let my eyes follow the straight, slowly sluicing path of water, partly clogged with ice floes, as it meandered into the heart of the city.

"Way it looked, she left the bridge about 20 feet thata way."

I hadn't heard the cop approach. I saw him nod toward the other end of the structure. A few cars sloshed by behind us. The air held a raw wet chill, rubbing my cheeks like steel wool. I shook my head, leaning out to look at the sluggish swirl of water, lugging ice along under the bridge. I thought of how cold it must have been when Janet took the tumble. "There were never any signs she struggled before she went in?" I asked.

"None."

"Did she leave anything behind?"

Rodriguez stood next to me, facing downtown. Michigan's second-largest city hung out there, the lights flickering on, the buildings held in the rushing movement of homeward-bound traffic. "Actually, she did."

"Oh?"

"An old Bible, belonging to her mom."

His face was obscured by shadows, the eyes set back in their sockets, the stubbly chin stuck in my direction. His hands were buried in the side pockets of his coat. He was full of surprises. "Any significance?"

He snuffled, wiped a forearm across his nose. Made a sound in his throat, hacked a gob into the water. Faced me again. "Looked like she gave it to Janet when she made profession of something."

"Faith?"

"Whatever."

"There was an inscription?"

"Words to that effect."

"What did they say?"

Another sniff and assorted throat clearing. "Way I took it, mom was telling her kid to hang tough."

I don't know why it hit me so hard, but it did. I turned and leaned on the rail, my stomach aching, my head pounding. I thought of Audrey VanTol offering her daughter encouragement on the teen-age day in which she stood up to be counted in her church. I thought of the Janet I'd met a couple times. Once at a potluck Monica held. Janet came early, looking freshly scrubbed, her long hair still wet from a shower, a pot of vegetarian chili as her offering. Around the table, as we prayed, I peaked and noticed the expression of intense fervor on her face. Another time I'd gone to pick Monica up after class. Janet had been outside the room, reading a leather-bound book, maybe that Bible. I'd said hello. She gave me a quick nod and returned to reading. Drawn back by whatever lived on the page.

"Her mother?" said Rodriguez, turning it into a question.

I didn't respond, figuring he had more good news to vent.

"We have a sheet on her. Shoplifting three times, once at Woodland, the other two at Jacobson's."

I shook my head, looking at the water, wondering what demons lived in that family. More to the point, what had driven Janet? Maybe it was a suicide. Maybe she followed Rene and answered a call that rose from the water. For a moment, I had the wild urge to take a plunge, to drop into the cold embrace of the Grand River. By going deep, by letting the water sweep over me like flames, the answers might come.

"Turkstra?"

I glanced over at the cop, who had huddled inside his leather coat. The tough guy single parent. "You want a ride?"

I could feel the river move, unfolding below, flooding on. A dip in there would drive me into hypothermia in no time. "One more thing."

His mouth opened a half-inch, letting steam leak my way. "What?"

"How come you never told me about your son?"

His eyes glistened in the dusky light. His arms folded across his chest. "What's to tell? He's a good kid. But he's never going to play for the Yankees."

CHAPTER TWENTY-NINE

If anything my mood plunged, locking me down with knotty fingers as we rolled into downtown and the detective dropped me off at the Amway Grand Plaza. Rodriguez made a couple snide comments about Monica recovering on the nose job floor, but I didn't have the heart to sass him back. Blackness had its hooks in me.

"Reverend," he said as I started to climb out. When I paused, he went on: "I'm hoping you can leave it right here."

Cold nipped in through the open door.

"Take care of Monica, go back to being a minister. Leave the rest to us."

"Us."

"The police."

There he was being bossy, just when I thought we were starting to be bosom buds. I waved a hand behind me, shoved on out and shut the door. He jerked away, tires catching the road and making sounds.

Once inside and flopped in a chair on the 22nd floor of the hotel, I small talked with Monica awhile. Then I watched her write at the shiny wood table stationed next to the window for a bit before looking upriver.

At the far edge of my vision on the east bank of the Grand stretched Riverside Park and the beginnings of Comstock Park, an old railroad town, on the other. Closer in spread the tinkertoy bridge I'd just been standing on. I tried to imagine again, what happened that night. If it had been suicide, what had Keester and Tina Martin seen? It must have been something.

I remained mesmerized a few minutes by the roll of the wintry water, the way light lolled across it. Then I turned back to Monica, sensing a tug in me that began with Dorie Klock, grew in that bar and got a good grip on that bridge.

More or less ignoring me, she wore a gray-and-white Redeemer College sweatshirt and sweatpants, cut off at the knee of her broken leg. Covered by a fiberglass cast, the leg was propped on a fancy footstool. Her hair hung curly and clean on her shoulders; her round, pink face was scrubbed and lively. She wore pale pink lipstick, some rouge and her blue-green eyes caught the light sifting through the large window. "Great view," I said.

She looked absently behind me at the riverscape. "It is."

I had meant her, but didn't tell her. The attempt at intimacy misread, I sighed, imaging myself stuck in mud, unable to move, unable to help.

"What's wrong?" she asked.

I took in the room around her: The taut, diamond-patterned spread on the double bed; the prints of English setters chasing foxes and hunters speeding along atop horses on the wall by her bed; the disguised hospital cart containing a tray of medication and some other medical doodads by one wall; a shiny dresser, topped by an array of her toiletries, by another wall, and walk-in closet. "The Hound of the Baskervilles is howling in my head," I said.

She frowned, setting her pen on the pad on which she had been writing. A phone sat next to the pad. Cupping her chin in one hand, she said: "You've had a long day, Mr. Holmes."

"And not too fruitful."

"I don't agree."

I hoisted myself out of the chair and stood at the window. Wind riffled across the cold water, chunked with ice, that spread north and east. To the left, just visible around the side of the glittering Bridgewater Place, was the onion dome of St. Adalbert, a Polish-Catholic church whose Romanesque features had earned it the special title of basilica. I touched my forehead to the glass, thinking about that cow being hoisted from the swamp of garbage and then dropped on the belt, moving toward the flames. For a moment, I thought of a topless bar I'd visited in San Diego. Men had been pounding on tables with wooden joysticks, to the beat of a Bob Seger tune, as the women twisted in cages. It struck me as a horrible vision of hell. Thing is, back then, I'd been attracted to that. To fire, to flames that kept me away from anything solid.

"Seems to me, you've filled in more of the story," said Monica. "Plus, there's what I learned this afternoon."

"Which is?" It seemed a heavy weight had settled on my shoulders, drawing me down, darkening my outlook, forcing me to talk slowly.

"I tracked down one of my former students, a friend of Janet's. Sharon Fitzpatrick. She's in graduate school at Berkeley. I should have thought about her before."

I leaned my shoulder against the window and looked down at her, noticing the hopeful expression on Monica's full Slavic mouth and wide probing eyes.

"Sharon's certain Janet was dealing with repressed memories." She watched me carefully. I had more than once told her I thought it was bunk that someone would be able to totally obliterate traumatic memories from childhood, only to have them march back in the adult years with prodding by a counselor. I almost groaned, but held it in. Too simple, Monica, I thought. Too simple.

"She thinks Janet was remembering sexual abuse by her father and possibly Max Wierenga, too. Sharon says Janet told her how Max was always over, like a doting uncle."

I looked back outside, feeling the unspoken groan spread out like a kind of liquid poison in my gut. I was no psychologist. Who knows if repressed memories are truly that —a way to save oneself under awful circumstances. What I did know is that Max and Branson, either together or separately, had wrecked their homes and the women in them for years. Or so it seemed. But joining together to rape Janet I found hard to believe.

"Truman?"

I bounced my head lightly on the window. I thought not of women battered and bruised by hungry men. Instead, the image came of that infamous Holocaust picture. The one of the Nazi henchman blowing away a Jewish prisoner's head. The Jew was standing in a ready-made grave, along with a bunch of bodies. In the moment after the photo was snapped, the poor man doubtless dropped to join his brethren. "However it happened, where's God in all of this?" I faced her.

Monica blinked, wiping back strands of hair, her face tilted up, her own lumps deftly covered by makeup. "He's at work, as always."

"Where?"

She smiled. "Through you, through me, even through Manny Rodriguez."

Now I smiled. "He'd be pleased to know that someone considers him a channel."

"The Lord works in mysterious ways, in many places, through the strangest of circumstances."

"I think I said that."

"But you stole it from me."

I stepped behind her, rubbed her shoulders. Her head bent and leaned against my thighs. "Lay down with me a second," she said.

On the bed, her cast arranged on a pillow, she nestled into the crook of my arm and turned her curious eyes on me, as if seeking answers. I touched her forehead, kissed it. "What next, Reverend?" she asked.

"Carnal pleasures?"

She chuckled. "My mind is still on the business at hand."

"Mine too." I realized what I was proposing wasn't feasible. Even so, I liked talking dirty. It bolstered my mood.

A knock sounded at the door. Then a key scraped in the lock. By the time the nurse stepped in, I sat upright, my legs dangling over the side of the bed. Monica had a hand to her mouth.

The nurse bustled around the room, asking questions, explaining more for me, than for Monica, that she had a little room down the hall and it was her job to look in on the patients. All of the patients, except Monica, had had some type of plastic surgery in the clinic in an attached building. "If you need anything just hit the button on the stand there by the bed," said the nurse. "I'm on until midnight, then someone else takes over. Since you seem to be doing pretty well, Miss Smit, we won't bother you unless you ask."

Monica thanked her and asked if room service could bring me dinner, too. The nurse, a wide woman in a pantsuit, said of course. I held up a hand. "They were going to eat with you. I told them I'd take Bob out."

We fiddled around with a few more particulars of who was going to do what or who was going to go where and exactly how this hotel-quasi-hospital room worked. The nurse then slipped out, clicking the door behind her. Monica jerked her head. "Sit back down, mister, tell me more about your lack of faith."

In a flash, I realized it wasn't God I wanted to talk about. I looked down at her. A lump of memory crawled inside me, scrabbling with anxious fingers to get out. I suddenly wanted to fill her in about Ruth. I'd never been totally honest about it. If we were going to build a life together, I had to cross that barrier. Somehow the day had conspired, with all of its messages about what men and women did to one another, to force revelation out of me. Or, at least, a fairly uncharacteristic urge to set aside sarcasm or theological explanations or just my Dutch reticence came over me. Basically, I wanted to come clean. So I sat and began to let it spill. And she listened. And I talked.

When it was over, Monica sat there, looking stunned. I wanted to reach out to her, to get her response. Maybe my actions surprised her. Maybe she saw me in league with the rest. But I didn't have time to do any of that. Far too much was about to happen.

CHAPTER THIRTY

Florence met me at the door of the church. On her way out, she stopped to fill me in on the status of the several small fires she had been just barely able to keep from smoldering into flames. As she spoke in the lobby leading in, Bob slipped into the sanctuary where he stepped over to the banner next to the cross, bent back his head and stared. Just gawking, he dug his hands into the side pockets of his puffy blue parka. Outside, the temperature hovered at freezing. Spring was edging in, with Easter, my busiest and yet most joyous season, not too far behind.

Buttoning her coat, Florence glanced in the sanctuary. "Boy's been through the wringer," she said.

As if aware she'd just spoken about him, Bob looked over and pointed at the cross. "Baby Jesus," he said in another of his moments of lucidity.

"That's right, sugar," she replied, giving me a glossy-faced smile.

I felt an odd pang, thinking how not a half-hour ago I'd gone on to Monica about Christ, and how if he was God, and he was, how could he allow men to beat up their wives, abuse their daughters, jointly father a child, and so on. For that matter, how could he allow me to act as I had?

"You sure do need to call Henry Biggs soon as you can," Florence went on. "That man's seeing kangaroos in his head again." Florence was in her early 50s, a transplant from a storefront Church of God in Christ congregation. The mayor had helped her gain custody of her twin grandsons from their mother, a crack addict, awhile back. At first, she served as church secretary, then slowly started coming to services. She was great on the phone, but still considered computers the spawn of Satan.

"Did you call his doctor about his medication?" I asked.

"Gone on vacation. Skiing."

"There's no backup?"

"Didn't seem to be."

I scratched a mental note. Florence wore a purplish worsted wool coat with dark piping on the sleeves and collar. Her husband, Clarence, was a city bus driver. "I appreciate all your work, especially this week," I said.

Bob returned to the doorway. "Checkers," he said.

"In a bit," I told him.

"The pastor taking you to that awful place again?" Florence wondered.

Bob looked at me cross-eyed. If it was up to Bob, he'd live on the chili dogs you could buy there for a buck apiece. I again wondered, given the occasional clarity of his mind, what he could tell us about the other night if we could just flip the right switch. But then, again, what had he seen?

"Oh that's right, Pastor Turkstra," said Florence, holding a handbag as large as a small suitcase in her hands. In the street, Clarence pulled up in their almond-colored Riveria. The boys, Seth and Sam, were buckled in back. Clarence beeped the horn and waved. "That man's wife stopped by to see you," she said.

"Who?"

"Skinny woman with the wrinkled tan."

I shook my head.

"Said she was here night before last."

Audrey VanTol. "She say what she wanted?"

Florence made a face, as if to ask who's to know what white women with Arizona complexions were up to. "She waited in your office, it was so crowded out here. Health Department was signing up people for cancer tests."

Another beep. I turned and noticed who else but leather-coated Ramon standing in the street jawboning with Clarence, who had rolled his window down to talk. I held the door for

Florence, let her go first and stepped out myself. "Ramon, you hassling the paying customers?" I called.

Florence opened the back door, futzed with the boys, pulling straps right, gave me a good-bye wave and climbed in the front, slightly rocking the shocks as she settled her bulk beside her husband.

"No, sir, Rev. Be talking with my man about the Hoops."

Clarence was an usher at nights at the Welsh Auditorium for the local semi-pro basketball team, which was playing in Fort Wayne that night. He had gotten me and members of my church many free passes. I nodded pleasantly at Clarence as he once again waved, nodded and pulled off. Florence had already turned and started giving him a hard time about something or another, probably loose belts on the baby seats.

Ramon swayed in the street, hands stuffed in the deep pockets of his storm trooper's coat. Hair oiled back, he gave me a wolfish grin, which drew the skin tight all the way down his bony face. "Got a message."

I shivered, feeling wind rake my neck. Bob, I noticed, loomed behind me, breathing hard. "You're going to pay back the five I lent you the other night."

The grin dimmed, but didn't die. "First of the month for sure."

Cars whooshed by in the center lane. One honked. He ignored it, his body tilting this way and that, his dark eyes glassy. "Preacher says when you going to see him?"

"He knows where I am."

"Says he stopped by."

I rubbed and blew on my hands. "What's he want?"

"Remember the van?"

Streetlights threw sickly yellow light onto the clotted asphalt of South Division. A block or so down on the other side of the street I saw folks lining up to file into the Guiding Light Mission. The mission, loosely run by our church and soon to be under the wing of my congregation, was appropriately housed in a former Michigan Employment Security Office. A place, that is, that once handed out checks to people without work. Looking at Ramon, I could tell he knew he'd snagged my attention by the loose smile on his face. I had forgotten about the van. "What about it?"

"He seen it."

"Where?"

"Got to ask him."

"Where's he now?"

"Hotel California."

"You're sure?"

Ramon pulled his arms in and did another quick jitterbug, this time dancing dangerously close to a pick-up truck which swerved away and then slammed on the brakes. "Hey, Rev, I gotta split."

A fat bearded guy stepped out of his truck and started swearing at Ramon, who huddled into his coat and slid off along the side of the road. "Hey, spic, I'm talking to you," said the fat guy.

Ramon flipped him the bird. The guy swerved away from his truck and started toward him.

"Partner," I said.

He paused.

"My friend carries a large gun."

The guy paused, his mouth dropping as he looked from me to Ramon and back, unsure. Other cars had started to honk. Ramon paused in the gutter by the side of the street, spun, got down on one knee, gripped a wrist with one hand and used the forefinger of the other as a barrel. "Blam!" said Ramon. "Blam, blam!" Ramon cackled, blew on his finger to cool it off.

The fat guy looked at the belly of his flannel jacket, possibly checking for blood.

Behind me, I heard Bob: "Don't leave home without it."

For the first time that day, I laughed. But I kept it pretty much to myself. I didn't want the fat guy to get any more angry than he already was.

209

Ramon sidled off, proud of himself. The fat guy shook his head, gave a mean look. I shrugged. Then he got in his truck and left. Thank God. Most altercations in these parts rarely ended so smoothly.

Back in church, I did what I had to do and then piled Bob in the car for a quick run for chili dogs and then a trip to look for Preacher. I thought of Rodriguez telling me to back off, to tend to my own knitting. I figured I would, soon as I talked to the crazy man in the wheelchair.

I'd just pulled out of the lot onto Division when I thought of Ramon and his finger gun. It made me wonder about my own, supposedly secure in my office.

CHAPTER THIRTY-ONE

Slices of shadow flicked on the sides of the concrete pillars holding the freeway, on which cars and trucks rushed and rumbled. Not too many hours ago I had ridden with Rodriguez through a snowstorm on the same road. We'd traveled to the far northern portion of the Lower Peninsula to hear a story that still resonated in me. A story that I knew held the truth that would lead to the two men to blame. The cop threw out other names, but even he believed, I strongly suspected, that either Wierenga or VanTol, or most likely both, were the buzzards to blame. What was needed, he had said, was better proof, the sort of evidence you take to court. He gave me the impression he was going to lean on them. Soon. Even so, I was sure the more goods on them the better. Which is why I was stalking through a pile of trodden snow, down a makeshift path to the open cavern under the expressway that was home, even in this weather, to Preacher and his pals.

Bob followed, his heavy shoes tromping through snow. He clutched the bag of chili dogs to his chest. "You all right?" I asked, peering over my shoulder.

"Slipping into darkness," he answered.

Bob had a mischievous grin on his face. A smile that reminded me of his sister. Back at the hotel, she had settled in for the night. Her dad and stepmom ate dinner with her. Monica had told me she looked forward to an evening largely alone, watching TV, writing and maybe making a call or two. Maybe she wanted me gone, after what I'd revealed. "You getting hungry?" I asked Bob.

"Time for the picnic, Boo-boo."

I chuckled.

211

Up ahead, flames leapt and danced inside a rusty barrel, around which a couple people toasted their hands and let warmth wash their face. Flames had been a big part of the confession I'd made to Monica. I felt no great relief in the telling, only sadness.

The sky above the expressway held a pale dusting of faintly winking stars. The full-faced moon hung behind me, peering down like a drunk grandfather about to play a practical joke. We emerged onto the edge of the open area under the concrete roof of the road, which continued to thunder and bump with traffic. Bob stopped next to me, the hot dogs leaking grease through the brown bag. I thought of having him pull it away from his parka, but figured that would make him mash it tighter.

"Who wants Coney Islands?" I asked.

A couple faces turned my way, fire crackling between us. I tried to spot Preacher, feeling wary and wondering if this had been a mistake.

"Preacher around?" I added when no one responded, except to offer me blank gazes.

"Back in the cheap seats," I heard.

I stepped around the blazing barrel, noticing the way ragged clothes hung on the bodies of those huddled around the sole source of heat. Mostly, they ignored me as I found Preacher in his wheelchair on the far side of a pillar, wrapped in a sleeping bag, his stringy hair a tangled mess on his shoulders. "Welcome to the Hotel California," he said.

Such a lovely place, this hovel under the road, I thought. "Who's your friend?" he asked.

I told him.

"Hey, bud, what you got there?" Preacher's face was smudged and charred-looking, his nose carried a bandage on the tip.

"Hot dogs," I said, taking the bag from Bob, who gave them up willingly, his large body hulking in the shadows of the viaduct, his hands moving up to cup his ears, probably to ward off the sounds of rumbling traffic.

212

"Health food," said Preacher, grabbing the bag and rummaging inside. He dug one out, took a whiff and made a face. "Deadly," he observed.

Bob bumped me. "Bob needs a couple, " I said.

"Have at it." He tore off the wrapping, stuck half in his mouth and ripped off a huge hunk. I took the bag from his lap, handed one chili dog to Bob, looked over at the others. "How about your friends?" I asked.

"Bunch of bloodsuckers, sucking up heat."

I gave Bob another, took one out myself. Set the bag on a small shelf of the pillar, near Preacher. I took a bite, then squatted, so that I was eye-level with him. Bob rustled above, grunting as he ate. "What about a van?"

Preacher swung his hair. Even in the chill, I could smell him. "You got suds to go with the mutts?"

"No beer."

He shrugged, shoving in a final bite. "Gimme another."

I nodded at the bag. "You aren't helpless."

Preacher snarled and wiped an arm across his mouth. When I didn't respond, he leaned over and fished one out. Bob was, of course, ready for more. I handed the bag to him. "Two more," I advised.

"Somebody stop me," he responded.

Preacher coughed up a laugh, his chest heaving inside the tattered, oily sleeping bag. "Bob's a card," he said.

"Make my day," Bob added, pleased to be the center of attention.

I waited for the hilarity, such as it was, to peter out, which didn't take long, and then tried again. "The van?"

Preacher shoved his head against the pillar. Movement from the fire, the twisting of shadows, circled his head. His eyes glowed, dark and ominous, watching me from deep places in his skull. "Devil gave me a visit the other night," he said.

"Rodriguez?" I asked.

"The real McCoy. The main man, pointy tail and all."

213

Aware he would toy with me before getting down to it, I gave him room to wander with his would-be vision. "Know what he wanted?" asked Preacher.

"No idea."

"Wanted me to help you out, not the scumbag cops."

"Why me?"

"Have to ask Mr. Lucifer."

My legs ached from being in the catcher's position. I knelt one knee on icy ground. For a second, I recalled Keester's head. Square, simple, removed from its moorings, there on the pavement. A stupefying Halloween fixture. The chili dog floated on bile in my stomach.

Bob was rummaging. I let him go. We'd deal with his chili dog overdose later.

"He told you where the van is?"

"Made me go look."

"In your wheelchair?"

"He rode me around on his pitchfork. You want to check, you can see the holes in my ass."

I sighed and nodded and noticed one of the barrel people, a woman, had stepped closer, arms at her sides. "Can we have a couple?"

I stood, grabbed the bag from Bob. A half-dozen still lay there, awash in juices. I handed it to her. She took it quickly, as if I might change my mind, and returned to the fire. Bob stared after her, as if she'd just stolen his prize comic book. Back to Preacher, I wondered: "Why don't we call the police and tell them?"

"No police."

"Why?"

"Devil said."

"What's it you want me to do?"

"Take me for a ride. I'll show you where."

"What if I then give Rodriguez a call?"

Preacher rubbed his chin, as if he was a rabbi making a judgment call on some esoteric section of Torah. "Wait till I'm gone, then don't tell him who told."

"Fair enough."

"One more thing," he said.

"What?"

"I want a new wheelchair out of this."

"What's wrong with that one?" I gazed at the contraption in which he sat.

"It's a heap."

"How am I going to get you a new one?"

He tapped the side of his head with a finger. "Ask God. Way I hear it, he listens to you."

The expressway rumbled overhead. I wanted to tell him to ask his pal the Devil for wheels. "Look, take me there. We'll deal with the wheelchair later."

CHAPTER THIRTY-TWO

Squeezed into the front of my trusty black Ranger, we cruised down Ionia Avenue. I had to crack my window to rid the cab of the smell of chili and onions. I used my hand to help it out as I headed toward the tunnel under Wealthy Street. Wondering about Preacher's demon talk, I tapped the steering wheel, anxious, aware of how dark it was in the old railroad warehouse part of town. Graffiti scarred the sides of the blocky bricked buildings; scrawny trees poked out of cracks in sidewalks.

I didn't buy Preacher's explanation about the devil. As far as I knew, he was as nutty as they came, but he didn't have visions or hear voices, as did some of the folks who shuffled through Heartside. Nonetheless, I knew he was plugged into the streets and what went on in ways that I never could be. "Who do you think you saw the other night?" I asked, leaning beyond Bob to look at Preacher, jammed against the passenger's door.

"Told you."

"Besides the Devil."

"Didn't see anyone. Just the van," he replied sourly.

"How do you know the one we're going to see is it?" I wondered.

"Just is."

I cut across Wealthy, bouncing along the cobblestone road. A large food processing plant loomed on the right, a couple trucks pulled to loading docks, steam pouring from roof vents. On the left, just beyond McConnell Street, ran several more, mostly abandoned, turn-of-the-century-era storage structures. They seemed strangely alive on this night, their broken windows staring back out at us with a kind of blind malevolence.

216

"So when exactly did Satan appear to you?" I asked, noticing that Bob had fallen asleep, his chin buried in his bulky coat. Preacher had leaned the side of his face against the window.

"Saw him twice."

"In your sleep?"

He looked over, angry, his face striped by shadows filtering in from outside. "You got to turn at Grant."

The road bumped underneath my truck. Dirty mounds of snow lined the gutters. A block or so ahead, at the top of a short rise, I saw traffic shoot by on Franklin Street. A fire station was up there. I thought of stopping and making a call to Rodriguez, which would no doubt spook Preacher into an even more distant silence. "Here?" I asked, slowing as we passed a modern, flat-roofed, aluminum-fronted metal coating factory. A few lights shone in its tall square front windows. Cars were parked in a side lot. Preacher grunted a response that I took to mean make the turn.

The road led into deeper darkness. Large trees, their branches bare, reached out from both sides. Bob bobbed awake. "Busted," he said.

"Not yet, bro," added Preacher.

I stopped where Grant dead ended into Buchanan. Across the way, through a row of bare trees, stretched the CSX railroad yard. Many tracks fed this yard from the south, most rolling in from Chicago, a couple hundred miles to the southwest. I saw the bulky shapes of freight cars moving like slow, oversized buffalo, trying to hook up. Red lights dotted the dimness of the yard. Beyond the tracks, elevated up a bank, swooped the bottom edge of the S-shaped curve that configured a path directly through the heart of the city. "Now where?"

Preacher leaned forward, pushing his face almost to the windshield. Stale warmth beat from my heater; a puff of it made strands of his hair wave. He touched them back with fingers poking out of his ratty wool gloves. "Try left."

217

"The Devil was unclear on his directions?"

Preacher flopped back in his seat. I wondered if Satan had greased his palms to bring me here, with the understanding that he keep the smarting off to a minimum. I was feeling increasingly anxious about this.

We passed a railroad switching station, a two-story structure on the left, and rolled parallel to tracks. I remembered something. "Is this where those two idiots took that jail guard and killed her?" I asked.

A couple years back a woman was getting off work at the jail and stopped at a convenience store for coffee. Two coked-up teens climbed in her car when she came out, drove to the railroad yard and killed her.

"I don't keep up on the news," replied Preacher.

Not too far up, the road twisted right, across the tracks and back under the freeway. Patches of ice on the cobblestone road made my tires spin in spots. "Gone too far," said Preacher.

"Turn around?"

"Looks like."

"Staying alive," Bob chimed in. Not a bad idea, I thought, reaching over to pat his arm. It felt like a log inside the feathery softness of his coat.

I backed up and drove north on Buchanan. Headed this way, I could see the tops of downtown buildings. Barely visible was the sketchy, towering frame of Eastbank Towers, Max Wierenga's reclamation project. Once again, I felt a shiver of fear, wondering where this was leading. A thought edged into my mind, something from the conversation last night. The train sounds.

"Slow down," commanded Preacher. He shoved his face against the windshield again. He was looking out at a patch of ground on which a snow-covered couch and easy chair sat. "Keep going," he said.

"Pee," said Bob, hands rooting near his crotch.

I told him just a second, thinking I better hurry. "Through there," said Preacher, pointing at a rutted, icy path that led straight where Buchanan bent right toward Pleasant Street. I geared the truck down, heard it whine into low, and started along the makeshift road under a loop of the expressway. More graffiti, this announcing Deke's love for Janice, was scrawled on cement walls supporting the overhead girders. "Not far," said Preacher.

"All of this the Devil told you in the dream?" I asked.

"Wasn't no dream," he responded.

"This was a personal appearance?"

Preacher grumbled.

The road started to curve left, back under the freeway, winding toward Century Avenue and the scores of furniture factories that lined the edge of the expressway in this part of town. "Slow down," said Preacher.

Straight ahead beyond a huge pile of shoveled snow stretched a massive, empty lot, a place where downtown workers left their cars and hopped shuttle buses into work. Florescent lights, attached to flower-stem poles, dropped lonely powdery light onto bare asphalt. Preacher had me stop near the pile of snow. I noticed now a couple saw horses, topped with blinking orange lights, on the lot side of the mound. Near them stood a backhoe, its large metal frame making me think of Midnight, the slumbering horse. "There," said Preacher.

"The hole?"

"Other side. Over there." He leaned across Bob and pointed out my window at a tangled web of underbrush and trees. Squinting, I saw a dark slash cutting through the wintry vegetation. Another path, or a driveway of some sort. "What's back there?" I wondered, hands on the wheel, as if still driving. Although we were close to downtown, he'd led me into a fairly remote spot, bordered by the expressway, factories and railroad yard.

"The van and some building."

"You've been back there?"

219

Preacher slumped in his seat, arms folded over his chest. "I took you here, now take me back."

Leaving the truck running for heat, I slapped open the door and stood in the crisp, biting chill. I felt the air rush around me, biting my ears and nose like tiny teeth. I took a couple steps toward the skinny, bare-branched trees and the twisted, tangled bushes. Down the rutted path, I spotted a wall of blackness. I squeezed shut my eyes, trying to make them adjust quicker to the dark, opened them and could make out the outline of what looked like a vehicle and a small building. I combed fingers through my hair, trying to make out sounds, but all I heard was the steady thrum of traffic. I turned to my truck, its headlights blocked by the hill of snow. Above a shoulder of the pile came the faint flickering of orange, warning intruders away from the hole.

The door on the driver's side of my truck popped open. "Hey, Turkstra, take me home."

I stepped over, leaned in the bed of my pickup, grabbed hold and yanked Preacher's wheelchair out and onto the ground. Once I'd pulled it open, I pushed it on bumpy snow to his door. Tapped the window. He looked my way, a tiny man with dripping hair. When he didn't respond, I thumbed the button on the door and tugged on the handle. "Out!" I ordered.

He shook the hair on his head, flopping it back. "No way, man."

Bob leaned my way, smiling. "Make a wish," he said.

"Either I drag you out or you go willingly."

"Why?" he asked.

"I'm not going back there alone."

"Take Bozo with you."

I reached in and grabbed his coat. He twisted back. Bob, apparently getting the drift, shoved from his side. He was, as always, a powerful force when he decided to move. Jammed by Bob and hauled by me, Preacher didn't do much resisting. He wasn't much help either. As he tumbled out the door, I had to quickly loop my arms under his and heft his scrawny body into the cold night air. He weighed 100 pounds or so. He tumbled out into my grip, complaining but not much. It struck me, with sudden sadness, that Preacher was probably very used to being manhandled, either by friends helping him in and out of his chair or by others who used him for their own forms of twisted fun. I was trying, with effort, to shove him down into his seat. "Let me," he said, reaching for the sides of the chair and settling in with a crumpling rag-doll like plop. "There," he said, glaring up with flashing eyes, "you happy?"

I took a place behind the chair, shoved forward and made for the orange lights and the hole. "This ain't the way," he said, turning and trying to grab at the sleeve of my jacket.

We jounced along the side of the snow pile and down a slight slope to the ring of sawhorses. Their lights were spattered with snow. I felt wind ruffle around us, swirling up dusty dabs of white powder. I left my place behind the chair long enough to move one of the sawhorses, got behind Preacher and muscled us to the lip of the hole. Light poles, coupled with the glow from the orange lamps, gave the area substantial, if sickly, illumination. I leaned over and down. It was hard to tell, but the gouge in the ground looked plenty deep. I suspected they were putting in a storm sewer for this large parking area. "Hey, Bob," Preacher called, "found a place for your piss."

By the soft splattering I heard behind me, I figured it was too late. Zipping up, Bob waddled toward us, the pumpkin grin slicing across his mug. His shoulders dipped side-to-side as he walked. I inched closer, gave the wheelchair handle a little lift, enough to bring Preacher back to business. "What?" he said.

"Tell me what's there and who told you."

Crunching snow, Bob walked the last couple feet and stopped next to me. He was humming in his throat.

"Man," said Preacher, "what kind of Christian are you?" He was an easy nudge from the abyss.

"Talk to me," I said. I heard something crack and scrape behind us and swiveled to see a quick shape, a big rat, dart from around my truck behind the snow pile.

"Already told you," he grumbled, sitting still, peering into the pit made by the city workers. I figured it was a 10-foot drop onto a floor of icy mud. I hefted the handles again, tilting him up an inch or two. He swung around, jerking his face up at me. "You crazy?" he asked.

Twenty yards or so out into the lot, I noticed a pyramid of large cement pipes, stuck there like a pile of tiny caves. For the utility work, I figured. Beyond them and across the curve of the freeway, I spotted the skeleton of the new arena and the dim, hovering forms of other buildings. "No," I told Preacher, "just cautious."

"Dump me in there, I'll die."

I doubted he'd die, but he'd probably get plenty hurt. "Who told you about the van?"

He sighed and settled back in his seat. "I need to know. You going to tip me in there?"

"Just answer it," I said.

The muted, murmuring presence of the city spread around us. I heard the echo of freight cars coupling, the clink and clanging of metal, a screech of tires on tracks. "You drop me, I'll scream," he whined.

"For what good that will do."

Bob shuffled his feet, still humming, digging in his pocket for something.

"It was that builder guy," said Preacher.

Which is what I thought. "Wierenga?"

"Guess that's his name."

"What'd he want?"

"He seen me on TV that night when they interviewed me about the dumpster. He come by, told me about the van and said he wanted me to tell you where it was."

"Why me?"

"Ask him."

I stepped back. Bob was turning in a circle, head craned back, mouth open, marveling at the stars, what few of them there were. I reached out to stop him from getting too dizzy. He came to a standstill and stuck his fingers over his ears. I jacked back on the wheelchair, drawing Preacher from the brink.

"He pay you for this?"

"Few bucks."

"Which you were drinking up in Kale's?"

"He found me after."

I swerved him around, so he faced the mound of snow. From where we stood, we couldn't see the path leading to the van and the building. "When's the last time you talked to him?"

"Last night, about midnight. Wondered if I talked to you yet. Was pretty blasted, you ask me."

He had to have called from that building. What did he want me to find? "What surprises does he have for us in there?" I asked.

"Us?"

"You're going, too."

He coughed a couple times. "I don't need this grief."

"What else did he say?"

"Said there'd be a folder or something in the van that would explain everything."

"Explain what?"

"Nuclear fusion. Man, I don't know."

I rolled him toward the snow pile. "Why didn't he just go to the police?"

"Look, Turkstra, I'm freezing."

I stopped as Bob slipped a cap out of his pocket, messed with it a second and then dragged it onto his head, over his eyes and down to his chin. A black face mask. Again, things got clearer.

"You plan to rob the place?" asked Preacher.

The hat, it was new. The same one he'd been tugging on in the plane. He'd lost his other one, and Monica planned to buy him another. Maybe someone at the home got him this, but there was another explanation. "Did you get that the other night, Bob?" I asked.

He gazed at me, twisting a finger in an eye socket.

"When you went into the house and came across the guy, you grabbed his hat from him, didn't you?" I asked. "You saw his face?"

"Turkstra, I'm in suspense, but mercury's dropping," said Preacher.

I turned to Bob and rolled the hat up so that his face was showing. "That's what happened, isn't it?" I asked.

Bob gazed intently at me. He stuck a hand, palm down on the hat. "Fish bones," he answered.

"C'mon, Turkstra," said Preacher, rocking forward in his chair. "Let's get the show on the road."

CHAPTER THIRTY-THREE

Calling the cops and letting them look was certainly an option. I still wasn't convinced that Max and Branson, and possibly a couple others, weren't lurking back there, ready to buzzsaw me into oblivion.

But at that point, I wasn't thinking clearly. First off, I hadn't been smart enough to have the cops let Bob go through pictures or mugshots, hoping that would get us to the killer. Besides that, I'd done a little tap dance around the boundaries of my own conscience when I pried information out of Preacher by threatening to dump him into the hole. I wasn't sure if I would have done it. The mere thought that I might made me aware of how close to the edge I was. I felt as if I'd been swirled into this thing and would be sucked along until I went down the drain or came up into fresher air. I was in it and had to keep going.

As for the smell of things, I detected a foul odor, something on the line of garbage left out too long, even as we approached the van. Likely it was in my mind, I told myself, it being the tail end of winter. Stink was almost always masked by the outdoor refrigeration provided by Michigan in early March. Even so, something slipped into my nose and gagged back in my throat. Probably my fear.

"Who cut the cheese?" asked Bob, next to me. Preacher rolled up the rear, his wheels crunching ice.

A few feet in front of the van stood a flat-topped, cinder block building, its front facing us and the back shoved close to the railroad tracks. I grabbed the back door handle of the Dodge van with one hand. The other held a flashlight I'd stuck in my back pocket earlier.

"Keeps on ticking," added Bob.

I shushed him. Then I leaned back and jacked on the door. It didn't budge. I tried again; nothing. Ready to give it up and call in the cops, I angled the flashlight in one of the double back windows. I couldn't see anything. Lifted up on the toes of my shoes, I peered harder and thought I made out the long lumpy outline of something stretched on the floor to my right. I tried to aim the cone of light in that direction when I heard a pop and the bend of metal up front. I immediately stepped back and swerved toward the sound, wishing I had a weapon.

Bob stood by the passenger's door, looking in, the face mask rolled all the way down again.

"Old Bob's a relentless bugger," said Preacher.

I joined him, flipped the shaft of light around on the front seats. Fast food bags, a few empty beer bottles, a coil of rope, and some crispy curling newspapers littered the seats and floor. Bob bumbled next to me, working on the cap again, tugging it off. I let him work it alone as I climbed in farther, again smelling a faint but distinct odor. Metal. Copper. Of blood, it came to me.

In my years as a paramedic, I had smelled it many times at scenes and in places where death had occurred in a violent way. It was an undercurrent here, largely masked by the weather, but noticeable. That acrid, gluey stink. Clotted and rank. I shoved crud off the passenger's seat and hoisted myself onto my knees. From that perch, I swept the van with the light, holding my breath as I did. Back there was a large wad of sheets, stained dark and grimy with frozen fluid. I wedged between the seats, touched the crusty, brittle material. Swallowed hard, noticing what looked like flecks of frozen tissue.

Once in Denver, we'd been called to an upstairs apartment off Colfax. Word was a guy had shot himself. When we got there, we found no body. But there were bloody blankets and sheets that had been used, we later learned, to clean the place after the guy, not dead at all, had sliced up his son, stuck the

226

parts in grocery bags and stuffed the remains in an abandoned refrigerator two blocks away. The frozen sheets, glued to the carpeted floor of the van by runoff body juices, reminded me of that time. I waited a few moments, allowing my stomach to settle. Then I wiggled the light across the rest of the area. Not much caught my eye, except for what looked like a manila envelope by the back doors. Head bent, I duck-walked to it, trained the light down, not wanting to touch anything. Facing up, the front of it read: For Reverend Turkstra. I knelt and nudged it open with the tip of the flashlight. It flipped over easily. I punched down on it with one finger, felt its thinness. There was nothing inside. If there ever had been, it was gone.

"Hey, Turkstra, better get out here!"

"What?"

"Little buddy's got something to show you."

Slipping back to the front and craning out, I looked for Bob. Preacher sat below me in his chair. "What?"

"Take a look."

Once I'd stepped outside, Preacher spun his chair and aimed toward the building, where Bob stood in the open doorway. "Careful. He's already messed up the tracks," Preacher said.

"Tracks?"

"In the snow. Was only one set a few seconds ago."

I checked it out with the light, saw ribbed stripes leading up and back. "Looks like you made the trip, too."

"Couldn't let Bob get all the glory."

Bitter cold, the kind that feels like sharp rocks on your skin, shot through the open doorway. Bob stood a few feet inside, hands on his cap; maybe worried it would blow off. I slipped around him, hearing the trains couple in the near distance. Again, it took a couple seconds to grow accustomed to another shading of light. But it didn't take long before I saw it.

A real one this time, not a lump of sheets. It hung from a grappling hook in the ceiling, a large sack of dead flesh and bones, directly in the center of the room. I let the light crawl up

227

from the floor, where I saw an overturned stool, to the paint-splattered work boots, the baggy jeans, the dangling hands, still as blue marble, the brown denim coat, and the twisted square of face. The large nose, open mouth, gawking pellet eyes. "Good God," I said.

"Must've slipped and caught himself," Preacher said from the doorway.

"This the man who told you to bring me here?" I kept light on the face, this one more anguished than Keester's.

"Well, he was alive then."

The rope had been looped inside the hook and attached to the neck. He'd probably done it from atop the stool, which he kicked away so he could swing free. Or maybe, someone drugged and stuck him there.

Again, the past rushed back. Denver again. Out near the airport. We got called to a tawdry split-level in a lousy neighborhood directly underneath the path of one of the main runaways. Someone thought a guy had cut himself with a saw and called us. When we entered the garage, there he was, naked and dangling. A scrawny, 60-year-old with spiderweb tattoos all over his chest. He'd taken his false teeth out and set them on the work table next to carefully folded clothes before doing himself in.

Bob hovered by my shoulder, staring up. Taking the light away, I suddenly was aware this was a woodworking shop of some kind. Large saws and stacks of wood stood in corners and on the other side of the room. I let the circle of yellow again play over the twisted, agonized features, the drawn-down mouth, the half-open eyes, which were turned to the right. So much carnage; the bile in my stomach bubbled to life. "Recognize him, Bob?"

"Flashy flippers," he responded.

I let the light drop to the floor, thinking of yet another suicide. Of a car racing in the desert, driven by a woman full of booze.

"Looks like he crapped his pants," said Preacher.

I caught that smell, too, always the worst odor when you raced into a home to find someone, often elderly, dead in their own fluids. The chili dog churned, a snake uncoiling, and I stepped outside into the chill air.

The white noise of the city filled my ears, like hands jamming in. I thought of the dark, dried blood in the van, the empty envelope with my name, the tattoos on that naked guy in Denver, the horror-stricken look on the face of Max Wierenga. All of it made me weak-kneed and woozy. Try as I might, I couldn't keep my chest from quaking as the snake unfurled itself with wide fangs and puked out its venom.

CHAPTER THIRTY-FOUR

A Grand Rapids cop cruised by on Century moments after I finished upchucking. Swallowing back gastric juice, I trotted out to flag it down. When the cop pulled warily to the side of the road, I hurriedly explained what we'd found. She didn't seem too thrilled at first, giving me the once-over behind wire-rimmed glasses, but got out and followed me across a barren stretch of land, over the railroad tracks, and through a mass of leafless trees to the building in which Max Wierenga hung like a side of beef from the hook.

From there, the wheels of misfortune spun fast. Within ten minutes, three other cruisers bounced in on the road we'd taken awhile before. Not long after, Rodriguez showed up. By then, Bob and I had climbed into my truck. My stomach was still hardly functioning.

As luck would have it, my heater had decided to use that time to turn into an air conditioner, something I would have appreciated in July. So together we huddled, the windows skinning with ice. Through a spot I kept clear with my hand, I watched Rodriguez talking to the street cops. A few had already checked the building, as well as the van. All of it lit by sweeping blue-and-red lights, the scene was quickly turning surreal. As for Preacher, he spun around and around in the chair, his arms gesturing, showing the troops the high points of his amazing, case-breaking discovery. Only when Rodriguez showed up did he tune it down and drift off to the side, soon to be joined, however, by a night TV crew and reporter and photographer from *The Press.*

"From the looks of it, everyone must assume this is it," I said to Bob.

230

Stocking cap half down on his head, shoulders slumped, he shivered so hard I could hear his teeth clicking.

"Only thing," I said, "what was in the envelope?"

Bob gave me a preoccupied, sidelong glance, his mouth moving, steam swirling from his mouth. I smacked the dashboard, hoping that might reconnect bad wires to bring us heat. The heat didn't return, but pounding helped clear my head, to get me thinking again. "Is Max him?" I asked Bob.

Bob stared at the windshield.

I heard a tap on my frosted window. I tried to roll it down, felt it catch from the cold, so I snapped open the door, moderately careful not to bump the knocker. "Hey, watch it," said Rodriguez, stepping back.

I got out and shut the door behind me. "Sorry."

The detective shook his head. "You leave the doo-doo back there?"

"Maybe you should bag it and test its DNA."

He sniffed and wiped under his nose. Rolling his shoulders, he stared at the van, beside which an evidence truck had parked. "You left your mail in there," he said.

"Someone took what was inside."

He slid a finger along the side of his nose. His hair was mashed down by a Grand Rapids Police baseball hat. He wore the leather jacket with the snake on the shoulder, zipped to the collar. "How do you know that?"

"I poked it."

"This before or after you slipped the contents?"

I turned away, gazing at the pile of snow, the blinking orange lights around the hole and the parking lot beyond. A few vehicles had pulled in there, drawn by the circling circus of lights and official cars.

"Turkstra, I got to know this."

"If I took anything, I sure as heck wouldn't leave the envelope."

231

"Unless you were trying to throw us off."

"For what reason?"

"Search me. I haven't been able to figure you out yet."

I breathed the cold air. "Wierenga told Preacher I'd find the van here."

"He mention the body, too?"

"As far as I know, he was alive at the time."

"Why you?" demanded the cop.

"Only thing I can figure is because I'm a minister in his church."

"What, he wants absolution for stringing himself up?"

"Wrong denomination."

Now it was his turn to stew. He scraped the ground with his boot, shifted his shoulders like he wanted to box, scratched the back of his neck. Then he leveled a dark, cruel gaze at me. "You figure you got the whole thing capped, don't you? The killer yanks himself in his butcher shop."

"You think that's where he cut up the body?"

"It's looks like the meat department at D&W," he said, giving me an "I'd-like-to-squash-you-like-a-bug" look.

I leaned against the side of my truck. "Preacher said there were tracks in the snow leading up to the building. Fresh ones. Went right in the door, when we got here."

"Thanks for blowing dinner all over them."

I stood and faced him, our noses inches apart. "Whyn't you do your job, Manny."

His chin rose, his breath smoldered out in thin fingers of white. "I'm trying. You keep screwing it up."

"Try harder."

"I've had about enough of you, Turkstra."

"Gentlemen." It was the mayor, wearing his dark overcoat, his hair flopping in the wind, a sad expression on his mug. "What's wrong?" He separated his hands, as if detailing the size of the fish he'd just caught.

Neither of us responded. I felt like a school boy in a playground standoff, which was amazingly stupid given the circumstances—that is, a contractor's body hanging nearby, a van and woodworking shop smattered with the blood of a West Side blackmailer. My stomach started to twist again. I stepped away, turning in a half-circle, noting the way the sky held its handful of stars in a vastly oblivious manner.

"I got to get back," said Rodriguez.

"Wait," said the mayor softly. "What you've got here?"

"Ask Captain America."

"Manny, I'm asking you," Pete Hathaway commanded, still in the gentle voice but with unmistakable authority.

I turned to see Rodriguez, hands on his hips, flash me another one of his nasty looks. "What's it you need?"

"The body in there. It's Max Wierenga?"

"Unless he has a twin." To the side of the building, Preacher sat in his wheelchair in a flood of TV lights, his face animated, arms moving.

"Is he our culprit?"

Bob opened his door and climbed out of my truck, gazing at me with a pained, half-frozen expression. No spotlights for him. He wanted to get somewhere warm.

"Seems he wanted to cough up all his rotten secrets to Mr. Turkstra here, but someone ran off with the confession."

"Oh?" Now Pete trained his intense, microscope eyes on me. Beard dotted his chin. His hair still danced in the breeze.

"We don't know about that," I told him.

"Cop a plea," Bob said from the other side of the truck. Rodriguez rolled his eyes and started away.

"Manny," said the mayor. Rodriguez stopped, turned. "I know this isn't the best time, but I'm sorry. About Janet." I saw the remorse on the mayor's face. He'd made a mistake and would flog himself for it.

The cop pulled the brim of his cap down. "No matter."

"It does to me."

A sardonic smile cut across his mouth. "Why don't you two breastbeaters go someplace warm?"

233

I wanted to argue, but Pete touched my arm and inched me a step or two away. Meanwhile, the lights from the cop cars swirled. An emergency rig now jounced through the parking lot. Preacher was still washed in the glow of TV strobes. My stomach did a little rhumba.

Rodriguez waved at another detective, indicating he was coming. Gave us both one more warning glance and stalked off. But a few feet into his exit, he stopped one last time. "Turkstra, we need your statement."

"Let me take Bob back and I'm all yours."

"Now."

"I'll be back in a half-hour."

He frowned but headed off, directly toward the one-man press conference. Rodriguez stepped to the side of a reporter and sliced a finger under his neck. The reporter gave him a questioning glance. Then the cop said something, emphatically, and the lights went out. Preacher got the hint and backpedaled into the shadows. I then noticed the reporter, a tall man with a helmet of black hair, squinting our way. "Looks like we're ripe for the picking," I said.

The mayor ignored me. He was staring at the flat-roofed building, its small rectangular structure now ringed by cops, medics, a medical examiner, and evidence technicians. "I wish I would have known before," he said, ignoring my comment.

I didn't respond.

Bob leaned his chin on the roof of the truck, looking sick to his stomach. The mayor continued to gaze at the activity around the building. He shook his head solemnly. I saw the reporter and camera man slide our way. "I hate to think this has come out of our church," he said.

"Don't kid yourself," I retorted.

He turned to me slowly, as if my words had taken awhile to register. "What?"

"This is far dirtier than that," I said.

He shook his head, still not with me.

"It's about incest, among other things," I said. "I don't want to blame this one on God or the CRC."

Confusion still smoked up his face. But he then noticed we had company. In short order, a sponge-tipped microphone floated between us. "Mayor, Reverend Turkstra, what can you tell us?"

I left the telling to the mayor, climbed in my truck with Bob and started off. Halfway down the road leading under the freeway, a car pulled up, stopping next to me. The window shot down, revealing a familiar face. Blonde hair, less makeup than usual. My window cranked this time, giving me space to look out.

"What's going on?" she asked.

I knew Rodriguez would hate it if I identified the corpse for Crystal Franklin before an official press release was issued. But I didn't care. I was sick of him. More than that, she had a right to know. Images of those horrible photos, lousy porn, set on her desk flickered through my mind. "Max Wierenga," I said.

The TV reporter shook her head. Stared out her window. I bet she felt as soiled as I did by these rotten doings. "Dead?"

"Yes, ma'am."

"You think he's the one?" she asked.

I wasn't sure. I wished someone hadn't taken the confession. "Maybe."

She continued staring out her window, beyond me, at the scene with the circling lights. "I sure hope so."

So did I. But as I started rolling again, I had a feeling there was more. The body left hanging only told part of the story.

CHAPTER THIRTY-FIVE

Powerful weariness slugged into me after I dropped Bob off in his dad's room, just down the hall from where Monica holed up. I had thought of leaving Bob at the foster home, but that would take too much time, since Rodriguez was hot to get the particulars of my side of the story. Or so he had led me to believe. So I gave Bob over to his dad, who answered the door with tousled hair and a bleary, sleep-drugged face. He didn't really ask many questions, and I wasn't up to filling him in. I told him I would check back in the morning.

Then, leaning against a wall in the hall outside the room, I took a rest. All the way here I'd been trying to dislodge a thought from my mind. What was it that kept nagging me?

I stuck my hands in the pocket of my coat, felt the soft material of the face mask I'd taken from Bob, sometime during the last hour or so. My hands gripped it, dragged it out. Then it hit me: Bob at the museum. On the rail, by the whale bones. Why hadn't I figured this out before?

Hadn't Bob been in the room featuring the history of furniture makers in Grand Rapids? I scoured my brain from the couple times I'd been through there. I was almost sure that a huge photo of Branson VanTol hung from the museum wall. He was standing outside his factory, a grim smile on his face, arms over his chest. That was it! Bob had seen it and gone nuts. Ran out of there, onto the rail.

I stretched the hat, gazed at the holes where his eyes had looked out at Monica, at Bob, at Tina. Damn! If Bob had recognized Wierenga as the killer, he would have blasted off tonight. Gone ballistic. I was sure. So, it wasn't him. It had to be VanTol. Not the sort of information to take to the prosecutor, but enough to draw some clear conclusions.

Rubbing my face, I wondered if I should look in on Monica and tell her? I didn't want to wake her. Her dad said she fell asleep at dinner. But she ought to know.

I gazed three rooms down, to where Monica stayed, still unsure that I should bother her. But then I noticed her door slightly ajar. Or was it? I felt my heart kick start and fear flicker to life as I stepped over.

I squelched the urge to bust in. I shoved an ear against the door to listen. Tried to pick up sound and heard muffled voices. Which was enough for me. I shouldered it all the way open.

At first, I couldn't see a thing. The wall to a closet blocked my view. The door to the bathroom was open as well. I immediately sensed tension in the room. Smelled liquor and wet clothes. I stepped in, shoved the bathroom door shut, and came face-to-face with Audrey VanTol.

She looked wild-eyed. But that's not what grabbed my true attention. The gun in her hand, the .38-caliber Smith and Wesson that had been in the bottom drawer of my desk, did that. It was the weapon I stuck there the other night as she sat in the office under Thomas Merton, wanting to know about her daughter. So that's why she made a visit earlier and then used my office.

"Howdy," I said stupidly, noticing Monica sitting up in bed, her face pale. Branson VanTol stood alertly by the window, hands folded over a hat protecting his crotch.

"Step inside, please, Reverend," said the woman with my gun.

I held up my hands. The balled face mask was in one. "What's going on?"

She swiveled as her husband started from the wall. "Don't!"

He gave her a sick grin and froze. I reached out for her arm, only to have her swing back and stick the steel barrel about level with my clavicle.

"Truman," said Monica from the bed. She patted a spot next to her. It wasn't the sensual invitation of a few hours be-

237

fore. It was a command, muted by fear. I edged between Audrey VanTol and the wall and settled on the edge of the bed, feeling Monica's hand dig into the small of my back. "You all right?" I asked.

"I've been better."

Branson gazed at his wife, who wore a dressy outfit, replete with red heels and a linen garment decorated with quarter moons. Hooped earrings dangled from her ear lobes, partially hidden inside her sprayed fluff of white hair. The makeup she wore defined her face. Her eyes and mouth were set in hard, serious lines. She eased one hand up under the wrist holding the gun and pointed it at her husband.

"You know," I said, "I don't think I gave you permission to borrow that."

She ignored me, but Branson swung a glance my way, as if asking me to intervene. "We were just getting to the purpose of this visit," she said.

"Dear," interjected her husband. His body was a study in coiled, controlled fury.

"Shut up!"

He wore a natty three-piece blue suit and a white shirt and tie decorated with diamonds. His coat had been neatly folded and set on the window ledge. His skin looked scrubbed, lightly freckled, and a little raw around the eyes. His mouth kept twitching, as if trying to turn the situation around with a nervous smile that just couldn't quite get there. But his eyes, the ones that probed through the mask, were cold, lifeless.

"Mrs. VanTol, I'm sure whatever you know would be best turned over to the police," said Monica.

Gun still trained on her husband, Audrey VanTol replied: "I really wish it were that simple, dear." I saw a glitter in her eyes, a trembling in her hands, and heard a strained, about-to-burst quality in her voice.

"I resent you bursting in here, whatever your intentions," Monica said.

"You answered the door, Miss Smit."

I stood, which made the woman move my way. Branson took the opportunity to lean in, ready to pounce. Again, she swung at him, then at me, and stepped back to the wall. "Both of you men, get back!"

"Audrey, I command you to stop. Put the gun away and we're going to leave."

Her face focused on him. Her mouth pursed and chin poked forward. "You pig. Who are you ordering around?"

"You, honey, for your own good. You know that." He used a soft, almost singsong voice on her, a practiced hypnotic tone meant, I suspected, to bring her back from wherever she had gone. "We were coming back from a nice dinner. I had no idea Miss Smit was the friend you had to visit here."

"Stop," she said as he took another step in her direction. "I mean it."

"No, darling, you don't."

"I do!" she nearly shouted.

Branson, trying to get the upper hand, glanced at us with a slightly apologetic look on his face, as if saying he was sorry for her behavior. "Do you have any idea what this is about?"

I let the face mask unfold in my hand. It hung from my fist like a limp sock. "This."

He squinted. "Another of your games, Turkstra?"

"No, the hat you wore when you killed Tina Martin."

His lips twitched, the eyes flicked to his wife.

"See?" she said. "You viper."

VanTol hunched up his shoulders, his face hiding all emotion. "This is ridiculous. Give me the gun, honey."

"Apologize to Miss Smit first."

"For what?"

Against the wall, Audrey VanTol breathed hard, her full chest moving up and down. It struck me again that her tight, tanned face and almost perfectly formed chest were likely results of a plastic surgeon's craft. I wondered if she'd been a patient in this place in the hotel herself. I could see questions racing in her eyes. But her hands had grown steadier. She could turn the gun on Branson or me easily and with lethal results. A woman warrior from the Grand Canyon state. "Mrs. VanTol," said Monica. "The only apology any of us need is the truth."

Her eyes shifted for a second, but then flared back to her husband, who was licking his lips, a little less sure of himself again. "It has to start with him," Audrey VanTol spat out.

"Dear, I don't know anything about the hat."

"How about killing our daughter?"

"Don't be silly."

"Silly!" Her voice was a screech. "She came to you to talk but you pushed her in the river!"

Branson leveled his eyes at me, as if trying to figure my response. "Can't you talk to her?"

"Max Wierenga is dead you know," I told him. I suspected he knew by the way his face failed to register the information.

"I didn't kill Janet," he said, edging toward me, perhaps hoping I was an ally. "Max did that, which is why he killed himself."

"Liar!" Her hand trembled. "Apologize!" The skin on her face was so tight that it made knife-sharp edges of her bones, sketching her skull and making her eyes appear bigger than they were.

"Audrey," he said in a calm voice, "that is enough. You had too much wine at Cygnus."

She threw back her hand and laughed. But she brought it right down, narrowing on him a hateful, chaotic gaze.

"Who took the papers from the envelope?" I asked.

Branson blinked, confused. His wife let her face swerve in my direction, serious and deadly. "I made a trade. Max's confession for your gun."

"In the drawer?"

"That's right."

"Why did you leave the envelope?"

240

"An oversight."

Branson looked to her and to me and back. It seemed to be registering that his partner in family crimes had probably sketched it all out for the world to read. I saw his body tense. His features closed in as he realized this was it. I wondered if he had seen Max hanging and left him there. Certainly his wife had.

"You see, Brandy, dear, I went over to that horrid building looking for you, and found Max instead."

"What building?"

"The one in which you and Max cut up Johnny Keester's body," I interjected.

Branson VanTol's face grew flushed. He hardly reacted to my words. "You disobeyed me?" he said.

His wife stared, as if a little surprised.

"You went against my orders?"

"Branson," she said, her mood suddenly shifting. "You destroyed our family."

He licked his lips. His head, nearly bald, glowed softly in the light in the room. "Nonsense." He stepped toward her.

"Please," she said, more meekly.

"Don't you see, Audrey, it's not me who is wrong. Don't you?" Again, his voice was soft, scolding, his gaze nailing into her. "Why are you blaming me?"

If I wasn't mistaken, she shrunk into herself even more. The gun hand wavered. But not enough for me to make a move. Monica had scooted to the side of the bed and sat right behind me. "Mrs. VanTol," she said.

As the gaunt, too-tanned woman in a dress that reflected a kind of mystical bravery turned to my fiancée, Branson VanTol made his move. Quick as a cat and just as vicious, he swiped the gun from her hand. Barreled her against the wall with his shoulder. Swung back around at us, his gaze fueled by hatred. He raised the weapon in our direction. I started to duck and fall back on Monica when his wife shoved from behind, mak-

241

ing him stumble. "God will damn you, Branson VanTol, he surely will," she said as she pounded his back with her fists.

Righting himself, VanTol turned, took quick aim and fired into her face, immediately sending her back to the wall in a splatter of blood. The sound was huge and quick and would draw attention.

I climbed from the bed as he swung back at me, the gun expertly pointed. I paused, held up my arms. Veins bulged on his forehead; his teeth showed white and glossy inside snarling lips. "Turkstra, this is your fault."

His wife moaned, slumped on the floor, head awash in red. Monica had struggled to her feet behind me. "Lord God," she said, "you animal."

VanTol's eyes shifted, as if Monica's words had touched him and actually found a place in his conscience. But, no, they hadn't. An ugly, off-kilter grin appeared, making him look as deranged as he really was. "You and Max, " I began.

He shook his head, his face flushing. He glanced at his wife and back at us, ready to kill us as well. "Someone will be here soon," I said.

As if in answer, the door pushed open and Bob burst into the room. In the same moment that VanTol turned, I crossed the carpet and grabbed for him. Erupting in a scream, Bob ran at us, his large arms open, and we all crashed, swaddled in Bob's massive bear hug, to the floor. I could hear Monica on the phone as we squirmed and jammed into one another. In the confusion, I felt VanTol slam us with his elbows and slip up onto his feet. He'd clipped my nose good. Blood spurted as I tried to grapple onto my knees, worried about the gun. Shaking my head and dragging a forearm over the blood, I tried to get my bearings.

"Bob, don't," I heard. Monica wobbled next to me.

Standing, I saw what she meant. The two of them were gone. They'd blasted out while I was worrying about my nose. "Truman, bring him back. He'll shoot Bob."

242

CHAPTER THIRTY-SIX

I nearly smashed head-on into Monica's father. As he stepped out of the doorway, I was about to ask where Bob had gone. But I saw him, down the hall to the right, shoving through a door, over which hung an exit sign. "Check on your daughter," I said.

"Calvin!" he yelled.

Smearing blood with the back of my hand, I raced to the door, slammed it open. Then I paused to listen. Hearing no steps on stairs, I noticed a doorway a half flight down. Once there and through, I detected the clattering of feet to my right and the sound of a metal clanging.

"Bob!" I yelled. No response. I trotted to a nearby door, pushed it open and saw they'd run through a dimly lit operating room. The odor of disinfectant, and the lingering stink of burned skin made me pinch my nose as I circled the empty stainless steel table and left through a door that led to another hallway, this one more institutional. I figured it was the entry area to the plastic surgery suite.

Again, I stopped, listened hard, then realized only one way led out. I took it, rammed through two swinging doors down a shiny marble tile hallway and once again caught a glimpse of Bob. A shoulder, his legs racing.

"Hey!" I called. He stopped, looked back, his face flushed and fearful, but he twisted open a door on his right and disappeared. A kid on a frantic scavenger hunt.

This time the racket of shoes on metal stairs echoed clear. Bob's head bobbed a flight below. I bent and peered through a space between the curving of the iron-railed steps. I thought I could spot a bald head, a flight or so beyond Bob. "VanTol! Give it up!"

He was in no mood to listen either. As I started down, I heard Bob make a wild, keening sound, a war cry.

"Bob!" I called helplessly, winding down, using the rail for support, wondering where the stairwell led.

Legs pumping, I remembered it was a year or so ago some-one else stole my gun. That incident had ended in two deaths, one caused by a bullet from my .38, although not fired by me.

Below, maybe two floors, I heard a crash and a bell clang loudly. The noise bounced off the ceiling and reverberated against the painted cement walls. I took the steps two at a time, dropping quickly to the bottom, where the sound beat hard and an emergency door stood open, its red handle jammed in and causing the terrible ringing.

Outside wasn't really outside. I stood panting in another hallway that led right to a skinny spiral stairway. I headed that way, trying to escape the horrible sound.

I wound maybe three times in a corkscrew to yet an-other doorway, through which I saw a large open room, filled with hampers and carts. My eyes swept the area, a basement, and caught movement on the left, beyond a row of large laundry buckets. Then on the right, another flash of activ-ity.

"Hey, buddy!" I heard from that direction. It was a man in a blue work uniform. Jogging my way, he wore a white cap and had a belly the size of a ripe watermelon.

"Where's that lead?" I said, throwing an arm toward the spot where I'd seen Bob bobbing.

"Whata you doing here?" As he approached, I knew I'd have to do some fancy explaining before he'd tell me a thing. So I shot off, my chest aching, my bad knee a little wobbly.

"Hey!"

I ignored him, navigating through hampers, flipping them aside. I heard the guy swear behind me. A couple carts had rolled into him. "Call the cops," I shouted as I entered a long, brightly lit hallway.

Straight ahead, I saw Bob. If I wasn't mistaken, VanTol was thirty or so yards beyond him. This hall was a straight shot. Brightly lit, more a tunnel than anything else. With effort, I picked up my pace, figuring we were running through a long connecting corridor of some kind. My ears still rang, but I assumed that was now from the blood rushing along, trying to keep pace with my heart. Pushing myself, I gained a little on Bob. I knew he had the stamina to keep him going. In the Special Olympics last summer he ran forever. Event after event. Not fast but sturdy as a mule.

VanTol, however, was older. How long could he last? For that matter, what about me?

Ahead, I saw Bob jog left as the hallway ended. My breath coming in jagged gulps, I reached the spot at the end and saw that an arched door led into yet another hall, which ran straight for a ways and then cut back right. Above me I noticed pipes attached to the ceiling, some fairly large. Lights here were stuck in the wall and protected by chicken wire in glass. It had to be a utility tunnel, feeding under the hotel to who knew where.

Bob had already made the abrupt turn to the right by the time I forced myself down yet another tiled stretch of tunnel. My feet hit the cement floor hard; my chest felt as if it was being pumped with burning air. My nose leaked gooey fluid.

As soon as I cut around the next corner, I came to a complete and painful stop. I ran smack into Bob's shoulder with my neck, driving him against a wall, and sending myself flopping onto my butt.

Sparks and tongues of flames flew in my head. Darkness swirled in from the edges. I was breathing like a steam engine, sweat poured down my face, it felt as if someone had rammed a knife into my throat, angling for the windpipe. I tried to talk, but couldn't get out the words. Staring at me, face red as a lobster, Bob jerked a finger toward the ceiling. He grunted something I couldn't understand. His square face peered intently at

245

me, sweat dripped from his nose. His chest heaved. His finger kept jerking upward.

Finally, I got it and I looked to where he pointed. I noticed a ladder, starting about three feet from the floor and climbing, along with the pipes, straight into darkness. VanTol had scrambled in that direction. I waved a hand, my throat locked, making it hard to breathe. Bob nodded. I tried to tell him forget it, hang back, our part was over, the police would take it.

But I couldn't get it out. I gargled for breath, still on the floor, my head woozy. Maybe taking my silence for agreement, Bob grabbed the bottom rung of the ladder and hoisted himself up. I tried to say: "Let him go." It came out as a croak.

Bob ignored me, his legs rising out of view.

I massaged my throat, digging fingers toward my voice box, wondering if I could make it work manually. Again, no dice.

As best I could, I stood and swayed against the wall for support. It felt as if a Mack truck, carrying gravel, had crashed into my head. I had to stand there a minute, fighting off the sharp urge to collapse and let the world unfold as it would. But it was the thought of Monica, in her room with a bloodied, possibly murdered woman who tried to make things right, that forced me to turn and reach for those metal rungs. I tugged twice, hardly able to lift my weight from the ground. Which is when I took another few seconds, to mumble a prayer, to ask for intervention. Maybe God heard; maybe God didn't. Even so, a jolt of energy slipped through me—hot enough to lift me up and onto the ladder. Craning up, I could see only black.

CHAPTER THIRTY-SEVEN

Moving up the rungs didn't take long. Soon enough, my head bumped to a stop. I reached up, felt a latch hanging down and fumbled with it a moment. Then, realizing it was loose, I pulled on it and the ceiling, actually a hatch, slid open. I heaved myself up and through, quickly aware of wind and fingers of cold. I had to bend because my head whammed a hard surface that felt like concrete. I reached up and touched curved hardness. Another rotten tunnel.

Rubbing my head, I realized it was still dark, but I was outside or close to it. Cocking my head, I thought I heard footsteps, but wasn't sure. Looking each way, my eyes adjusted to pale light. I stepped forward carefully, smelling a faint fecal odor, a hint of decay. My foot met only air, so I paused, my eyes getting a better profile of shapes. After a second, I saw I stood on a small ledge, three feet or so from the bottom of the new tunnel. I'd just climbed out of a chute or access point that brought me into this chilly tube of cement, a ledge really, just above the floor of what looked like a huge pipe. I suspected it was a storm sewer. If so, I calculated it led to the river, which wound by the west side of the hotel.

"Bob!" I yelled, my voice bouncing back. Maybe VanTol had shot him and now waited for me. I could drop back down the tube or go on.

I slipped off the ledge onto the floor of the tunnel. Even now, I couldn't stand easily, but I noticed a circle of light, not too far on the right and went for it. Wary. Expecting any second to stumble over Bob's body or to get a slug in the spine.

My feet slid on a skin of ice underfoot and my mind conjured images of a huge flood pouring in from behind. For a moment, I wondered if they'd gone the other way. If so, I'd lost them. I didn't plan to retrace my steps.

The light grew as I approached. It went from pale gray to fuzzy white. I reached out and used the concave sides of the sewer for support. Wondering if rats kept busy in the midst of winter, I reached the end. Two thick bars were stuck in the lip of the tunnel. Luckily, they were placed about one foot apart. Out there, I saw liquid blackness, a shimmering.

I checked behind me again and saw more dark. There was no movement; it seemed to go on forever. I turned back, sucked in my gut, and with some effort squeezed a shoulder through the pipes. Then, stomach still tucked tight, swiveled my hips to the sides, used my feet for traction on the pebbly floor, and got the rest of me through.

I found myself once again on a ledge, this a dozen feet from the frozen face of the river. I could feel icy blood under my nose. "Great," I said to no one in particular, wondering now about the other way, hoping Bob wasn't sprawled back there.

The Gerald R. Ford Museum, a triangular building bathed in harsh flood lamps, stood directly across the water. A pedestrian bridge, glittering with rows of Christmasy lights, loomed out of the river on my left. Turning, I noticed a sheer wall of concrete rising twenty feet to the ground above. But I also saw I could make a quick leap to the side, onto banked snow and climb up. That is, as long as the snow wasn't too hard and slippery.

Before jumping, I checked the patches of inky water that showed through chunky ice for bodies. Had they emerged where I had and plunged in? I didn't think so. Taking a breath, I pushed off and onto the snow, which was softer and wetter than I had imagined. Grateful it wasn't hard as a slide that would tumble me into the river, I scooped my hands into the slope, grabbed hold and, legs straining, scrambled to the top. Once I could stand, I felt nausea wash through me and had to take another break.

Leaning my hands on my knees and still struggling for air, I let the seasick sloshing in my belly subside as I got my bearings. The back of the Welsh Auditorium was in front of me. The river below; the president's museum on the other side. OK, I had it. I could figure where I was. As the geography came clear, I knew I'd lost them. My best bet was to circle the hotel and look for help.

Slogging to an open area between the auditorium and the hotel, I tried to figure how I'd ended here, because Monica's room was probably visible from where I stood. Gawking up at the black glass and muted yellow illumination inside the Amway, my mind clamped on a far more chilling quandary. Did I leave Bob down there in the sewer? God, I hoped not.

Then, coming around the north face of the hotel, I noticed, on Monroe Avenue, the flashing of blue lights, one patrol car whipping by, followed by another. I jogged out, shoving my queasiness aside, to find lots of cops in front of the main entrance to the hotel.

"Where's Manny Rodriguez?" I asked as I ran up, lungs quaking, voice hoarse.

A cop turned to me, rubbing a gloved hand over his chin. "You're the reverend?"

"Where is he?"

"The fact is he just ran out. We got a call that a couple guys, one matching the description of . . ."

"Where?"

The other cops huddled, emanating a serious unfriendliness. The guy I'd been talking to I now recognized as a sometimes beat officer in Heartside near my church. "Over by the Eastbank," he said.

I took off, hearing him shout: "Other cruisers are on the way!"

CHAPTER THIRTY-EIGHT

Huffing along stores between the hotel and the Eastbank, I wondered where they'd climbed out of the sewer. As I approached the fenced-in construction area surrounding the apartment and condo complex, I could see a wedge of cop cars and lights sweeping by a gate leading in. My voice, as I tried to scrape it out, wouldn't go louder than a frog's cough. My throat and neck felt swollen as my nose. I gave up trying to get anyone's attention and ran in high gear to the barrier of cruisers. Two officers, both swinging red-coned flashlights, barred my way. I tried to dart around them and into the construction zone, where I saw more activity. Both stuck reddish light in my face, making me turn away. "I need to get back there," I was able to say.

"Who're you?"

Beyond them, at the base of a huge white crane, the one that had been hauling heating ducts the other day, I saw the leather coat and baseball cap. "Manny!" I tried to yell, the sound strangled in my throat.

But it was enough for him to turn. I shoved forward. The pair of cops closed ranks, presenting a solid wall of dark-uniformed authority. I reached between them, stuck my head between theirs. "Rodriguez!" I got out through a windpipe scraped by sharp stones.

Rodriguez detached himself from the others and stepped my way. "Let him in," he called.

The two eased apart enough for me to slide through sideways. "What's going on?" I croaked.

"Your boy's following VanTol up the sky crane." Rodriguez stepped back, as if to give me a better look and angled his jaw skyward.

The grid of metal, enclosing a ladder, rose and disappeared somewhere by the huge arm of the boom and the invisible roof. "Where?" I asked.

Rodriguez' arm shot up, the finger approximating the spot. "Fourth floor I'd say."

"You've got to stop him." I made out a hunchbacked form, moving slowly, relentlessly up the ladder that crisscrossed inside the framework of the crane tower.

"Fire department's on the way," he replied.

"Christ," I said, almost as a plea, moving past, ducking under a bar and finding the platform to the ladder. I felt a tug from behind, tore away and started up, the cold iron rungs cutting painfully into my hands. My voice useless, I didn't call for Bob. I just climbed as quickly as I could.

"You're nuts," I heard behind me.

Probably true, I thought, feeling a wet icy wind splatter my cheeks. I hadn't been working my way up for very long when I became aware of someone not too far behind, only a few rungs below the heels of my thick-soled running shoes. I checked briefly over my shoulder and noticed the dark wavy hair and white fleece collar. Rodriguez, hatless, come to get me, or to help.

Hand over hand, my skin sticking to the hard cold metal, my nose aching, wind battering my forehead and slicing into my eyes, I tried to get a look up a few floors.

"What's he trying to prove, Turkstra?" I heard not too far below.

Flurries of snow smattered all around me. I didn't want to lose whatever voice I had left by answering his stupid question. "Doesn't he realize, VanTol's not going anywhere?" the cop called.

Tell him that, I thought, feeling the cold fill my soggy lungs. Taking a step up, I nearly slipped on a rung. I had to stop, get my bearing. As I did, I glanced behind me at the expanse of downtown, the buildings unrolling east, their lights winking cruel and calm. I thought of the article I'd read somewhere that said this crane rose nearly 450 feet, making it the tallest piece of machinery of its type to ever work in Grand Rapids. From the top on a sunny day, that article said, you could see smokestacks along the Lake Michigan shore at the end of M-45. I was about to start going when, from above, I heard metal hit metal and saw something, I had no idea what, drop past my face.

Whatever it was didn't hit Rodriguez either. I tried to peer straight up the chimney-like network of triangular piping. I saw movement, scurrying, and then it was gone. Below, I heard Rodriguez struggling for air.

"Let's hop in there," the cop said, reaching a spot just below my feet.

"Where?"

"There."

I hadn't noticed before how close we were to the open face of the stripped building. As part of the revamping, whole walls had been ripped off. We were only a few feet from a floor that led to what had probably once been one of the apartments.

"Can you yell at Bob?" I said hoarsely.

"I think they both slipped in a couple floors up."

"Yell at VanTol not to hurt Bob."

"Right."

"Do something?" I hung out and looked at his grimacing, snow-dabbed face.

Below I heard the rush and roar of fire engines, saw the bouncing strobe of red lights. I figured we were up about ten floors. "We don't need to do this alone," he said.

"Who else?"

"Don't be a hot dog."

I clung there, my hands tight on the rungs, my side aching. He was probably right. Even so, I couldn't live with myself if something happened to Bob and I wasn't there to try to prevent it. "You go," I said.

"Too late for that."

We started up another few feet. Stopped. Hacking for air. Snow stabbing at us, the city slumbering below. About ready to go on, I saw movement in the gutted building. Out of the shadows stepped a compact figure with a bald head. I saw the silvery glint in his hand. His face was etched with fierce lines. "Turkstra, you're worse than a girl."

I made out the snarl on his mouth, the self-confident leer. "What the hell's that mean?" I asked.

"You tell me."

"You hate women."

He laughed, a shrill cackle.

"To rape your own daughter!"

The gun reached out. The laugh turned into a stricken sound. "She didn't like it from men."

"You're sick."

His body shook, the face twisted, the eyes sparking with water, or was it more hate.

"Where's Bob?" I demanded in my awful voice.

Light touched his polished cue-ball dome. I could hear him heaving in and out, his chest giving off a steady wheeze. But the rest of him was deadly still, powerfully in control. A figure on the edge, ready to take us with him. "In the hall," VanTol said.

"What'd you do to him?"

"Killed the retard."

"You asshole!" I swung away from the ladder, reaching a leg toward the exposed floor. As I did, sound and fire exploded from my gun, forcing me back, jamming hammer heads into my ears. Swinging free for a moment, I was sure I'd fall. I had to. The surprise and whiplashing away from the shot had to have left me out of control. And they had. But I was lucky; my hands had frozen themselves to the metal rung. They held even as the rest of me flopped into thin, snowy air. In the same surreal, dangling moment that I realized I hadn't tumbled from the ladder, I wondered what part of me had been hit. At the same time I worried about that, I prepared for yet another shot, for another chunk of hot lead to come careening through tissue and bone. But there was nothing like that. I hadn't been shot, or didn't appear to have been. Even so, my legs felt like sandbags being torn from my hips.

VanTol stepped back into shadow.

I tried to move my legs and free them of a tremendous weight. Maybe, I thought, the bullet had got me there. "Watch it!"

I looked and saw Rodriguez with his arms wrapped around my thighs, as if he'd tackled me. My hands dug tight into the rungs. I thought of kids on the playground who licked their tongues on cold metal and got stuck in the dead of winter. The both of us definitely were stuck. "You all right?" I asked.

"Don't ask me to dance."

VanTol emerged again, like some black vapor, looking annoyed. He glanced at the gun, as if to thank it for shooting. "Help us out," I croaked. "He's hurt."

VanTol stood silently and gazed from the platform of the room, his attention on the world out there. He shook his head, a raging rooster of a man in a business suit with lots of blood on his hands.

Rodriguez dangled, dragging on me. "You weigh a ton," I said, my upper arms straining their sockets, hands fused with the ladder.

"Sorry," said the cop.

VanTol edged closer. "Why didn't you leave us alone?" he asked.

"What made you kill Max?" I wondered.

His face turned to me, his expression hidden in the shadows cast down by this massive wreck of a building. Snow fell between us. "Max was weak," he replied.

"Why'd you hang him?"

"He did that to himself."

"Why'd you shoot your wife?"

254

"Audrey disobeyed me."

"How about Janet and Rene and the girl you strangled on her bed. Or Dorie Klock, what about her?" Or Monica? I thought.

Rodriguez swung from below.

"Or Bob," I said, almost gagging, "what about him?"

"Pastor," VanTol replied, "you have no idea." I wanted to ask what happend on the bridge that night. But with that, he raised the gun and carefully leveled it toward my head.

"Just tell me . . ."

He shook his head, as if rebuking a child who wanted another cookie. I could feel his finger tense on the trigger. "Nothing more to say."

"Did you push your daughter in the river?"

"She was a lesbian whore."

"But why? It makes no sense."

"Ask God if you get there." As he spoke and got ready to finish me off, I saw a rolling, stoop-shouldered movement behind him. Then, again, there was a thunder-drumming sound. Not too far from my face, forcing me to twist and my arms to wrench their upper joints. In the instant of the explosion, I forgot about the shifting shape behind VanTol.

But soon enough, I looked back to see the completion of the swift, solid body block. In that second, freeze-framed in slow motion, I found a sturdy spot for my feet and felt my hands flex, having torn themselves loose, and watched as VanTol's face registered the sudden impact. Like a rag doll rendition of the angel of death, he flung out his arms. He flew straight toward me, his pinched face smacking the piping of the crane tower, and then he dropped, his body sideswiping along the edge of the building.

It didn't take long for him to hit, bounce and flop to a stop on the ground, around a circle of firefighters who had scattered.

"Sweet Jesus!" said Rodriguez.

I glanced over my shoulder to see the detective gathered in the arms of another cop who had climbed to his rescue. Even in the dim light from the hazy night sky, I saw slick, dark wetness on his lower leg, a mash of blood. But Rodriguez didn't look to be in pain. If I wasn't mistaken, as I hung there from weary arms and burning hands, it looked as though he was smiling. A big grin strung itself from side-to-side on his face. He wasn't beaming at me. He was offering it to Bob. "King Kong, my man!"

Swiveling around, I noticed Monica's brother hulking on the lip of the wall-less room. His arms were bent out and down, as if he was about to lift weights. A splash of blood glistened on his brow. He wasn't looking at either me or Rodriguez. His blocky body was turned groundward and he was staring curiously at the sprawled result of his handiwork. He did remind me of a benign but powerful gorilla.

"Hey, Bobbo, good moves," said Rodriguez. "Tell him Turkstra. The guy's a hero."

My body drooped, wind-splashed and wrung out. I wanted to say something, but couldn't make the words work.

Turning his square, lumpy face on us, Bob did my talking for me. As he did, he chugged out more syllables that made more sense than I'd heard him say in awhile. "Hulk's got 'em good. Made the Prophet pay."

CHAPTER THIRTY-NINE

"Want a slug, bro?"

"No,thanks."

"Good stuff."

"I thought you were going back on the wagon?" I asked, wearily leaning against the wall in my office, my body numb and bruised.

Preacher peered at me, one eye half slit, and showed me a sloppy smile. "I got to relax. Been a hard day's night." With that he raised the bottle of Early Times, flung back his head and gulped an inch or so of the fiery fluid. Finished, he winced and ran the back of his gloved hand over his mouth. "Kills what ails you."

I doubted that the whiskey would do that. I recalled the last time, more than a decade before, when I polished off the better part of a gallon of booze. I think it was Early Times, too. It had been my last day with Ruth. When I drove her away for good. I closed my eyes and rested my head against the wall, seeing the familiar flames.

I'd been in my office for awhile, reading Max's final words, when someone, it turned out to be Preacher, pounded on the door outside. I'd reluctantly let him in a couple minutes before.

"We'll probably make CNN," he said.

I opened my eyes, shaking the fire from my mind. "Maybe you'll win a big movie deal."

Preacher leaned forward over the bottle in his lap and twisted his head to the side, aiming bleary, burning eyes in my direction. "Think Pacino will play me?"

"Don't count on it." I sat heavily in my chair directly across from the publicity hound. Wierenga's confession, if that's what

257

it was, sat on the desk in front of me. Three pages of explanation and self-justification. I placed my torn palms on either side of it. I had descended from the crane without much effort. When I got down, I noticed I'd left layers of skin behind.

"How's Bob?" Preacher asked.

"Twenty-five stitches in his head. Possible concussion. They're keeping him for observation."

Preacher scratched his skull. "Youch! What'd that guy do, bust him in the noggin?"

"Looks like." I assumed VanTol didn't shoot him because he didn't want to draw our attention. But I didn't know. That man's motivation was hard to reckon. Likely, he slammed Bob with a board or hammer, planning to finish it off once he'd dispatched with us.

Preacher nodded and sloshed back more Early Times. I smelled fumes, billowing toward me. "He's like Forrest Gump, ain't he?"

"Who?"

"Guy in that movie who mooned LBJ."

I idly touched Wierenga's handwritten pages. They sickened, saddened, but didn't surprise me. "I never saw it," I replied.

"Won some Oscars."

I shook my head, showing him I could care less.

Sipping booze, he got off the movie kick. "Rodriguez gonna pull through?"

"He won't walk for awhile, but he'll be OK."

"Bummer." Preacher wore his ratty olive drab fatigue jacket over a couple plaid shirts. Baggy sweatpants were pulled over his useless legs. Cracking a watery, yellow-toothed grin, he tipped the bottle and slopped in more.

"You're a sensitive guy," I said.

He splayed his upper arms in a shrug.

I picked up Max's papers, tapped them straight on the desk. One of the paramedics had sprayed some sort of disinfectant on my hands. I figured I'd get them looked at later.

By the clock near my phone, I saw it was going on 7 a.m. Gazing at Wierenga's sloppy handwriting, I thought of what he wrote. Much of it rambled, making me wonder if he'd been tanked up with his own version of Early Times when he put it down. In it, he talked about Dorie Klock, this woman he and VanTol met. He mentioned Rene and he touched on the death of his wife. I somehow got out of it that his wife never forgave him, or Rene, for the circumstances that had brought the girl into the world. Sounded from what I read that he was arguing with her, in front of Rene, shoved her aside and she walloped her head. The supposed accident.

I also learned it was VanTol who pulled some strings to get the cops in Saugatuck to lay off on the investigation into his wife's supposedly accidental death. Which, I gathered, was why Max was so willing to intervene when Janet died.

As for Rene's death, I didn't get the idea that Max, or anyone, was in on that, at least in the sense of shoving her off the pier. The last part of his discourse was especially hard to figure. But what I discerned was that he reluctantly threw in with VanTol when Keester started in on blackmail. I don't think he was the one who strangled Tina or threw Monica down the stairs. I had the impression he may have helped chop Keester up in that woodworking shop. But it was after that, and just after my visit with him, that his conscience erupted, or so it seemed. The last part of his letter said: "There's been too much blood in our church. Pastor, pray for me as I burn in hell."

On the Promise Keepers he was vague. He wrote that he had been involved with VanTol in his group, the one buying off votes, but that he joined the PKs soon after they came to town. In a way, I got the feeling his involvement with them put a wedge between him and VanTol and may have even brought his conscience back alive.

"How about the dead guy's wife?" asked Preacher.

I sighed, my skull aching at the temples, my throat still raw, the image of VanTol falling still locked in my head. He

259

had said Max was weak, probably referring to his defection to a group whose foundation was love, not fear or hate. "Which dead guy?"

"One Bob sent flying."

"When I left, they were saying time will tell. Damned bullet got into her brain."

Preacher chortled, sliding a hand over his brow. His nose, sharp as a hawk's, had a map of broken purplish veins. "Man, you crack me up, Turkstra."

"Why?" I asked, thinking of Monica with her leg cast and paling bruises. We'd stayed side-by-side all night in the emergency room, keeping a vigil over Audrey VanTol and Bob. VanTol's wife was in a coma. I was amazed at the courage or foolishness that brought her to the hotel.

"I mean," said Preacher, "you don't talk or act like any other minister I ever met."

"That's bad?"

"Makes me wonder what God thinks."

"I thought you didn't believe in God," I said.

"He's not the one who signs my check."

My eyes fell to the crabbed, twisted handwriting. I felt a painfully empty spot in me, a place where my faith had rested for several years now. The business of the last few days brought me up against the wall of doubt I had hoped I had gotten over. It was the tired old saw: How come the Lord, if this was his world, let such awful things happen? Even worse, how could he let persons who professed his name act like such jackals? I wondered just how, given my own faulty hold on faith, I ought to take Preacher's comments. I shoved them aside and asked a question of my own. "When'd Wierenga come to you?" I asked.

Above him Thomas Merton, himself a bastion of doubt for much of his life, looked down. Preacher shook back his hair and gazed at me with booze-bashed eyes. "Told you."

"Right off the bat, he mentioned the van and wanting you to lead me there?"

Preacher shrugged, staring in his nearly empty bottle, an aura of depression, a pause in the bender, leaking from him and wafting my way. "Pretty much," he said.

We sat there, him sinking down into his booze. Bleakness of another kind gripped me. I wanted to hear more about Wierenga, but figured I could wait. In the silence between us, I saw how shattered this man without legs looked. I had to admit, he had helped. Without him, who knows what would have happened.

I thought, too, of Wierenga. His hanging was testimony to his faith, however twisted. As for VanTol, I couldn't fathom what motivated him. Calling his daughter a whore. Maybe killing her because of her sexuality.

"You know," Preacher said after a time, "I got a problem."

"What's that?"

"I'm not sure if Pacino or DeNiro should play me. What do you think?" He looked up hopefully, as if I could solve this problem. But, my spirits lifting a half-inch or so, I had my own problem.

"Fine enough, but who's going to play me?" I wondered.

Preacher sipped the whiskey and thought a second. "Easy, if he's not dead."

I waited, aware that sun had started to shine through the blinds and wash against the glass, behind which Merton also waited to hear.

"Bob Denver."

"Who?"

"Gilligan."

I shook my head. "I was thinking more of Kevin Costner."

"The one who was dancing with those wolves?"

I gave him a weary smile.

Preacher's head bounced up, as if I'd shot a ping-pong ball his way. He fixed his drunk's expression on me. "In your dreams, minister man. In your dreams."

261

EPILOGUE

It was an odd place for an ordination. A spacious, faceless warehouse room above an indoor basketball court in Forest Hills. But that's how Monica wanted it. If she was going to pastor the fledgling church in the fast-growing suburban area southeast of Grand Rapids, she wanted the ceremony to be in the upstairs room in which she planned to do her preaching, at least for the time being.

As it turned out, for any number of reasons, I wasn't officiating the service that would make my soon-to-be-wife the third female minister in our denomination. Over the last few months, we'd quietly agreed that the man to handle the words on this important day would be Pete Hathaway, the mayor, and the man who worked behind the scenes to make this happen for her.

Many road blocks, too numerous to mention, appeared throughout spring and summer that initially made it look like no women were going to be made ministers this year. But Pete, in his fierce political way, had helped twist the rusty gears, talked to all the right people and forced all of the final items to be faced, taken care and put behind, not only for the denomination but for Monica and the other women who were making history in our small conservative denomination. Most of this happened at our annual Synod in early summer.

The first two women, one in Toronto and the other in inner city Grand Rapids, to be ordained in the summer had made headlines. This affair, coming in early October, wasn't such a hot news item. Even so, given all that had happened earlier in the year, the local paper and TV stations were going to do something. In fact, they waited outside for interviews. One of the reporters, Crystal Franklin, was inside, but as a guest. She sat

262

demurely in the back. She planned to drag out the mike and crank on the TV lights later.

So, there I was, glad to be muzzled for a change, two rows from the spot in which Monica sat alone, in front of the small stage and podium, behind which Pete Hathaway had been passionately preaching for going on twenty minutes. Memories were still eating at me, but not as hungrily. Even so, I kept looking around to get my mind off me.

From behind, I saw the proud, square shape of Monica's shoulders, the full sweep of her blonde hair, the white liturgical robe, tied at the waist with a black rope belt, that she had chosen to wear for this special event.

Next to me sat Bob, in his tight-fitting blue suit, with his large scrubbed face, bisected in the forehead by the scar from the pipe that Branson VanTol had used to knock him silly that night we had chased the both of them up the crane. Bob had his eyes closed, as if praying, but maybe daydreaming his way into some wild raging world all his own. Beyond him was Monica's dad, looking straight-backed and grim. Next to him was Monica's stepmother, wearing a floral outfit that made my eyes ache just to think of it.

On the other side of me sat Manny Rodriguez, one leg extended under the chair ahead us, his black cane settled in his lap. He was now Lieutenant Manny Rodriguez and head of the homicide squad. When he hadn't gotten an invitation to what he called this shindig, I told him I had no idea he wanted to come. Which is when he held a hand over his heart and acted hurt. So I said come along and sit by me. His son, Jared, sat on his right, a wispy child who kept sticking his knuckles in his mouth. Manny leaned over every minute or so to gently take them out.

Others were there as well, including many of Monica's students. For them, she was an inspiration. I suppose she was to me as well. As for Preacher, he'd moved to Florida for the winter. In a new wheelchair.

In his sermon, Pete spoke out of a scripture from Matthew, in which the apostle talked about the command of Jesus to "make disciples of all nations, baptizing them in the name of the Father and of the Son and of the Holy Spirit, and teaching them to obey everything I have commanded you."

He also talked, powerfully I had to admit with some envy, of the historic movement in our denomination that, through great trials, tribulations and storms, had brought us to this place in which we were rightfully giving women their ministerial birthright. It had been a massive struggle that manifested God's grace. Even if that grace was thwarted, I thought, for more than a little while by men, some of them definitely psychotic.

"Our church has had to look in its own dark places on the journey to this day, and days like it," the mayor said. "We have had to face ourselves and who we are, and we are coming out stronger, happier, and more powerful Christians, all with a bolstering of God's support, commitment and grace."

As he waxed on, he reminded me of the prophets. Even though he wore a slick three-piece suit, he had those wild eyes, that booming voice, the driven, God-ordained energy that I always associated with the men and women who spoke out for the faith on the far fringes of society. If God wasn't at work in his words that afternoon, I would turn in my own credentials.

But powerful as he was, and as strong and lovely as Monica looked, my mind drifted back to Ruth. Somehow that day in the desert, now that I had shared every bit of it with the woman who would be my wife, did not hold such power over me. Much of the pain was gone. Still, it came back at times. As it did now. Like a wound about to heal, it itched and grabbed my attention. For years, I'd shoved it away, stuffed it aside, paid it no mind. But now, with some ease, I could bring it back—and in that way assure myself it no longer haunted me.

So I pictured the night before it had all erupted. The argument happened in my apartment in Gallup. At first, as many times before, it was more sniping than anything else. The two of us were continuing our painful and yet enticing secret life. Her husband was that night, as most nights, at home, probably working on the latest of his many books, in which he heavily, angrily and articulately defended his fundamentalist faith. That night, however, turned out different, for Ruth and me.

Maybe it was the drink, or more likely just the accumulation of it and the seesaw nature of our relationship. I'd spent the day with friends watching a baseball game on TV and drinking. She came over after dinner. For whatever reason, I told her I'd had it. It was time to decide. I couldn't play second fiddle any longer. Either leave him, and bring her two children, then in their teens, or I was going. Even then, I was thinking about returning to college in Michigan. To go to seminary. I think I was flailing out, trying to find solid ground for myself. One word led to another. We were both screaming. I got up to leave my own apartment. I was going for more to drink.

As I lurched for the door, she grabbed me, called me a faithless coward, asked how could I abandon her, and that's when I ripped away, swung out an arm and slammed her chin. She'd fallen in a heap on the floor, crying, saying I was now the same animal as her abusive husband. I didn't want to listen. There had been too many times like this, although I'd never hit her before. I went to a bar and when I got back she was gone.

I went to work on the ambulance at noon the next day, nursing a horrible hangover from booze and remorse and emotions I couldn't control. At two, we got the call. A car had spun off the road in the big mesa north of town. We raced to the scene, arriving even before the state troopers. Running out with my bag of medicine and starting down a steep rocky slope into a gully, I could see the flames and black smoke. Right away, it didn't look good. Then the car, a red 1978 Escort, made my heart pause and my mind sway. But it couldn't be, I told myself as I went down the embankment. No way.

Closing in on the car and the large rock that it had smashed against, the truth slammed home. I knew it, even before we got

265

there. It was Ruth's car, and the fire was raging inside. Through a cloud of smoke, I could see movement behind the steering wheel, the body reacting to the heat and fire. She'd done this then and there, I knew, because she was pretty sure I'd be one of the ones called out. I had no idea what her motivation was. If she wanted to cause me nightmares for many years, she succeeded. Not until Monica could I approach another woman with anything more than superficial intentions.

As soon as I knew it was her Escort, I flung my bag and ran full-out for the car, ready to plunge through glass if necessary to drag her free. I'd reached the car and grabbed the searingly hot door handle when my partner tackled me from behind. He knew about Ruth and me. Probably everyone did, including her husband and kids. He also knew, or strongly suspected, who was inside the car. I fought him, but he was a big bruiser, a Zuni Indian and former football player for the University of Arizona. He wouldn't let me up. He kept me down as the cops and firefighters arrived. I was still on the ground when the entire front of the car exploded, flames guttering out and heat swirling out like a great lopping tongue there in the dry, desperate desert.

Up front, I heard Pete Hathaway say: "Sister, do you promise to be a faithful minister, to conduct yourself in a manner worthy of your calling, and to submit to the government and discipline of the church?"

My mind snapped back. The big moment was here.

As Pete spoke, I thought of how Monica had held me the first time I got the whole story out for her. Not in the hospital, when some of it showed its face, but after. It was she, over time, who said I had to forgive myself and Ruth for all that had happened. Without forgiveness, I could never go on with anyone else. Which was true.

Coming around the podium, stepping down and approaching Monica, still seated alone up there, Hathaway asked: "Monica Smit, what is your answer to these questions?"

266

Raising her face to him, her body still and poised inside the robe, she answered: "I do, God helping me." She was so different than Ruth. She would survive, with or without me. I hoped, however, it was with me.

Pete found my eyes and beckoned me forward. I checked on Bob next to me. He was playing with his thumbs. Getting up and slipping by the detective, who gave me a punch in the thigh, I stepped down the aisle behind Monica. The mayor nodded at me, a hint of a smile on this mouth.

Around us the large open room, with non-descript walls and a pale yellow-tiled ceiling, seemed to hush. I could feel the eyes of everyone turned to the front, on us, and especially on Monica. As I stood close behind, she craned up, showing me her round, pink face and the wetness in her eyes. A hard pit of a lump caught in my throat. Many years before, in church in Chicago, I'd been through this. I felt very proud of her. For a second I thought of VanTol, an evil man who got what he deserved, and his wife, who didn't. She was paralyzed and living in a nursing home.

"Please, let God's grace be manifest" said Pete, laying his hands on the top of Monica's head, which she now bowed.

I reached out, tenderly, carefully, and set mine on either side of her hidden ears. My palms felt the silky sweetness of her hair and my nose picked up the soft perfume she'd dabbed on earlier in my apartment. My fingers felt the muscles in her shoulders, the strong ground of her.

"God, our heavenly Father, who has called Monica Smit to this great office," Pete went on in his sonorous voice, "enlighten, strengthen, and govern her by your Word and Spirit that she may serve, faithfully and fruitfully in your ministry, to the glory of his name and the coming of the kingdom of his Son, Jesus Christ. Amen."

I could feel a weighty power move through me as he spoke, circulating through my body and pouring into Monica. This was a tremendous time, a moment of splendor and fear. God was making her, in significant and lasting ways, one of his own prophets, one to speak and teach and minister for him in the world. My own eyes filled, my chest burned, my hands, long healed from the night on the crane, allowed grace and strength to seep into the body of my beloved.

From behind, I had heard the folks in the audience intone: "Amen."

Then, as I swallowed hard and felt love warm through my chest, I heard rustling. Someone getting up. Without turning, I figured who it was. When he spoke, I knew. "Big Hulk, stomping face. Tell it to me now."